Now the Day is Over

— MARION HUSBAND —

Sacristy
Press

Sacristy Press

PO Box 612, Durham, DH1 9HT

www.sacristy.co.uk

Published in 2014 by Sacristy Press, Durham

British Library Cataloguing-in-Publication Data
A catalogue record for the book is available from the British Library

ISBN 978-1-908381-81-1

CHAPTER 1

~

In my more lucid moments I know I'm dead. I'm frightened then; I panic over what is to become of me. I can't keep still and quiet as I usually am so I go to the station and talk to strangers. I don't have to say very much, a comment on the weather or the lateness of the train will do. The station is a safe place because I know I've done no wrong there, although it has changed, it's not so busy nowadays and the soldiers that stand on the edge of the platform are fading. They are ghosts too of course, but the kind that lack awareness, *lucidity*. I'm afraid of them; I hate their gunmetal stink. The urge I have to push one of them onto the tracks makes me clumsy with shame.

Often, however, the matter-of-factness of my death is easier to bear. Lately things have changed for me and I'm no longer as alone as I was. New people have come; they are called Gaye and David. I am becoming used to them; I am making them my interest.

Take today, for instance. Today I watched Gaye plant mint and chives and lemon balm in a terracotta pot outside the kitchen door. After she'd pressed each plant into the compost she crushed a leaf between her fingers and held it to her nose. I watched her chest rise and fall; her nostrils flare and her mouth turn down as it does when she's satisfied. Her mouth turns down when she grasps a handful of sheet from the washing line and realises that it's dry, or when the credit card bills torn from their envelopes are less than she'd expected. Sometimes her mouth turns down and she nods. She is happy. Gaye thinks happiness is simply an absence of remembering. I think she sets her sights too low.

The lemon balm she planted made me remember a field hospital in France. It wasn't a bad memory; I had this feeling of tremendous calm as I saw myself smoothing sheets that curled my patients' toes tight as fists. The smell of lemon in the air was warm and sharp and mixed with the spoiled meat stink of the lieutenant in the last bed. His name was Evans. I made myself remember that when Evans woke he spoke with a stutter and that I hoped his last word would be pronounced perfectly, that I would have the honour of hearing it, and that he would have the satisfaction of knowing that at least in this his life ended well. That was all I wanted for them: a satisfactory ending, for there to be no going on and on so pointlessly. There is no purpose in suffering, nothing to be gained or learnt. But perhaps I am being disingenuous and I shouldn't make excuses for myself, because beside the beds of men such as Lieutenant Evans I was not a philosopher but a conduit. I can only say that I did what needed to be done.

When Gaye had finished her planting and had gone inside the house, I tore a leaf from the lemon balm and ate it, concentrating, my jaw working steadily. It tasted green, of nothing very much. Memories come and go; it's no use trying to capture them.

I followed Gaye into the kitchen. She lives in the house I lived in. It's a square, detached house, Victorian, three stories and a cellar and a garden with lawns and a vegetable patch. There's a summerhouse and a small orchard of plum trees my brother Peter and I planted the year before the war. Gaye keeps the garden tidy. She's not a gardener but a labourer, a would-be killer of weeds and slugs that are, of course, immortal if she only knew. Gaye mows the lawn and plants the flowers her father planted: snapdragons and sweet peas and London Pride, dahlias that run with earwigs. She bought a sculpture for the centre of the lawn, two metal herons entangled with one another so that their gangling awkwardness is emphasised. She worries that she paid too much for the metal birds because now, without the gloss of the catalogue's page, they are ordinary.

Much of Gaye's garden becomes ordinary after her first flurry of enthusiasm. Often her plants melt into the ground and often she doesn't notice their passing. She pays men to come each spring and paint the summerhouse, choosing a new colour each year. This year she chose a pale blue that sometimes looks grey and makes the summerhouse disappear in the rain.

In the kitchen I sat on one of the mismatched antique chairs at the pine table. Lately the table has been covered in an oilcloth patterned with blue and red cherries. It's an ugly cloth, a lapse in taste I think, old-fashioned and too jarringly cheerful for such a dark room. The kitchen of this house faces north and has always been gloomy, although Gaye brought in other men to modernise it, knocking down the walls of the scullery and the sitting room so that it's all one big, draughty space. The men painted the walls cream to soften the cold light.

Above the deep recess where the kitchen range used to stand she's hung a print of Picasso's coffee pot. Unfashionably, Gaye likes instant coffee— Kenco from the blue-lidded jar, almost the same blue Picasso used in his painting. Every morning she sits at the kitchen table in her dressing gown and drinks strong, milky Kenco from a mug decorated with childish drawings of Easter bunnies. Her cat comes in from its night's hunting to become a pet again, curling innocently on her knee. Later, still in her dressing gown, Gaye will tour the lawn, noting the positions of headless mice or small, brown birds that hardly have a mark on them but are just as stiffly dead. Her cat is quite a killer and there's a part of her that takes pride in that. Dressed, protected in her gardening shoes and gloves, she will dispose of the corpses beneath the shiny, artificial-looking laurels. She imagines their quick decomposition, remembering the speeded-up film she saw of a rat breaking down into the earth. She thinks she remembers this film every time she throws a little body away but she doesn't; often there are more pressing things on her mind.

Often enough she thinks about David. David is her husband. He's a dentist, and he hasn't time for any of this.

Seeing David for the first time is like coming across a masterpiece by a favourite artist in a junk shop. Like all beautiful men he seems familiar. You begin to imagine you've met before because the characteristics of beauty are always the same: square jaw, straight nose, full mouth, dark hair and eyes. Beautiful men have high foreheads and firm, clear skin. They have small, tight ears and are clean-shaven, although they need to shave often.

They are intelligent and they don't suffer fools; they are hard and driven and ambitious. Their shoulders are wide and their hips are slim, their bellies and backsides taut. David seems familiar, then, but only superficially; he's quite singular, really, although his ideas of happiness chime too harmoniously with Gaye's. Like her he would prefer not to remember; like her, he's unsure if this wanting to forget is the right way to go on.

From my vantage point at the table I watched as Gaye prepared supper, a risotto to use up the dark chicken meat and the half-glass of Chardonnay left from Sunday's supper. She doesn't drink very much. Sometimes Gaye becomes hung-over after a single glass of wine. She would like alcohol to have the same effect on her as she imagines it has on others: a relaxed, pleased-with-the-world feeling that would make her body forget itself. Wine causes David to fall asleep. Stretched out asleep on the couch he looks earnest, as though something important is going on in his dreams, and she remembers how pompous he is. Years ago she would cover his sleeping body with a quilt. Now she thinks that such small, caring gestures were just play-acting.

She met David at a nightclub called *Bentley's* in the summer of 1980. She was eighteen, dressed in a red, knife-pleated rayon dress she wore only that once. The dress clung to her hips and thighs and breasts; the disco lights made it almost transparent; sweat marks appeared beneath her arms as she danced. David watched her from the gold metal rail that separated dancers from drinkers. He liked her slim ankles and small breasts and the fact that she smiled as she danced. Also he liked that her face was flushed with exertion. He guessed she would be good in bed, lithe and uninhibited, and that she would care less about the trivial things he imagined most girls cared about. David was nineteen and anxious to lose his virginity. He put his pint of beer down on a nearby table and walked onto the dance floor just as the music changed. He stopped her as she was about to dance with someone else, tapping her shoulder and smiling shyly, old-fashioned, courteous; when she remembers that meeting now she imagines that he bowed.

In those days she drove a sky blue Fiat 126. She drove him back to his parents' house and took his virginity on a draylon sofa as chipped mugs of tea cooled on the floor and Donna Summer played quietly on the stereo and his mother and father slept in the room above. The parents were professors of history and philosophy and their house was dirty because what were houses, anyway? Who with any intellect cared about hoovering crumbs from carpets or buffing the stainless steel sink to a shine? The sofa creaked and sagged when David climbed on top of her. As he finished and she turned her face away from his, she inhaled a smell of stale biscuits from the cushions.

Driving away that night she knew that she would marry him. She knew without any doubt she would be Mrs David Henderson, that she would settle for being his wife and it would be OK. She knew he was steady and sure of the future, although she didn't think he knew yet that his future would include her. She imagined it dawning on him gradually: he would believe it was his idea that they should be married. I know that she was happy then and it wasn't only that she had less to forget.

I seem to have absorbed her memories as if they are my own. I know that when she was a child she was afraid of causing damage, a fear that made her timid. If she said too much secrets might be given away: words were dangerous as a still-glowing match dropped into a waste paper basket. She didn't believe in accidents; everything, in the end, could be blamed on her wilful negligence. Someone might die because of her.

I know all about negligence, of course.

I was born in 1897. When I was a girl my father took my brother Peter and me to the seaside every summer. We'd take the train from Thorp to Saltburn, a little town with grand hotels and a long pier and a lift that was like a miniature railway carriage that carried holidaymakers down the cliff to the beach. Donald, my father, insisted that we three walk to the beach, carrying our picnic and seaside paraphernalia down the many steps cut into the cliff face. The steps zig-zagged gently, we were protected by a wooden rail that I grasped obediently, whilst Peter, older than me by three years, ran ahead. Peter galloped to the sea, hopping from one leg to the other to take off his shoes and socks as he got closer to where the waves sucked at the wet sand. I stayed behind to help Donald spread out a tartan rug and erect the windbreak. The sea had to be ignored for a while, my excitement at the sight of it subdued. My pleasure wouldn't be snuffed out in a gush of enthusiasm as Peter's was. Later I would swim in the freezing water, far, far out beyond the suicide cliffs where the only sound was my own steady breathing; I imagined how it would be to drown.

My mother drowned. She drowned in her bath when I was seven. Peter and I were alone in the house with her, as far as I remember. If memory serves me correctly, Peter and I were quite alone; she had left the bathroom door unlocked, as though she wanted us to find her.

What am I to make of this now? Sometimes I imagine how it would be if I was to see her around the house; I wonder if she would be dressed (not all of us dead are clothed—even shrouds are sometimes lost). Perhaps I would try to help her; or perhaps I would, as always, abdicate all responsibility, just as she did when I was a child.

I was a slight, gangling child. Other parents might have imagined I was delicate but Donald was not that kind of father, not when we were children. His practice took him to the poorest back streets where children my age were stunted from malnutrition, their chests rattling beneath the carefully warmed metal of his stethoscope. Despite our mother's death he told Peter and me we were lucky. Until the war it was this luck of ours that kept him distanced from us.

After a day on the beach we would climb the cliff to the promenade and stroll to the Queen's Hotel for afternoon tea. There would be salmon paste sandwiches and cakes decorated with sugared violets. We drank scalding, pale tea from cups delicate as razor shells. The Queen's dining room had a high ceiling painted with naked cherubs puffing at sailing ships and the white tablecloths seemed to take on the blue of the cherub sky. I was tremendously impressed, even my crush on the head waiter seemed noble in such surroundings. I ached to impress him but the only time I dented his fantastic aloofness was when I turned up in my WVS uniform in the winter of 1916. My new shoes creaked and gave away my half-baked intentions. He served me tea and smiled at me as I left, wished me luck and called me *Miss*. At once the stop-start train journey, the solitary walk along the November beach was worth it: he had noticed me. I wasn't quite as invisible as I'd imagined.

In those days I looked in the mirror and saw a plain Jane whose eyes were too big and hungry, at odds with her mousiness. Beneath that decadent ceiling my greed could almost be excused, though it was there, in the Queen's Hotel dining room, that I would catch my father watching me, his face ugly with concern. I remember my own face distorted in the silver teapot as I studiously avoided Donald's eye, relieved that Peter was there to diffuse the embarrassment that surely would have been unbearable if we'd been alone.

During our last visit to the hotel together, Peter's voice had risen as the tiered plate of fancies was brought to our table.

'Pa, could we have teacakes, too? I could eat a mangy horse.'

Mildly Donald said, 'Don't call me *Pa*, Peter. It makes you sound affected.'

To the waitress he said, 'Could we possibly have toasted teacake? Three rounds?'

Peter watched the waitress walk away. She had been making eyes at him, as many girls did. When she'd disappeared through the swing door into the kitchen Peter grinned. 'I heard that if you tell them you've joined up they throw themselves at your feet.'

It was August 1914. I remember how tanned Peter was, his dark hair still damp from the sea. His long, brown fingers tap-tapped his teaspoon against his cup and he bowed his head, his grin slipping a little because he was shy, really. I dared myself to look at Donald and was relieved to find he'd turned his concern onto my brother.

'We need to think about what you might need when you go away, make a list.'

Peter glanced at me as though I might share his amusement at our father's faith in lists.

'There's bound to be something you've forgotten,' Donald said.

'Hankies, headache powders, syrup of figs.' Peter laughed. 'What else? Vests. Ear muffs? Damn noisy those guns.'

Donald poured the tea. 'We'll go shopping before you leave.'

Peter said, 'Wilson and Tilsley have joined up, Duggan, too.'

I thought of Wilson and Tilsley, that double act of dullards. Duggan too, captain of the rugby team, squat and vicious. I pictured them killed and lingered on the image of their corpses and their fat, weeping mothers. Peter kicked me under the table.

'University will seem pretty dull with all this going off, Edwina.'

I looked at him, a look I had perfected only recently, a coolly interested gaze. It only made Peter grin.

'Think of it Eddie—all those men in uniform—you'll hardly know where to look first—'

'Peter, that's enough!' Donald's face had coloured. I don't think I'd ever seen him so angry. Only the arrival of the teacakes saved us.

Gaye doesn't know about me. There are some that are sensitive, those who glance towards me when I enter a room; those who shiver theatrically and rub their arms. Years ago a little girl used to talk to me. 'I know you're there,' she'd say, 'I'm not afraid of you.' Once she laughed, surprised at her own perceptiveness, 'Are you afraid of *me*?' I sat on the floor beside her, amongst the furniture she'd taken from her dolls' house and arranged in doll-sized rooms on the rug. She looked a little to the left of me, as the blind do. 'Daddy says I make you up.'

Her Daddy had white streaks in his hair. He'd lost half a leg at Dunkirk. He dragged memories after him weighty as a sack of limbs.

When Gaye first came here I had been alone for years. I remember watching her from the attic as she stood on the drive and looked up at the dark windows. I willed her to go away, just like all the others who had trailed after the estate agent. Most of them had only liked the idea of such a broken house, the idea of making it whole again, wholly theirs. Prospective purchasers had to wear yellow hard hats supplied by the estate agent whose name was Martin. Martin blushed as he handed out the hats, all the same insistent that they should be worn. 'Health and safety,' he'd say, almost the only words he'd utter. He led them up and downstairs, from cellar to attic, thinking of his lover, Graham, who only called in the early evening, an unromantic, unsatisfying time of day to Martin's mind. As he watched his clients tap pointlessly at the flaking plaster, he thought about things he'd said to Graham the evening before and cringed, all the time keeping his face dully polite. He hated these clients, these wasters of time; he believed the house should be demolished. No one was more surprised than Martin when Gaye and David bought the house, no one except Gaye herself.

On the day Gaye and David moved in, after the removal men had left and the house resounded with silence, Gaye slumped on the stairs, imagining she might cry. But it seemed too self-conscious an act, too mannered and too much expected of a woman in her position. She could hear David walking from one bedroom to another and she thought of a cat marking its territory, acknowledging the ordinariness of the thought even as she wished him dead. I sat beside her and she stared straight ahead, her face blank. Then she turned to me and for a moment I believed that she had some understanding, that she had recognised me. She shuddered and wrapped her arms around her; she began to rock back and forth on the stair. 'It's all right,' she said softly, 'all right, all right. Everything will be all right,' and I thought for a moment that she was talking to me because her voice was wheedling, the kind of voice the living use when speaking to the dead.

I was so convinced that she saw me that I touched her face. She jerked away, shocked for that instance it took for rational thought to return; and then her expression became that of someone who does not believe in ghosts, only in draughts or the twitching of nerves below the skin, disconcerting but ultimately explainable. All the same, she went on staring at me. I found it hard not to speak her name, to test her further because some of the living are like tightly folded buds, clenched against what they won't acknowledge until finally they allow themselves to see. With some of the living it is only a matter of timing.

I'm not sure that I want Gaye to recognise me. As I said, I am making a study of Gaye and her husband, they are my subjects. It's best they behave normally, without the distortions of suspicion.

CHAPTER 2

～

My brother Peter was sent to France very soon after the war began. He wrote nonsense home, the same nonsense I was to write myself, knowing as I wrote that Donald wouldn't be taken in, that in time worry would transform our father into an old man we hardly recognised. During that time Peter discovered he was a coward, although he told no one but me. Half-way through the war we sat opposite each other in a London pub strung with patriotic bunting and loud with the half-drunk voices of enlisted men.

'I find myself *watching* the others, you know?' Peter leaned towards me, his face intense with the effort of making me understand. 'Watching to see how they behave, trying to work out what they're truly thinking. I can't be the only one who watches for signs, can I?'

To sudden, explosive applause, a woman sat down at a piano and began to play some musical hall song. Peter winced. He sat back in his seat and his eyes lost their focus. 'I can't be the *only* one.'

In the blue, smoky light of the public bar, his face was translucently pale. He was thinner, his wrists sticking out sharply from his tunic sleeves. His hands were disfigured with eczema and his breath was familiarly rank. He repelled me. I'd been sitting on the edge of my seat, better to hear him above the noise. I sat back. I felt that I might catch something.

Peter snorted, his nose wrinkling in that expression of disgust he often used on me. 'Look at you. Miss Florence Nightingale. Hold out your hands.'

I obeyed. Without touching me, Peter examined my hands as my cigarette wasted smoke between my fingers. Eventually he met my eyes.

'You're ruined, you know that, don't you?'

He looked away towards the group at the piano, all soldiers, all singing or pretending to, as the woman banged at the keys and the black feathers in her hat quivered. Watching the men, Peter snorted. 'Dead, all of them. And me. Even you. *Even* you. I bet. Six months tops.' Then he said quickly, 'I've been thinking about Mother, how it must have been for her.' He turned to me. 'I've been thinking rather a lot about that.'

I thought of her, too, how her long dark hair was made even darker by the bath water, how it floated around her face as though it had taken on a life of its own now that she was dead. I thought of how pale her skin was, and because I had never seen her naked before, how different she looked so that I could almost believe she was someone else, *something* else—a sprite that had crept into the house and slipped beneath my mother's bath water as though it was a portal to her own world. Her wrist rested on the bath's side, her hand limp. A puddle of water soaked my stockinged-feet and I became aware of the cold as I stared and stared; such a numbing cold, making me witless, voiceless. I think I would have turned to stone if Peter hadn't found me.

'Did you kill her?' Peter asked, although I think he timed his question badly because as suddenly as he had begun the piano playing and the singing stopped, even the voices and laughter too, as though everyone in the pub was holding their breath, shocked by my brother's nerve; their silence trembled, desperate with the fear that they might miss my reply. And so I opened my mouth to speak, to put them all out of their misery, but my mouth was too dry and it felt as though there was something wrong with my tongue, my teeth, all getting in the way of the words I might have come up with. The music started again—*Tipperary* although I know you will find that hard to believe—the men began to sing *it's a long, long way* and it was as though the question was never asked because Peter indicated our empty glasses and said, 'Another, I think,' and went to the bar.   ·

I can't say how Peter died, not yet. There has to be suspense otherwise it's just death after death with the lives in-between going from one experience to another with all the false suspense of join-the-dots. All I will say is that I did my best for Peter, more—I did what I would have had done to me.

I followed Gaye today. I sat in the hotel room watching as she took off her shoes and coat, skirt and blouse and lay down on the bed to wait. The man she waits for books the room under his name so today she is Mrs England. She likes this name—it sounds anonymous to her, like the name on dummy cheques in lottery promotions.

The hotel room is full of dry, electric heat. Outside its window an extractor fan whirrs and there is a clatter of pots and pans and a smell of gravy from the kitchen. Gaye's room has a moss green carpet as rough as pan scourers, and paler green bedding and curtains. The curtains are drawn and the sun lights the room as though it's filtered through pond weed. She waits, smoothing her hands over her satin slip, still as Ophelia beneath the water. Her toenails are painted pink, neat as shells. After a while she raises her knees so her feet are flat on the bedspread, and cups her breasts in her hands. Her underwear isn't new, he's seen it before, but it still retains the feel of newness, of its expensiveness, she's still surprised by the way it transforms her. She breathes in deeply, trying to catch her scent. It's still there, faintly, the *Youth Dew* perfume she dabbed between her breasts and on her wrists, but all she can smell is the peach air-freshener masking the stink of the previous guest's cigarettes.

Her perfume will be the first thing he takes in from her. As always it will take him back to the day they met. His name is Noel England—a ridiculous name, he thinks—a name that sounds invented for a B movie actor. On Christmas day he will be thirty-five. Adultery is against his nature. He thinks Gaye is lovely and sexier than his wife. He has two children and he reads to them in bed sometimes. He reads *Peter Rabbit* or *The Gruffalo*, a little girl under each arm, their blonde heads smelling of Johnson's Baby Bath. He turns the pages and his worry flits in and out of the story as his mind wanders to Gaye. Noel senses me watching when he makes love to Gaye. To Noel I am a freezing draught; he used to look for an open window, block the crack beneath the door with the hotel's towels. Now he's decided I am Guilt. I have changed his mind about the nature of his own sanity.

Noel taps on the bedroom door before pushing it open. He smiles at Gaye; he sits beside her and takes her hand and lifts it to his lips. 'My darling,' he says. They don't have many words for each other. Perversely she wants to ask him about his little girls. She wants to know about his life. There's not much for him to tell, and I think she guesses how little there is to him but won't admit it to herself, not yet.

I watch as Noel undresses in the under-water light. He wears white underwear, pristine, smelling of the detergent his wife chooses for its mildness. His body is soft, used to its comforts; in a few years he will look in a mirror and will be cross for allowing himself to become so unremarkably middle-aged. Now though he imagines he's not like other men but will remain youthful. All men imagine this, all the men I've ever known.

I think of Gaye's husband David as Noel lies down on the bed. I compare the way Noel looks at Gaye to the way David looks, the way Noel cups her face in his palm and frowns, his eyes searching hers as though he has to pick out a speck of dust. I can't help thinking he's acting-up the part of adulterer. *This is how adulterers look at each other! With intensity! With a passion that transforms their ordinariness!* All acts of adultery are sordid, all but this one—that's what his look says. No, not says, questions. He needs to be reassured and it's this need that lets him down because Gaye is thinking that he looks like a pleading, spoilt little boy. She wonders how at this moment it is possible to be bored and repelled and to feel such pity all at once. She lays her head on his chest and allows him to stroke her hair. After a while she closes her eyes. 'Gaye,' he says, and then quietly, 'how can we go on like this?' His hand rests on her head; he is holding his breath. Perhaps he will finish their affair, Gaye thinks, but he only exhales and pulls her closer. His hand moves beneath her slip.

Oh—but this is just adultery! Do I care what she does to him, to David? Except this woman has caught my imagination, my sympathy; I thought I was beyond such feeling, but I witness her affair and it's all I can do not to weep with shame.

All the same, I watch. That's wrong of me, isn't it? But wouldn't you watch too, if you had no fear of being seen?

◆　　◆　　◆

I return home and walk in the garden amongst the plum trees. I see through the kitchen window that Gaye has returned home and is unpacking groceries. She would have pushed the supermarket trolley wearing her adulteresses' clothes and I wonder how she could bear to go from being Noel's lover to David's wife without changing from her silk knickers. I find myself staring at her, wanting her to sense my disgust. But Gaye is oblivious to me. Besides, my disgust is hypocritical.

I sit down beneath the trees that are so old now they barely fruit. Peter and I planted these trees the year before the war—did I tell you that? In France Peter used to think about these trees, about our garden. 'After the war—if there is an *after*,' he wrote to me, 'I'll build a summerhouse. It will be my quiet place.' Peter craved quiet, of course. 'I think it would be marvellous to be deaf,' he wrote. I wrote back that yes, deafness would be a blessing. As I wrote the bombardment that had been going on for days stopped. I realised my ears were ringing.

That was in 1918. 1918 was my year of grace. In 1918 I met my one true love. His name was Michael Hardcastle.

Don't you think that's rather a noble name? I wrote *Michael Hardcastle* on Saltburn beach, scoring the letters deeply into the wet sand, and then waited until the sea erased them and the salt water came over my knees and dragged at my skirts. I wanted the sea to finish me off, dissolve me as though I were solid, corruptible flesh. On that beach the other dead watched as if they might learn something, or at least have what they already knew absolutely confirmed: that we can't do away with ourselves so easily.

In 1918 Michael sat in his wheelchair in the hospital grounds, smoking a cigarette, his face raised to the December sun, his eyes closed. He was smiling. I walked past and wondered what he might be smiling about, so I stopped to look back at him. I blocked his sun and he opened his eyes, only to shade them with his hand as he studied me. At last, holding out his hand, he said, 'Hardcastle. Hello.'

I stepped forward. 'Sister Johnson.'

'I know who you are.' He went on studying me and I looked away, squirming. He knew who I was, knew my reputation. My face burned.

Michael said, 'You were going for a walk?'

I nodded.

'Take me with you.' He tossed down his cigarette and looked at me expectantly. He was used to his orders being obeyed without hesitation, but I only stood there, desperate to get away from him but paralysed by anxiety. Major Michael Hardcastle knew who I was. My hands began to shake, my knees; my teeth began to chatter. He wheeled himself towards me. 'Push my chair,' he said, 'it will steady you.'

I get up from beneath the plum trees and go into the house. David has arrived home and I have a longing to be with him. I sit on the side of the bath and watch him bathe in green, pine-scented water. He cups his testicles delicately, resting his head back, and stares at the ceiling. After a while his hand closes around his penis but only rests there, nursing his half-hearted erection. Thinking of Gaye, he lifts his hands to his face and groans. He knows that what he did to her was terribly wrong, that what they go on doing to each other is worse. He loves her. It's his love for her that traps him in this marriage, the certainty that he could never love anyone else as much.

He remembers the first time he made love to her and how scared he was that his father might discover him. So he had been too quick, reaching his climax in seconds, hastening to cover up her nakedness, to zip his flies. Now he can't remember if he even took off his shoes and he winces to think that he might not have. He remembers that her mascara smudged, that she left lipstick on his shirt so that the words of that corny song rang in his head: *Lipstick on your collar—gonna tell on you . . .* He kept his secret, though: he threw the shirt away. He showered, too, as soon as she had driven off in her funny little car. He stood under the shower and soaped and soaped himself, thinking that he was ordinary now, like his friends; ordinary because he could make love to a girl (after a fashion); ordinary because, in the end, he had wanted to.

In the bath, David lowers his hands from his face. 'Ordinary! Jesus.' He smiles bitterly. I touch his knee that breaks through the water, wanting to calm him. He bows his head, stretching out his leg so that all of it is submerged. He thinks of Alastair, the new dentist that has recently joined his practice. Alastair has just married his boyfriend. Alastair passed around the photographs—two grooms in morning suits, pink cravats at their throats. *Pink!* David grunts. They probably thought they were being ironic. Gently I say, 'Perhaps they just like pink.' Sometimes the sound of my voice surprises me because mostly I'm silent, but now I only want him to hear. Louder I say, 'I'm sorry, David.' He closes his eyes, blind and deaf to me.

David looks like Michael. I think so, anyway. I'm sure I'm not just being romantic.

Michael was younger than David, of course, although he seemed older to me. Unlike me, Michael had done more than just stumble around stinking hospitals since he left school. Michael had worked for a man he called Uncle. He and Uncle bought and sold antiques, travelling around London's outer-reaches to clear tumble-down farms and country houses where sometimes, he told me, the dead were still on display, tidied into their coffins, impotent of course, but still somehow *owning* the objects he and Uncle had been invited to cast an eye over. 'I felt like a crook in those houses,' Michael said, 'even though I always apologised to the corpse.'

He told me, on that first walk of ours, that he had been watching me since he'd arrived.

'How d..d..dull,' I said.

'You stutter,' he said, 'I don't suppose you stuttered before the war.' He glanced over his shoulder at me as I pushed his chair along the path to the river. 'It's damnable, isn't it?'

He presumed it was all right to curse in front of me; he knew I wasn't like other girls, and not only because I was a nurse and had seen everything a man would rather hide. All the same I blushed and was pleased that he couldn't see me as I pushed his chair further away from the safe neatness of the hospital's grounds. Soon we were out of the hospital's shadow; I could look back and see its gargoyles leering from its Victorian Gothic turrets.

The hospital was once the home of a lord, a man who had lost his sons in 1916. He'd donated his house to the war effort and now the war was over he had no heart to reclaim it. I felt that we were forgotten, us workers and inmates of this sad asylum, inmates who were, it seemed to me, neither mad enough nor sane enough to be worth the army's effort. The war was over and few of us had visitors other than parents, men and women who were as cowed as we were. Sometimes my father Donald came, his arm through Peter's, guiding him. He brought me sweets. Those visits were fraught with danger; I might let something slip that would reveal the kind of person I had become and Donald and my brother would never visit me again. We talked about home, as safe a subject as could be.

On that December morning I stopped Michael's chair beside a bench and sat down. He took out cigarettes and offered one to me. Smoking, we watched the swift flow of the river. I waited for him to speak, anxious still, aware more than ever of my potential to stutter. And, of course, he knew who I was, he had been watching me. Odd that I hadn't noticed, I thought I took in everything, but then, he had only been with us a few days. Rumour was that he'd seduced a nurse in his last hospital and had been sent here to cool his ardour. Most of the other nurses in the lord's house were nuns. The nuns, and their supposed benign influence, were one of the reasons why they had sent me there, of course.

Exhaling cigarette smoke, Michael turned to me. 'You're not as I expected you to be.'

I made myself return his gaze. 'Oh?'

Michael turned back to the river. Flicking cigarette ash he said, 'I'd expected an angel-like creature. That's what they call you, isn't it? The Dark Angel?'

I laughed. I thought he was an idiot and was ashamed that I'd been awed by him. He was just like all the others; his imagination as limited as any dim corporal's. He had an accent, I realised, a cockney twang he tried to disguise. Far from being a gentleman, I decided he was nothing, nobody.

Finishing my cigarette I stood up. 'I'll wheel you back.'

'Leave me here. I can walk.' Looking up at me, he said, 'They don't like me to, not without their watching, but I can. So, now you think I'm a fraud as well as an arse.' He smiled a slow, beautiful smile. 'What's your first name?'

'Edwina.'

'Edwina, I'm sorry for everything that's happened to you.'

No one had ever apologised before, I had only ever been blamed. Yet here he was, taking it on himself to say sorry. I sat down because my legs were shaky.

Eventually he said, 'I wish I were dead, don't you?'

I had never wished that, not even in the darkest time. I nodded.

'It's the boredom,' Michael said, 'and a longing for . . . I don't know—*purpose*. I would like an answer to the clamouring in my head.' He searched my face as if seeking understanding. 'I think we have things in common, don't you?'

What did we have in common? Death I think, as its witnesses, as its servants, willing or otherwise. I think most of all we shared a sense of responsibility; I won't say guilt; only Michael felt guilt.

In the bath, David submerges his head. When he surfaces, gasping, I reach out and touch his face, his hair; it's the first time I've allow myself to be so intimate with him. This is what David does to me, he makes me forget realities. David flicks at my hand as though a fly has landed on him. I stand up and go downstairs and out into the garden.

CHAPTER 3

~

Gaye has a visitor today.

Visitors are rare in this house. There used to be dinner parties for members of the golf and rotary club, those men whose wives and children may need expensive cosmetic dentistry. For these parties Gaye would buy armfuls of roses and lilies, fern and baby's breath, and her arrangements were over-blown and old-fashioned. There'd be candles and bowls of fruit—the most perfect bunch of black grapes kept back to grace the cheese board. That dining room was in another house and was painted ox-blood red, the mahogany table extended to seat twelve. Gaye wore a short black dress and pearls and pinned up her hair. Her knee would be squeezed beneath the table or late in the evening the club captain would proposition her in the kitchen where strands of her hair had escaped from its pins and her cheeks were flushed with the hassle of coffee.

Our visitor today, Ralph, attended such a party, one of the late ones when Gaye had lost interest. Ralph had been seated next to a dermatologist's wife who said how much skin bored her, and what did he do—could it be any duller? He told her that yes—it probably could, thinking of the tattoos beneath his shirt sleeves, the Chinese dragon with its breath of crimson fire, the mermaid coiling coyly on his left shoulder, and what a dermatologist's wife would make of such decoration. The dermatologist's wife thought how gorgeous he was, although that fat, greasy word didn't do him justice. She wished she'd seen him in his naval uniform, as a young officer, veteran of the Falklands War. She found her thigh pushing against his; he made her feel daring.

Ralph stands in the dining room (Gaye has painted this room cream) and looks at the garden. He's opened the French doors so he can blow out his cigarette smoke, and the smoke of next door's bonfire takes him back to his childhood, the memory vivid because the smell is so rare. He hardly ever reminisces; he likes to believe he looks forward. Even his nightmares have become rarer so that now when he wakes in the night, hot with terror, he wonders if the return of these bad dreams might be a portent. He is forty-seven and he paints impressionistic pictures of birds. His paintings have been called startling and joyous and *touchingly profound*, also confused, insipid, gaudy. They sell well. *Parrot* is being reproduced as a birthday card. Blowing smoke into Gaye's garden, he squints at the heron sculpture so that the stark metal blurs in the sun. Blue tits, small as tropical butterflies, flit in and out of the hawthorn hedge. He thinks of the blackbird he worked on that morning, its too-yellow eye more sinister than he would have liked.

Gaye comes in. She has made proper coffee and strained it into her Wedgwood pot. Cups and saucers, milk jug and sugar bowl are all in the same, discontinued design of peach-coloured cottage roses she once loved and now doesn't care for. She surveys the tray and moves the milk jug a little to the right so that it is half hidden behind the tall pot. She is almost certain he doesn't take milk, almost no one does nowadays.

'So,' she says, 'how are you?'

Ralph turns to face her. 'I'm well, thank you.'

He looks well. Still at the French doors and with his back to the light, his aura shimmers but Gaye can't see it. Unable to resist, I stand close to him and he glances at me, disturbed by the cold. His cigarette burns by my hand; as he brings it to his mouth it scythes through my body. He frowns as he inhales: the taste has changed.

'How's David? Still determined to save the world from decay?'

'Sit down, Ralph.' She inclines her head towards an armchair. Handing him an ashtray, she says, 'Sit down, please. I don't mind about the smoke.'

'David will mind.'

She pours the coffee, thinking that when Ralph has gone she will have to open all the doors and windows to get rid of his scent. Even so, David will know that Ralph has been here, it will show on her face, sound in the higher tone of her voice. David will be contemptuous of her inability to keep secrets.

Ralph sits. He takes the coffee cup she hands him and sips cautiously before smiling at her. 'You make the best coffee.' He'd set the ashtray on the arm of his chair and now he stubs out his cigarette. He would like to light another because coffee and cigarettes are a sublime combination, but of course he can't smoke so carelessly in this house. Instead he smiles at Gaye. 'There,' he says, 'filthy habit.'

He glances in my direction and for a moment it's as if he can see me. I hold his gaze but it is as pointless as staring into a mirror. He turns to Gaye. 'You still have the ghost.'

She laughs.

'I'm serious, Gaye.'

'I know you are—that's why I laughed.' Even as she says this she glances in my direction. I hold out my arms to her, my expression mocking those imploring ghosts I sometimes meet, those who can't tell the living apart. 'Gaye,' I say, 'help me, please,' and although I had meant to be ironic, I hear the whine in my voice and am ashamed.

I feel I have disconcerted her. She looks away from me quickly and becomes aware of how she is sitting, on the edge of her seat, knees together and angled away from him, her back straight. Her skirt reaches mid-calf but she wishes it was longer and that her scooped-neck sweater revealed less. She had dressed to go into town, she'd put on lipstick and mascara and blow-dried her hair instead of just raking a comb through it. If David was to come in now he'd think she had dressed especially for this visitor. David is jealous of Ralph; he thinks women are impressed by his easiness.

Ralph says, 'Maybe you should research the history of this house. Find out who's buried under the floor.' After a moment he asks, 'May I take you out for lunch?'

Gaye hesitates. She thinks how pleasant it would be to go to Santoro's with Ralph, to eat those big, delicious olives and sip iced vermouth as he entertained her. She can be lazy with Ralph, free of the obligation to be entertaining in her turn. With Ralph, all she has to be is his audience.

And there is the chance that other women will turn to look at them, and she would know that these women were jealous because few men are as astonishing to look at as Ralph. The idea of heads turning makes her smile.

'Lunch would be nice,' she says.

Ralph is David's brother.

I may have given the impression that Ralph believes in ghosts. He doesn't. He doesn't believe in God, either, nor does he have any moral code. He does what he believes he can get away with. In this he's like David; the only difference between the brothers is David is consumed by guilt afterwards. Afterwards, Ralph hardly thinks of his sinning at all. I find Ralph refreshing. He makes me feel better about myself.

Santoro's is half empty. Gaye and Ralph are seated in a corner, as though the waiter understands their need to be discrete. I sit beside Gaye so that I might look at Ralph—there's no harm in looking. The restaurant's walls display prints of posters by Toulouse-Lautrec, pictures of entertainers and prostitutes. Ralph looks at the posters and smiles, thinking how fitting they are. He looks at Gaye as she studies the menu. He remembers how little his mother thought of her, this girl her son brought home that lacked intellect or ambition, who wanted babies and a clean, bright, tidy home. And he remembers how his father fell for her prettiness, forgetting what he was supposed to think about such silly, empty-headed girls who let down the feminist cause. Ralph's father's infatuation had infuriated his mother above all else, cementing her hatred of Gaye. Poor Gaye, Ralph thinks.

He says, 'Is David well?'

'Yes.' Gaye places the menu down. 'I'll have the veal, I think.'

Ralph takes his spectacles from his pocket and puts them on. Scanning the menu he says, 'I shall, too.' He closes the menu, takes off his spectacles and smiles at her as he swings them from his fingers. 'I have to believe they make me look distinguished.'

'They do,' she says, although she thinks the spectacles make him look like his father, a sweet man. 'You could wear them as a disguise.'

Ralph looks puzzled. She is becoming odd, he thinks, and reaches out to cover her hand with his. After a moment she draws away. The waiter comes.

Ralph is a year younger than David. They share the same birthday, 8th

October, so that Ralph, when he first discovered the facts of life, used to believe that his parents only ever had sex twice: once on their wedding night and again on its anniversary. There is a part of his heart that still believes this. Once he shared his belief with David, who looked at him with an expression Ralph interpreted as disdain. But David was only shocked; he didn't want to think of his parents having intercourse. He began to think that Ralph was sick in the head.

David and Ralph went to the same boarding school. Ralph was the popular brother, captain of the cricket team. David was bullied, at first. He was so slight, so scared-looking, but angry, too, full of hell at being sent away so that the others weren't sure what to make of such a boy, except to try to knock all that fearful defiance out of him. In his first term, David had his nose broken. Such a lot of blood; and David didn't cry, but just stood bleeding. After that he was left alone: there seemed little point in tormenting someone so unnervingly stoical. The feeling was that David was too far beyond the pale. And his beauty didn't help—of course not: he looked too much like a malevolent fairy. Younger boys were afraid of him.

The veal arrives and Gaye and Ralph eat. Gaye regrets imagining lunch with her brother-in-law would be pleasurable and not the trial it's turning into. For once he is quiet and of course she has no small talk. She is desperate to ease the growing awkwardness between them and so she says, 'You really think the house is haunted?'

Ralph puts his knife and fork down and takes a sip from the glass of wine he ordered. 'It's an old house,' he says eventually. 'Full of memories. Perhaps something of the lives of those who once lived there gets trapped . . .' He trails off, thinking that what he's saying is nonsense but wanting all the same to say something, anything, which might make this meal more companionable. He makes his voice lighter. 'What do you think?'

I turn to Gaye, this is interesting to me.

'I think we should never have moved there.'

'You both needed to get away from the old place—'

She laughs dismissively. 'Away from each other! What was the point in simply exchanging houses? Besides, I was happy in *the old place*! Happy until . . .' Now she has strayed on to dangerous ground; she might even cry. Again, Ralph reaches across the table and takes her hand.

'Oh, Gaye,' he says. 'Gaye . . .' But what is there to say that hasn't already been said over and over? Words aren't any less useless now that a little time has passed.

He squeezes her hand and draws away. He allows her a moment to compose herself and then says, 'I thought I might paint your garden.'

'Oh?' She manages to smile, relieved that she has kept her tears in check, although her throat is burning from their suppression. 'Which aspect?'

'Looking towards the summerhouse. It could be my house-warming present to you both, rather belated, I know—'

She interrupts him. 'There used to be plum trees by the summerhouse. David cut them down. He hired a chainsaw . . .'

There were leaves and blossom everywhere, branches trembling on the ground, and such noise, such terrible noise I had to hide away. I had forgotten. David cut down the plum trees and I was so frightened I hid away.

My panic is suffocating. How could I have forgotten? How could I have believed that I was safe? I cover my face with my hands and try to breathe normally. The trees are gone; I have made a mistake over my realities, a critical mistake, terrible, so that I wonder what will become me, if I am to be found out.

Time passes. Gaye and Ralph finish their meal and go. Waiters clear the tables; they sweep the floor and turn the sign on the door to *closed*. I sit on. Eventually, in the dark, empty restaurant, I become calmer. After all, nothing seems to have changed, there has only been a confusion. I let my hands fall to the table and push myself up. I'll go to the station. I feel safe there.

◆   ◆   ◆

On the platform the soldiers are waiting for their train, the first stage of a journey that will end in France. I approach one of them, a boy of about nineteen with dark rings beneath his eyes. He hasn't slept for days. Even though he had longed for this leave, for his own bed, all he could think of was going back. He often thinks of a horse he'd seen lying dead in the road, close to Arras. Rats had taken up residence in its belly. He's afraid he lacks something to care so terribly about the horse and less about the human dead. I touch his arm, hoping I might reassure him. 'Sister,' he says, 'has the train been delayed?' His voice is no more than a whisper.

I am in my uniform. I too have not slept. My father Donald stands beside me, but he isn't still. He cranes forward to look for the train along the track; he stamps his feet and blows on his hands because it's November and he has forgotten his gloves in his anxiety. From time to time he will glance at me and if he catches my eye he will smile. I wish more than anything that he would go home. I want to be free to talk to the boy who stands on the edge of the platform; he looks so sad, so done-in. This boy has lovely eyes. Perhaps it's best that Donald stays. Perhaps he knows he is saving me from myself.

Donald says, 'I've packed some cake in with your sandwiches. An apple, too. A Cox's pippin. They've been plentiful this year.' He breathes out sharply. 'Will you be able to get a hot drink on your journey?'

I smile at him. 'There's always some grand lady manning a tea urn somewhere. I'll be fine.'

He nods. 'Now, you'll write—as soon as you get there safely?'

'Don't I always?'

'Yes. But let me know how that cough of yours is. If it gets any worse . . .'

The train comes. I watch the boy climb aboard. Donald is gone. I am alone and the people on the station wear the kind of clothes that Gaye and David and Ralph wear.

I am dead.

I had forgotten about the trees and that was a bad mistake. I shall go back to the garden and sit on the summerhouse steps and think carefully— remember more carefully. I shall stick to the truth, I promise.

CHAPTER 4

~

Michael was being treated in the hospital where we met by a psychiatrist called Dr Cooper. Cooper asked about Michael's mother.

'He wanted to blame her,' Michael said, 'but because I'd never met her he was to be disappointed, so I invented a mother.' He grinned at me. 'Oh, she was such a dear! She spoiled me to death! Never was a boy more pampered! The good doctor hung on my every word, making me feel rather guilty. In the end I couldn't bear it anymore and told him that she had died rather suddenly shortly after I'd enlisted. Poor man looked quite heart broken. He must have loved her too.'

I told him that my mother had died when I was seven years old.

'Truly?'

He believed I could lie about such a thing as easily as he lied to Cooper. 'Truly,' I said.

I barely remember her alive; she was so frail, a shadow on my bedroom wall. She didn't stay; in my heart I know she didn't, not as I stay; she must have been as blameless as she appeared. I imagined telling Michael about how I had found her body; I imagined describing how I had stood for so long and even when Peter came I didn't move; he had to shove me out of the way and he was crying and shouting, I remember; or perhaps just shouting, harsh with me as ever. I think the crying came later, when he was alone.

Of course I didn't tell Michael any of this; these were early days and I didn't want him to think I was any odder than he already believed me to be. Also I knew there would be questions—he would *have* to know the reasons, the details—no detail was ever too small for him. I would have to tell him how the skin on the tips of her fingers was wrinkled and white having been submerged for so long in the water; although the fingers of her other hand, that hand that fell over the side of the bath, were quite smooth, quite relaxed-looking. I would tell him this and remember that the bathroom smelt of roses that had been seeped in boiling water, and I would tell him of this peculiar scent because it was just the kind of detail he appreciated. The cold tap was dripping; there was no other sound except that drip, drip, drip.

We were walking by the river, Michael and I, my arm through his as I decided not to tell him about my mother, as he told me about his sessions with Dr Cooper. By then he had decided to walk again, allowing Cooper to believe he had made his break through. 'He's so pleased with himself,' Michael said. He laughed. 'Perhaps he'll write a paper about me. I'll make his name.'

He had decided to walk again and together we had decided to be married as soon as we were discharged. I imagined a little house on the edge of a village, a van with our name painted on its side: *M & E Hardcastle—Purveyors of Fine Antiques.* I imagined an unmade bed and Michael whistling in our kitchen as he fried bacon, collarless, his sleeves rolled up, braces hanging at his sides. I imagined it as though I was watching through a window.

Beside the river, Michael stopped walking and turned so that we stood face to face. 'Promise you'll never lie to me.'

'I promise.'

'I'll only ever tell you the truth.'

He told me then that his name was not Michael Hardcastle, but Alfred Booth, and that Uncle was not his uncle but a man who had picked him up one evening on King's Cross Station. Uncle had asked him how long ago he had eaten and if he had a bed for the night, saying, 'You're cold and tired, I know, and this isn't a safe place for a boy like you.' Holding out his hand Uncle had coaxed, 'Come. You've had enough of this, I'm sure.'

Uncle's last boy had died. Michael had seen the photograph of him that Uncle kept beside his bed. 'A weasel-faced creature,' Michael said, 'common.' Jealousy curled his lip and flared his nostrils and made him momentarily ugly.

That first night at Uncle's he slept in the dead boy's bed and in the morning Uncle gave him the dead boy's clothes to wear. Michael began to believe that Uncle had chosen him because he was the same size and shape as this boy. Because he fitted so exactly the empty place the boy had left, Uncle could fool himself out of his grief. Sometimes Uncle would call him by the dead boy's name: Michael. 'So I changed my name to his.'

One Sunday afternoon my father and Peter visited me in the hospital and rather than finding me alone as usual I was sitting outside on the lawn with Michael. I introduced them; I said, 'Daddy, Peter, this is Major Michael Hardcastle. The Major and I have become friends.'

I remember how formal I sounded, and yet childish, too, a little girl pretending to be grown up; I remember that I was shaking because I was afraid my father would see through Michael's bravado and would say something that would humiliate him so that I would have no choice but to detest Michael and feel ashamed. Even then I had an idea that most men would know Major Michael Hardcastle to be an imposter, and that Alfred Booth was more easily sniffed out than Michael believed. But Donald hardly seemed to look at him, only shook his hand briefly, preoccupied as ever with Peter.

I need to explain about Peter, how he had been blinded during the middle years of the war when it seemed that both the beginning and end of this ugly phase of our lives were too far distant to care about. At that time we became tourists into the future, taking comfort in an imagined survival; or we blundered around in the past, visitors to this or that important memory, inspecting it from the new perspectives inspired by recent experiences. Peter chose to visit the past, and in those hopeless middle years of the war his letters to me had become increasingly bitter.

He would write about our mother's death and had begun to pose a series of questions to me as though he was a detective from a penny dreadful. It seemed that the war, its depravations and terror, had given him leave to ask me straight: *why had I gone into the bathroom that afternoon? Why had I not run from there at once? You were soaked—why? Had you tried to save her? You didn't cry. I can't remember that you ever cried. Why?* I wrote back on postcards that bore hand-coloured pictures of soldiers and their sweethearts or that had been embroidered with baskets of forget-me-nots by local girls. *The weather here is fine,* I would write, *there has been a lull and I have had time to do some mending and even read! Father sent me a parcel; I hope this finds you as it leaves me—well.*

He wrote back, *You must tell me the truth, Edwina. Do you have no urgent need to confess?*

But then, in the middle of all this—the war and the questions it inspired—Peter had been blinded in some absurdly cruel way or other and had been discharged from the army into the care of my father. He did what Donald prompted and cajoled him to do and no more. His stubbornness was a great source of frustration to my father; Donald wanted him to begin to live the life of a blind man, to learn to read Braille and to find his away about in that mysterious way of the blind—counting steps, Donald supposed, perhaps recognising the different smells and sounds, the textures and shapes of a place. Peter would know where he was just by a taste in the air, Donald fancied, by the different ways the earth vibrated or gave beneath his feet. Peter used his white stick to probe his way around the house, but that was all. That day when he met Michael for the first time, he held onto my father's arm and this made him appear frailly dependant, but Peter didn't care about this. For all his timorous appearance he was fierce in his defiance, as though independence and bravery were for those who had not realised the hopelessness of their predicament.

On the hospital lawn my father settled Peter into a chair. At once Peter turned his face towards Michael. 'As you can see, Major, I'm blind as a worm. What toll did our great adventure take of you?'

Donald sighed. 'Peter . . .' To Michael he said, 'I'm sorry, Major Hardcastle—please excuse my son, he's had a tiring day.'

Peter sat forward in his chair, all at once animated. 'But he has the advantage of me! Now—*Major*—are you in a wheelchair? Limb missing? Are you recovering from a suppurating wound?' He paused a moment. 'Perhaps you're blind too? Or are you a deaf mute?'

Michael glanced at me but I'm afraid I was of no help to him; I had become frightened of my brother, of the licence he believed his blindness had given him to say anything he wished. I could only smile weakly, as apologetic as my father had been.

Michael laughed, embarrassed to find himself all at once without support. He cleared his throat. 'There's nothing very much wrong with me at all.'

'Touch of funk, was it?'

My father was appalled. 'Peter! Apologise at once!'

'It's all right, Mr Johnson, I understand.'

'There.' Peter fumbled in his pocket for cigarettes. 'There, you see? The Major understands.' He lit a cigarette and tossed away the match so that it landed at Michael's feet. 'Understands quite what, we're not sure. Oh, and by the way—he's not *Mr*, he's *Dr*. What do you think of doctors, Major?'

Michael glanced at my father, and it was quite an open, frank look, I suppose almost insolent in its way. Then he seemed to remember that this was my father, and although fathers were creatures he'd had no experience of, he knew enough to pretend respectfulness. 'My own father was a surgeon, Dr Johnson.'

Astonished by this lie I felt my face flush and it was as though Peter could feel this sudden heat from me because he turned in my direction, smiling archly. Turning back to Michael he said, 'A surgeon, eh? More or less of a butcher than any of the others?'

'Less, I would say. He's been dead some years. I barely knew him.'

Peter snorted. 'I can't quite place your accent, Major Hardcastle.'

'Please, you must call me Michael.'

'*Michael*. Tell me something more about yourself, Michael.'

'There's nothing to tell outside the usual: school, army—'

Peter turned to me. 'Is he really so dull, Edwina?' To Michael he said, 'Edwina couldn't put up with a dull man. She craves excitement, attention—'

Donald sighed. 'Peter, you're being tedious.'

'But Michael should know what he's letting himself in for.' He stood up. 'Michael, I think you and I should go for a stroll.'

Michael stood up too and allowed Peter to take his arm. He turned to me and I wanted his expression to say that he didn't want to go, that he was going for a walk with my brother only reluctantly and because he felt sorry for him; but he was smiling, as though this was all a great joke, as though whatever Peter had to say about me could be believed or not, but that all the same he would indulge him.

I watched them walk away and had an urge to go after them, to walk between them and keep up some empty-headed stream of words so that they wouldn't be able to talk to each other. But I only watched them cross the lawn, noticing how Michael was careful to match my brother's pace.

When they were out of earshot, my father said, 'He's very angry, Eddie. I hardly know what to say to him anymore.'

I think he wanted me to reassure him with some nurse-like talk of time being the best healer, that we must be patient and kind. But I couldn't speak; I was too afraid, imagining as I was all the malicious things Peter was telling Michael—how I had never been right, never would be right, that I was a wicked creature and that my reputation was deserved. I almost stood up; I remember I moved to the edge of my seat but fear held me back, cowardice I'm ashamed of now.

I wonder now if this is where my story should have begun, with Michael and Peter arm and arm, walking away from me. These two, Michael and Peter, are the ones that matter most, after all.

◆　　◆　　◆

Gaye and David are standing on the lawn. She tells him, carefully, shyly, that Ralph would like to paint their garden, that he would like the painting to be a house-warming present. David tries to imagine one of his brother's pictures hanging on their wall. Even though he knows that it will become invisible over time, he hates the idea. The picture will be too valuable; he will be humiliated by its worth and reminded every day of his brother's easy way with life, comparing his ease with his own awkwardness. He can't help thinking how unfair it would be to have his home invaded in such a way.

David turns and walks towards the house; he can't bear to stay; Gaye's enthusiasm for his brother's painting reminds him of how distant they've become.

In his study he sits down at his desk and opens his laptop. There are all the emails from people wanting to sell him Viagra and penis enlargers. He frowns at the image of a young Asian woman caressing a huge, fake cock. He presses the delete key, delete, delete, delete again and again, until he comes to Luke's message. There is no subject. For a while he gazes at the screen, and then deletes Luke's email along with the rest.

He imagines Luke's desk, its clutter of dirty coffee mugs, newspapers, notebooks and files; he thinks of the care he would have taken over that email, every considered word. Anyone reading his message would think nothing of it, he is certain of Luke's discretion. Only he would be able to read the code that after all was of his own devising.

He remembers one afternoon in Luke's flat, how there had been some argument that had begun over Gaye (almost all their arguments were over Gaye). Luke shouted at him, 'You relish the subterfuge! Christ, I can't believe I've only just realised how much you relish all this secretive crap!' Luke had wiped his mouth with the back of his hand because that's how his anger manifested itself, with too many words, too much spit and venom. David could imagine him dancing with anger, that same, funny little animated dance that his music teacher used to perform when he couldn't work out which choirboy was singing the flat notes. That queer man, that fat, kiddie-fiddler with his dainty hands and ankles, he couldn't bear Luke to behave like such a creature. So he had told him to sit down and to be quiet; he had pushed a glass of water towards him. 'I'm married,' he'd told him, as if he needed to be told.

'Leave her! They'll respect you for it, in the end.'

They: his patients; those men and women who, out of fear and nervousness made small talk as he prepared the drill. Some asked if he had a wife and he would answer too promptly as was his habit. He recognised how Pavlovian this promptness was and thought sometimes that he should be ashamed of himself, remembering back to a time when he and Gaye were young and he kept a picture of her in his surgery to prove himself. In that photograph Gaye looked like a good, sensible girl, dressed in her maternity smock with a pussy-cat bow tied prettily at her throat, and his patients would smile at her, satisfied.

Gaye would occasionally visit the surgery in those days. 'When is your baby due, Mrs Henderson?' A patient had asked her.

Instinctively Gaye had touched her belly. 'Two months,' she said, and she lowered her eyes like Princess Diana, and the woman who had asked the question was charmed.

At his desk, David takes out the diary he keeps locked in its drawer. He opens it on a blank page, writes the date then hesitates. Even though the diary is not meant to be read by anyone, he knows in his heart that one day it will be found and that its discoverer will be unable to resist their curiosity. Years ago, then, he decided to write in a way that might satisfy that reader, that man or woman sitting on the edge of the chair he sits in now, his desk drawers open and rifled, as they furtively turn the diary's pages. He wants that person to know the truth, or at least the truth as he saw it. David understands the vanity of this, but most of the time he thinks only of how much he wants to impress his clandestine reader.

He writes: *I think of her every day, every single day, and at night I dream of her, that she is here again and quite changed, or quite the same, but always in those dreams I am quite accepting that she should come back and am only disappointed in myself that I could have been taken in by her absence. Then I wake to the bleak reality, and it's back to my thoughts and memories.*

My memories are triggered by the most ordinary, random things. Today it was a yellow rose in a neighbour's garden. My mother sent a bouquet of yellow roses when she was born. On the card she had written Many, many congratulations. *This was before she knew, of course, before anyone knew for certain, when the doctors were only discussing her amongst themselves, when there was still a tentative question mark on her notes. The roses were half-dead when the doctor finally told us. Then, after he'd left us alone with our new knowledge, I felt as if a trick had been played on us, some terribly clever illusion that makes you feel as though all sound, all animation, all colour and light had been vanished from the world. I had an idea that if I were to move, to go to Gaye, to hold her, the illusion could be broken and everything would be as it was a few moments ago. But I couldn't bring myself to test such a theory. I only stood there, beside her bed, beside the cot where our daughter slept, staring at the dying roses. I remember thinking how they should be removed, that the nurses had been thoughtless in not taking them away. They were a symbol of something, or so it seemed in that moment, no longer merely drooping flowers but something representing all the pain and trouble in the world. I sensed Gaye watching me. I guessed what she was thinking.*

A yellow petal dropped to the floor and I imagined stooping to pick it up because there would be control and purpose in such action. Instead I lifted our daughter from her cot and she was silent, a good, placid baby, and I gazed at her, studied her, wanting to see something in her face that would prove the doctor wrong.

Her name was Emily. There are photographs of Emily on the sideboard in the dining room, the room used least of all. Although it's an unspoken agreement between David and Gaye that photographs of Emily should be displayed, neither wants to be reminded all the time. It's right that they should be allowed those moments of forgetfulness, brief as they are. So Emily smiles out into a cold, airless room, although I keep her company sometimes. She's not here, of course, but I feel the photographs of their child help me to know David and Gaye better.

Gaye and David were married five years after meeting in the nightclub, a church wedding and Gaye wore a white dress with a big hooped skirt and a fitted bodice and a ribbon sash tied in a bow around her tiny waist. She carried a bouquet of white roses and a rose thorn snagged her finger so that her rayon skirt became spotted with blood. Not that she cared, not that anyone noticed—Gaye was so vibrant (in the wedding photos Gaye believes she looks maniacal) everyone commented on how happy she looked. And there, at her side, is David, handsome man, a serious foil to Gaye's smiling. Few suspect him of anything other than a certain propensity towards introspection. But when he was on his knees at the altar, the scent of white roses sweetening the tired church air, he prayed with all his heart that his marriage would work and the prayer went *help me God, help me God, help me God,* so that he hardly heard the words the priest said, or Gaye's responses, or even his own vows; all was drowned out by that three word chanting, his heart racing along to its desperate beat.

And three months later, one wet and sullen autumn afternoon, a few days after his birthday, Gaye told him that she was pregnant. They gazed at the pregnancy test together and he could sense Gaye's excitement, although she tried to keep it to herself, still a little unsure of how things ought to be between them; but all he could think of was how it seemed to him that God had listened in church and that this was His answer: a child. He was to be a father and fatherhood would straighten him out, once and for all.

In his study, David picks up his pen again and writes *When Emily was a few weeks old I took her to the church where I was married. I thought that if I sat and prayed in the peace and quiet with Emily sleeping beside me in her pram then I might come to some understanding; but it was a Tuesday afternoon, and the church doors were locked and there was no one around. I felt like a fool, and my half-baked idea that I could find answers in a building became even more risible as Emily began to cry, already hungry again, missing her mother who I had left sleeping. I all but ran home and at least this speed, the pram's jolting, surprised her out of her crying. I wanted to think of the church's locked doors as symbolic; they weren't, or at least only of my shallow, self-centred faith. At home, as Gaye fed Emily, I didn't tell her where we'd been and I told myself that we had only been for a walk, that I had incidentally walked up the church path and that incidentally its doors were locked and I was only mildly disappointed. I would try again another day, but even as I told myself this I knew that the moment had passed. Because, after all, the locked doors were symbolic; for all my rational arguments I knew that I was out in the cold.*

I watch as David writes a little more in his diary. Then he closes the book and gets up, going to the window to look out on his garden. He knows that Gaye wants his brother to paint his picture of their lawn and flowers and trees, and if Gaye wants the painting then it shall be painted. He decides not to care; it's just a picture after all. He thinks of Luke; Luke once said that Ralph's paintings were representative of the crassness of the twenty-first century and that their popularity shouted of all that was wrong with British culture. 'His paintings are lazy and half-cocked,' Luke said.

That David might be offended by this criticism didn't occur to Luke, although he was offended, offended too by the bitchy note in his voice, the snide way he glanced at him. They had been in bed and perhaps the lunch-time sex had been too rushed, perhaps David hadn't been attentive enough, too distracted by the ordinary preoccupations of work. They were mid-relationship, after all; passion and excitement were over-with and the forced, false tenderness of a love affair that was dying was a little way in the future. As Luke denigrated his brother's art, David had begun to dress, thinking that he should say something to defend Ralph, or at least reassure Luke that he was still loved. But they were at the mid-point of their affair and so he said nothing.

I have seen Luke. He came to the house and there was a brief, quietly intense scene between him and David. Luke cried and David told him how sorry he was, although anyone could see that this crying, angry boy only scared him. 'Listen,' David said, 'you'll find someone else, someone better than me.' He meant the kind of someone who was certain of his right to make love to another man: someone who was shameless; David is certain such men exist. He took Luke's hands in his, squeezed his fingers and ducked his head to smile into the boy's teary face. 'I'm too old,' David told him, and although he hadn't meant to say this he knew that it was the truth. He belonged to another age, an age when men kept quiet about themselves.

He had never told Luke about Emily, only that he'd had a daughter and that she had died and the way he told Luke this—quick to the point of curtness—left the boy in no doubt that he wouldn't unburden himself further, much as Luke longed for such confidences. Such discipline David has! Such correctness and rigour! He is sure that one day this restraint will kill him. But that's all right: it's no more than he deserves.

◆   ◆   ◆

David leaves his study and I follow him into the bathroom. I watch him urinate and I feel like a small child, ghosting her father, keeping hard on his heels so that she might not miss a single word or gesture she could learn from, knowing that everything this grown man does is right. David shakes away the last drops and zips his fly, flushes the lavatory, puts its seat down and washes his hands. In the mirror above the basin I see him frown at his reflection; he believes he has lost his good looks because he is so gaunt now and so lined—he pulls at the skin around his eyes as though he could stretch the lines away, as though his face was made of some easy-going cloth that could be tugged into shape. He makes his distorted face smile because he has heard that if one smiles—no matter what one feels inside—then the soul is somehow tricked into happiness. He snorts and drops his hands to his sides. He wonders if he should start to dye his hair.

We go into the dining room where he picks up one of the photographs of his daughter, the one in which she is five years old and her hair is tied up into bunches with tartan ribbons. Her hair was so fine—fly-away-hair—and the ribbons slipped from it and were easily lost. He traces his finger along her hair's parting and he can smell her, clean after a bath, after he has spent time drying her unruly, peach-scented hair; she is in bed, listening sleepily as he reads about the Princess who lets down her hair from the tower. He is lying beside her, so tired he might sleep, and the book of fairy tales might fall from his hands and startle him awake; but for now he lies beside her, watching her eyelids flutter ineffectually against sleep. He should go on watching her, but he won't; he doesn't know the future and so doesn't appreciate what he has; so he edges away from her and prepares to stand up carefully, inch by inch in order not to disturb her. He wants to be away, to be free to get on with something else, and this is hard to believe now, with the terrible advantage of hindsight.

He looks down at the photograph and thinks about what he has just written in his diary, those pallid phrases that don't begin to express how it feels to be him in all his guilt and wickedness; for all his writing he is as lost as ever.

After a moment he puts the picture down again, straightening its angle a little so that it's in line with the others.

◆   ◆   ◆

With all his control, all his self reliance, David would have made a good army officer, just as I was a good army nurse, although that may be hard to credit when I am so terrified of everything. If I had met David during the war I would have recognised him as someone to compete against. I had decided from the very start to treat the war as a game I could win, to throw myself into it with all my energy and focus because I believed that's how I would survive. Half-heartedness got you nowhere; moaning, complaining, pretending to suffer from neuralgia—I was above all that. That was how my war began, anyway. By its end many of my colleagues were afraid of me, some of my patients too, those who had no understanding.

I remember that Michael frowned when I told him how afraid they were. 'How could they be afraid of you? Weren't you helping them? Couldn't they see how much good you were doing?' His expression became even more intense and he took my hand between both his own. 'Even before we met I loved you!'

'Yes,' I said. Yes.

'I mean it, Eddie! During the war . . .' *During the war.* He hardly ever said this. After a little while he went on, 'During the war I sometimes used to wonder what I would do if I survived—if I would marry and have children . . . But I couldn't imagine myself with some ordinary girl—someone who couldn't begin to understand. And even if she wanted to understand I knew I couldn't even try to explain. So then there'd be this gulf between us, and all the bloody mess would be on my side, the sweet babies and the warm hearth on hers and she would look across at me and wonder why she had married such a freak. And then I heard about you. I heard about you and thought that nothing would matter if only I could find you because you *would* understand—better than anyone. It wouldn't matter if I was a freak . . .'

'Because we are fellow freaks,' I said, and he laughed as if he might cry.

We had been discharged from the hospital, from the army. We were merely two civilians sitting in a café, the pot of tea we had lingered over cold between us. We had set our wedding date but there were bans to be read, a hiatus to get through before we could begin to be together, and we had nowhere to go except Michael's bleak room in a lodging house—where propriety banned us from being so absolutely alone—or my father's house where Donald watched us with a kind of puzzled irritation, barely able to conceal his suspicions of Michael. I had the feeling that he didn't believe his story about his father; I sensed that he listened hard to every word

Michael said, so that I would find my own ears straining to hear some quality in his voice that would betray him, and I think this listening of mine made my father even more suspicious.

Peter didn't care if Michael was a fraud or not; during his visits he became garrulous, far more animated than he ever was when he was alone with only Donald and me.

During one visit, close to our wedding, Peter asked, 'Is the Major handsome, Eddie? Should I be proud to be seen out and about with him?' Peter stood up and made his careful way towards Michael. Standing no more than a few inches away from him, the toes of their shoes almost touching, he said, 'May I?'

He lifted his hands to Michael's face, quickly and lightly feeling around his eyes and nose and mouth; then he held his head between his palms, frowning. 'Well, Major, I can't say that helped very much—I suppose I need more practice. But you didn't flinch, I like that—it tells me a lot, your not flinching.' Stepping back and allowing his hands to fall to his sides he said briskly, 'I've been thinking. Why don't you ask me to be your best man?'

Coolly my father said, 'Peter, Michael may have someone else in mind.'

'Do you have someone else in mind, Michael? And who might that someone be, after all? You never speak of family—apart from the dead surgeon.'

Donald snorted but Peter held up his hand imperiously. 'Ask me to be your best man, Michael.'

'Will you be my best man, Peter?'

'Yes, Michael, of course, I would be delighted. Honestly—I think we will become the dearest of friends! Don't you think so, Eddie?'

Of course, he didn't expect me to reply. His blind eyes were on Michael as though he could see him as clearly as I could. He was smiling and I realised then that the war had changed him in a way I hadn't noticed before: he had lost that lanky awkwardness of his adolescence; he was poised, as though blindness had made him the man he had aspired to be when we were children, when it seemed he had wanted some special edge over me.

Michael gazed back at him, such a look that you would think I'd had enough experience to interpret; but you would be forgetting how young

I was and that my experiences had been extraordinary enough to be worthless. I think, though, that my father recognised what I did not because he said, 'Peter, why don't you and I leave Edwina and Michael in peace?' And his voice was too sharp, not matching his words at all.

Peter turned to him. For a moment I thought he would dismiss him as he so often did in those days. But I think he realised that he had gone a little too far, given too much away—more at least than he had intended to. He sighed. 'Of course, father. Of course we must leave them be for now.'

CHAPTER 5

~

Shortly before Michael and I were married he leased a shop on Thorp High Street that had lately been a draper's and still smelt of new cloth. We were to be antique dealers, because, as Michael said, what else did we know? Above the shop—a single, large room with a smaller stock room behind—was a flat consisting of a bedroom, a sitting room and a kitchen. These rooms were gloomy, poky, there were mouse droppings along the skirting boards and a mass of dead flies on the window sills. There was a smell of miserable old women, I sensed the failure they left behind, the bitterness of it, and believed that their defeat would overwhelm me. During my first visit I turned to Michael, who was drawing back the dusty curtains in the bedroom. He was smiling; he grinned at me through the displaced, hectic dust motes and went into the kitchen. I heard him opening and closing cupboards; he turned on the tap, fiddled with the ancient-looking gas oven. I heard him laugh for no reason other than joy and excitement. This was to be our home. He didn't sense the ghosts.

He turned to me. 'What'd you think?'

'I think we need some furniture.'

'We don't need much—a table, a *bed* . . .' He stepped towards me and drew me into his arms. 'I'm trembling.' He laughed again and stood back. 'Trembling! My God!' All at once he held my face in his hands. 'Edwina, it will be all right, won't it?'

I remember that the floorboards were stained with white paint. Through their cracks I could see into the empty shop below as I lay on my side, nose to nose with him because he wanted to hold me, feel the full length of my body against his. Although we were alone, although no one was listening for any noise we might make, he was too nervous for anything but kisses. And he was trembling, and on a rush of breath he said, 'What they said about you was true, wasn't it?'

He was thinking of that creature his men had invented, the Dark Angel, a figure that might have stepped out on the stage of some silly revue with crow-black wings and an extinguished halo and a beatific, sweet, sad smile. She would walk the hospital corridors, through the dressing stations, taking in each man with a glance. If she reached out to you then you were a goner no matter what, but you shouldn't be scared, no, only relieved, even comforted, but not scared, although you showed all the signs of fear. No, you should just go along with her: she knows what's best, after all, knows, as you do, that some lives are not worth living.

But there was only part of the truth in this and of course the men had built me up and made me larger than life when really I was—and am— ordinary and rather plain and scared.

I held him closer, wanting to make him still and to put all thoughts of angels out of his head. I held him so close it was as though I could feel his heart beating in opposition to mine; I felt how slight he was, his hardness against my groin, and despite his fear I wanted him so badly and couldn't help but groan and press myself closer and closer, never close enough so that I cried out and my insides became soft as hot wax and my hands scrambled to undo his clothes.

'Edwina . . .' He drew away, his eyes so dark I saw my face reflected. How intent I looked! How determined not to be thwarted in this! Perhaps I frightened him because he held my face between his hands and whispered, 'I need you to tell me that what they said was true—'

I kissed him, silencing him. I undid his clothes and hoisted up my skirts and climbed astride him; I closed my eyes to shut him out and rode him with all my strength. Who cared about truth then? Sex vanquished all thought, all memory, just as I guessed it might.

◆   ◆   ◆

And so we made up for lost time, making each other bruised, sore; I got splinters in my palms, my knees, tiny daggers of paint-stained wood that he would pick out before kissing the wound with his pale, delicate mouth. He took the lead from me and we were pioneers; no one, ever, had done the things we did; I wondered how anyone could do such things and still go to work or be dutiful in any way; no one would want to do anything but this. We even banished the ghosts, or at least the stink of them; our new home came to smell only of sex.

My father came to inspect where I would be living, Peter accompanying him, because, as he told us himself, he wouldn't be left out. I remember how Peter's nostrils flared as he entered what was to be our bedroom. I imagine he pictured us naked on the floor, that he knew where Michael's hands had been on me—everywhere. There wasn't an inch of me he hadn't stroked or kissed or sucked. 'Keep your eyes open so that I might kiss them, too,' Michael had said. Impossible, although we tried; I remember how his face changed as it hung suspended above mine, how hard his expression was as he tried to judge the right moment to kiss my flickering, blinking eye. Frustrated, he would sigh, his breath warm on my face. 'It's a matter of trust,' he said. I nodded, mute with the anxiety that he might think less of me for my failure.

Peter's nostrils flared but he made no comment, except to say, 'Will you be happy here, Michael?'

'Of course!' Michael put his arm around my waist and pulled me to him. Earlier that day we had made love and the memory of it was still alive in him, crowding out any other thought or feeling he might have. For a few hours after the act Michael was impervious to ironic subtleties.

But Peter wouldn't give up. He said, 'Won't you be terribly bored?'

'No!' Michael laughed at the very idea. 'We'll be too busy. I'm going to buy a van—get out on the road again, auctions, house sales . . .'

Peter raised his eyebrows. 'How exciting—I only wish I could come with you.'

Because sex had made him forget himself, Michael said rashly, 'You could if you want to.'

'Oh, I'd just be a burden.'

'No, not at all—'

'Are you sure? Because it would be fun, I think—get me out of the house—'

As though bored of this exchange, Donald said, 'Peter, don't tease Michael now.'

'I wouldn't dream of teasing him. I could be Michael's mascot. People would remember the man with the poor, blind partner. Also, Michael could name his price for granny's old whatever and they'd be so desperate to get rid of the sad, discomforting sight of me they'd accept without a quibble.'

Michael grinned. 'Genius.'

'Sounds like dishonest nonsense to me,' Donald said. But he only sounded mildly exasperated; such an idea was absurd, after all. But I knew from Michael's expression that Peter would become his partner; Michael looked like a man who had been the brunt of a practical joke, the worrying repercussions of which had only just begun to sink in. Peter turned towards me and smiled as though he had won the first round of a long and complicated game.

◆   ◆   ◆

I walk round and round Gaye's lawn and my anxiety only recharges itself. Gaye comes out, her cat at her heels, and I stop as the cat arches her back, her fur standing on end as she senses me. I step towards Gaye and the cat spits and hisses. I hiss back. Gaye seems imperious to me, but then I notice that she is holding herself rather stiffly, her gaze diverted away from mine; she can see me, I am certain, but doesn't want to believe in me.

Ralph has followed Gaye into the garden. He says, 'At least pussy agrees that you have a ghost.'

Gaye scoops the cat into her arms and says with a forced lightness, 'Will you sketch the garden first? What's the procedure?'

'The procedure?' He laughs, only to glance around; his gaze rests on a horse-chestnut tree, his eyes narrowing as he draws on his cigarette. At last he says, 'I'll take some photographs.' Turning to her he smiles sadly, thinking that really he has no right to call himself an artist, he has decided that he is a fraud. Today he agrees with every criticism he's ever had, thinking how perceptive his critics are.

Gaye manages to smile back at him, thinking how handsome he is. After all, despite me—and of course she doesn't truly believe in me—she is happier today, as happy as Gaye allows herself to be. Later she is to meet Noel in the hotel she has come to think of as a kind of no man's land, neutral territory where sex with a man who is not her husband doesn't provoke the guilt it should. Thorp Travel Lodge does not exist in real life. Noel only exists in the brief hours of anticipation and then when he is actually with her, and later for a little while in her memory of the afternoon's sex.

She places the cat down and it runs into the house, away from me. Gaye says, 'Shall I leave you to it?'

Ralph nods, thinking about the light and shade the trees cast. I stand beside him; he would be in my shadow if I had such a thing. He is wearing a short-sleeved shirt and his forearms are very tanned; I can see the tail of the dragon trailing below his sleeve's neat hem. He has a memory of the tattooist's intent expression as he bowed his head to his arm; the man was so tough-looking, his head shaved, studs in his nose and ears and lips, there were runic shapes tattooed on his neck and curling around his ear. This man should have been a warrior, Ralph thought at the time, because he appeared so much scarier than him. Yet it was Ralph who had been trained to stealthily cut throats, him with his poster-boy looks. The dragon would fool no one. He remembers that the tattooist was gentle and so silent that the experience of having his skin decorated was dream-like and the pain of it hardly disturbed him at all.

Gaye goes into the house to prepare for adultery. I leave her be and Ralph traces my steps around the garden. We both think about our youth: sex and war; we have much in common, Ralph and me.

Ralph re-lives crouching in an alley in Belfast; there is a smell of dog piss and rain and of Sunday roasts; he can hear *Radio One is Wonderful* and he is tense and watchful and yes, afraid. This is the UK in 1981 and here he is, hard against a yard's red brick wall, alive to the idea of a bullet in his back. He stands up, makes his way out onto the street, keeping close to the wall, his weapon across his chest. He is ready but the enemy has slipped away, lost in the warren of back alleys. A mongrel dog sniffs at his feet. The rain begins to fall in earnest and he and his patrol move on. Now he is on his ship in the South Atlantic. There is to be a proper war and he wonders how he will behave, afraid that he may let himself down. Most of all he is afraid that he will feel as he did on the streets of Belfast, that nothing is worth so much. The world has become washed of colour. He thinks of birds he might paint to relieve the greyness, the first time he has thought of such an outlandish occupation.

It is 1918 and I am in a field hospital in France—no more than a large tent so there is a smell of sun-baked canvas and flattened grass and lemon-balm. And the lieutenant in the last bed stinks so badly that I know he must die. I, of course, am immortal. I won't die, I won't. I help the gangrenous lieutenant take a sip of water. He is afraid of me, as some of them are, although he is trying to be brave, even grateful, knowing as he does how dire his predicament is.

Ralph takes a camera from a bag he carries on his shoulder and begins to take photographs. He has left the South Atlantic and is wholly here, an idea of how he might portray Gaye's garden crystallising. There will be birds, of course, but dull, English, less abstract birds; these birds will not be what the painting is about; rather it will be about absence and loss. He grunts; it will be a painting of a garden, that's all. Nothing more, nothing less.

CHAPTER 6

~

Michael and Peter began their partnership shortly after we were married; going out together early each morning, returning late each afternoon in the van Michael had bought. I would work in the shop and from time to time I would sell a table or a sideboard or a figurine of a crinolined girl. In the shop there was a wall of clocks and each morning before he left Michael made sure that they all displayed the correct time. They chimed not quite in unison so that each hour there was a cacophony of ding-dong bells. I thought those bells would drive me mad as I waited for Michael to return, afraid that Peter had somehow spirited him away. I would imagine what it was like for the two of them alone together in the van, bumping along in the high-up cab as they drove to this or that house or auction room. I imagined the conversations they would have, the smiles they exchanged, the cigarettes they shared.

I should say something more about Michael's history, because that might help, an explanation might shed some light on what is to follow. He had been born Alfred Booth on Christmas Eve 1895, in a workhouse to a woman who was not the sweet wan thing of melodrama but a scrawny, hard-case drunk, and this was her fifth live child, one she hardly knew she was carrying until the pains came and the urge to push him out was so great, water and slime gushing between her legs so surprisingly and then this tough infant: a survivor, one who knew not to make too much fuss, who had secreted himself away for nine months and wasn't about to give up now. The woman from the next bed wrapped him in a torn strip of sheet, she being the only midwife; the workhouse staff were asleep or away somewhere else, this being Christmas and a time for those with homes to go to.

'I'll keep this one,' his mother told her makeshift nurse, and the woman agreed that yes, he was bonny and worth holding on to. But before the blood dried on her son's head, she was dead, her last breath warm and stinking on his face. Alfred Booth (*father unknown*) became an orphan and lived for fourteen years until the man he called Uncle found him on King's Cross Station, where he was re-born.

Michael told me, 'The second night with Uncle, shaking like a jelly, I crept into his bedroom. He'd given me pyjamas to wear—they were so soft, so warm and stripy and soft—and I stood in the dark by his bed wondering if I should take them off, or if that was something he would want to do himself. I stood by his bed and I thought that I could leave, that I could just run away. Except I had nowhere to go, except that Uncle had given me hot chocolate which I'd never tasted before. And he'd given me the pyjamas, and the sense that he was kind and wouldn't mind me so much as others seemed to mind, that we'd be all right together. He was snoring. When I climbed in beside him he rolled over and almost crushed me, and he cried out, these funny little noises—*oh oh oh*!

I remember Michael told me this on one long breath, rushed, wanting to get it out as though he was afraid I would interrupt him and cause him to lose momentum. But I didn't interrupt, just waited for him to go on, to trust me with every detail, but he stopped. I remember we were lying on our sides, face to face, and his eyes searched mine for understanding. At last he said, 'Do you think I should keep quiet? That I shouldn't tell you everything? But it seems to me that there was Uncle, and then there was the war, and now there is you. I have lived a series of lives, and each life is separated from the other, a discrete island where I live alone, surrounded by ghosts—'

'I'm not a ghost—'

He pressed his fingers against my lips. 'I think my life with you is different. I'm not alone now, and I can tell you about those other lives because I didn't live them—a stranger did. And he was quite brave, I think, but wrong-headed and I wish I could forgive him for the things he did, but I can't.'

I took hold of his wrist and lifted his hand from my mouth. 'What did he do?'

He moved away from me to lie on his back, flinging his arm over his face, his fingers curling around the bars of bed. 'Nothing, I suppose. Nothing I can truly grasp hold of.' He laughed, suddenly and harshly. 'Besides, Peter says it doesn't matter now. Nothing matters anymore.'

I gazed at him. He had closed his eyes to further shut me out I think, because despite all that nonsense he spoke about other lives he was embarrassed at his confession; he had gone too far; and by invoking my brother's name he had brought Peter into bed with us: Peter along with Uncle and all the men he had ever fought with, all those bright-eyed lieutenants he had cared for and failed.

I got up; I put on my nightgown and went into the living room to sleep in a chair.

◆   ◆   ◆

Ralph is painting in the garden when David comes home. David sees his brother through the kitchen window as he fills the kettle and watches him for a while, thinking how unlike an artist—his idea of an artist—he looks. Ralph is smart, his clothes carefully chosen and expensive; he is clean-shaven and his hair is cut cleverly to hide the fact that he is balding. But Ralph is not vain, nor self-conscious, only supremely confident, and David all at once feels proud of his brother, a feeling he sometimes had as a child, although then it would quickly breakdown into resentment. Now he allows himself this fraternal pride, even thinking that perhaps it would be better if he could do away with his personal pride and allow Ralph to become his ally. Idly he imagines going to him and saying, 'I need your help.' Ralph would be astonished; he would also be pleased and would fall over himself to do all he could. David imagines his brother's all-out reaction and knows he could never go to him; it would be more than his life was worth.

Sensing he is watched, Ralph turns, raising his hand to David in greeting. David does a little tea-drinking mime and Ralph smiles and nods. He walks across the lawn towards the house as David spills biscuits on to a plate.

Today David sat in a church yard summoning the courage to seek out the priest who had conducted Emily's memorial service. He has had the idea that writing in his diary is not enough and that he should talk to someone who will not judge him—or at least not betray his judging—a man that he can unburden himself to, a godly man, because David imagines he would like to find God again, that somehow God is a comfort. The man who conducted Emily's service seemed at the time to radiate calm and goodness and the more David thinks about him the more he believes he will have the answers. So, today, quick with nervousness, he left his surgery and walked to the church that he'd believed he would never be able to set foot in again without his panic killing him. Indeed, he couldn't go inside, but somehow hoped the priest would sense his presence and come to him, such a childish hope, so desperate in its passivity. All the same he waited, glancing at the church doors as infrequently as he could.

As he waited, a man came by, a shabby, shuffling boy who kept his hands in the pockets of his army greatcoat, his fingers twitching beneath the cloth. David wondered if he had a weapon; kept wondering as the boy's concealed hands moved so furtively. He sat down beside David and told him about the voices he heard, the relentless, pitiless whines. Then the boy looked right at me. Recognising what I've become, his eyes grew big and he laughed, delighted, his fingers becoming still around the bloody piece of jagged glass in his pocket. I told him to go home, that all would be well. All will be well and all will be well and all manner of things will be well. The boy took notice; he stood up suddenly, laughing still, he didn't hear David call after him, he was thinking of the voices and how they could be silenced if he only concentrated. He left a splash of blood on the ground. Gazing at the blood, David groaned. He was tired; he wished more than ever to be comforted.

Ralph comes in to the kitchen, sits down at the table and says, 'How are you?' He thinks David looks ill, done in, that he has lost weight. It crosses Ralph's mind once again that David has HIV Aids. He imagines the fuss his patients would make, how afraid they would be of contracting such an infection so undeservedly. Ralph realises how shallow he is. His first thought should not be about the foolishness of strangers but about his brother's welfare. But it would be almost irresistible to say, 'David, I know you're queer.' *Queer*. Could he use a less insulting word? *Homosexual*, then. Gay. Although not entirely gay, of course. Bi-sexual. He is married, after all; he sired a child. Ralph sighs, ashamed; he thinks of David's child Emily as he often thinks of her, in a way he refuses to believe is trite or sentimental: as a light that has gone from the world, leaving a more impenetrable darkness.

'That was a big sigh,' David says. He smiles as he places a mug of tea in front of him and Ralph thinks how like their father he looks; even his words are their father's, the *big sigh* phrase used to invite confidences, a spilling out of troubles. Ralph imagines telling him about the nightmares that have returned after so many years.

As David sits down, Ralph says, 'I've been invited to a memorial service. It's to mark the anniversary of the Falkland's War.'

David nods. 'Will you go?'

'Dunno.' He sighs again and thinks of Mark Walker, a fellow officer who was wounded during the conflict. He and Walker have kept in touch sporadically over the years; recently Ralph wrote to ask him if he would be there at the Cathedral to mark the passing of the years. 'Yes,' Walker replied. 'Shall we go together?' They were once close friends, but Walker was wounded and his blood soaked through the hasty bandages and his face became pale as blue-veined marble so that he was untouchable, an outcast; Ralph cannot think of him without shuddering. He shudders now, and wraps his hands around the mug, needing its warmth.

Gently David says, 'I would go, if I were you, if there is a chance that it might help.'

'You think I need help?' Ralph laughs painfully. 'It shows, does it?' Meeting his brother's gaze he says, 'I have a dream—a nightmare—where I'm responsible for everything, *everything*, all the confusion, the bloody cock-ups, the deaths. And I just stand there, wringing my hands. No one *wrings their hands*, except I do, in the dream. I wring my hands uselessly, feeling so bloody helpless. And guilty. This terrible . . . *guilt*. Then I wake up, but the guilt hangs around . . .' He laughs again, embarrassed now because David is frowning, such concern on his face, such compassion that he doesn't deserve. He realises he's afraid of this intimacy, that it may lead to confessions and revelations, and so he says, 'Listen, forget it. I'm fine. A few old memories have been stirred up with all this anniversary business, that's all.'

David sips his tea. He remembers war as most civilians do, in short, dramatic scenes starring jump jets and air-craft carriers, green-faced, camouflaged men wading from landing crafts onto barbed-wired beaches, the acrobats, elephants and tumblers of this war or that. He cannot imagine what it would be like to be so terrified, only imagines that he wouldn't be brave enough, that his legs would fold beneath him, that he would vomit and shit and be utterly shamed. But he knows Ralph jumped ashore; Ralph ran up the beach—or crawled, perhaps, mimicking that Action Man, belly-and-elbow-and-knees quick-slow motion, stiff and agile at once. Perhaps Ralph's fear would have transformed into rage so that he was only determined on revenge; perhaps his training kicked in, as his trainers knew it would, and he became that perfect soldier: an unselfconscious killer. This idea allows David to be kinder to himself: if he had been so trained he would have been equally as brave.

Ralph says, 'So, how are you?'

David considers the truth, that he has been lonely and afraid of the future without Luke. Also that lately, since he and Gaye moved into this house, he has grieved for his daughter as much as he ever did, and wasn't time supposed to heal, to corrode the sharp edges of pain? Perhaps he should tell his brother about his slowly dawning need of a father confessor. Quickly he says, 'I'm thinking of giving up the practice.'

Ralph frowns in surprise. 'Oh? What will you do instead?'

Leave Gaye, he thinks. Sell this ghastly, haunted house. Use the money to buy a little place somewhere he wasn't known. He imagines a bedroom with a huge, soft bed, a living room full of books and paintings; and Luke would be asleep on the couch, or leaning against the wall in the little, cluttered kitchen watching as he cooked supper, chatting in that relaxed, friendly way some couples have and that they had never achieved during their time of snatched and furtive sex.

David draws breath, aware of Ralph watching him. 'I don't know what

I'll do. I haven't thought it through, not yet.' Then, by way of reciprocal confession, says, 'I suppose I'm afraid to think about it too much . . . That in the end I won't be brave enough to make a change—that I'll drop dead yanking on a decayed molar.'

David won't die like this, I know. I sit down beside him and suppress the urge to put my arms around him, proud of my self-control that spares me so much pain. I only gaze at him instead, allow myself to be love-sick for a moment. He looks through me to the window, towards his brother's easel.

All at once he says, 'Emily would have adored this garden, this house—it would have given her such a thrill to explore all the rooms, the attics. She would have been scared of the cellar, though—the steep steps, the darkness. I would have kept the cellar door locked . . .' He closes his eyes briefly and sees Emily standing on the lawn.

Turning to Ralph he says, 'I've started to write about her . . .' He stops because he hadn't meant to confess this, it seems almost an irrelevance. Besides, he's not even sure if the confession is true; after all he's not writing about Emily but about himself. All the same he goes on, 'I've started to write about her. I want to write as honestly as I can, to see if it helps.' He wants to say that when he writes about her it feels as though his search for his true feelings is like trying to undo the knots in a fine, silver chain and it is so hard, and may even be impossible because his thoughts are so clumsy, so burdened with self-justifications; and also the truth might be too condemning. His reader might think he is a shit.

David takes a biscuit and snaps it in two; he eats it slowly and self-consciously, as though his brother can hear his too-noisy chewing and swallowing. He has exposed himself, although he has an idea that he has done this too discretely, that Ralph may not have even realised that he has given so much away. He takes a mouthful of tea to wash the biscuit crumbs down and says, 'Anyway, anyway . . .' and smiles to make even less of himself and his confession. He thinks of all the words that were said to him at Emily's funeral, so kindly meant and so meaningless; the sentiments were irrelevant because no one in the world was like him; no one had ever grieved so uniquely, so exquisitely, so surprisingly. That was the key to his wickedness: that he should have been so surprised at the fathomless depth of this grief.

Ralph doesn't know what to say. I watch him struggle to find the right phrase, rejecting each one for its triteness. Part of him believes that silence is best, that his expression speaks for itself. He does indeed look sympathetic, but also pained because he's not as good at hiding his feelings as he likes to believe. Imagining reaching across the table and touching his brother's hand, he curls his own hand into a loose fist. The brothers haven't touched for years, since they last fought as young boys: David once blacked his eye; remembering this, Ralph's sympathy withers.

'David, have you ever thought of seeing a counsellor?'

David is relieved that Ralph has said something so useless; he's off the hook, they can move on. 'Stay for supper,' he says. 'I'm sure Gaye would like to discuss the painting.'

◆   ◆   ◆

The atmosphere between them becomes ordinarily uneasy and so I go upstairs, to the empty attics to rattle around in the cold and dim dusk like a good ghost. I need to be alone sometimes, without the distraction of the living and the belongings they surround themselves with. These unfurnished, superfluous rooms are my refuge, where I come closest to the state of sleeping. The State of Sleeping! Heaven, by any other name.

But even in this refuge I hear Gaye come home, the closing of the front door, her too cheerful call of hello to her husband, the rattle of her car keys on the hall table. I know that she will look into the mirror above the table and check for signs that might give away her adultery. Her cheeks will be flushed, her hair greasy from Noel's increasingly despairing touch; David will notice these things, and also that she is behaving giddily: she is as brittle and transparent as a Christmas bauble, just as intoxicatingly, cheaply beautiful. Nowadays, the only time David desires his wife is when she is so strung out on illicit sex. He wants a share of her excitement, his cut. When she walks into the kitchen and her guilt makes itself as obvious as a starling trapped in a room, he will want to fuck her and it would be the rough and frantic sex he imagines she craves from him. Instead of course they will be polite and he will refrain from sniffing her; he will ignore his hard-on.

I sit down on the attic floor. The light is becoming poorer; I think of Michael and pretend that I am a spiritualist, messing about with an upturned glass, the alphabet arranged around the edge of a felt-topped table. This charlatan calls out his name and then listens, straining to hear, refusing to believe he won't answer because he is only hidden somewhere, put away, not quite beyond the reach of those with special powers. 'Michael,' I say more softly, and I become cold, then colder and the hairs on my arms stand up. I hold my breath, become still enough not to scare him away. When I exhale the air is warm again.

CHAPTER 7

~

As well as going out in the van with Michael, Peter would visit us every Sunday. He would feel his way around the shop, tap-tapping his stick against the cherry wood desks and mahogany escritoires, putting his fingers in his ears and grinning when the clocks began to strike. Together, Michael and Peter had bought a musical box from a woman who told them that her husband couldn't bear the sound of it since his return from the war—that even the sight of it disturbed him. I imagine that they nodded, understanding her husband's eccentricity even if she didn't. The box played *The Minute Waltz* too quickly and to hear it was to feel as if you were coming down with a fever.

During one visit, lifting the lid and listening to this noise, Peter asked, 'Do you mind me coming here?'

'No!' I laughed, embarrassed that he could be so direct. 'No, why should I mind?'

Peter closed the musical box gently and glanced past me towards the door he knew led to our rooms where Michael was still in bed. He had slept badly, not the usual combative nightmares but more a restlessness that had him getting up to pace around the sitting room. Just before dawn I heard him go downstairs to the shop and I had the idea of following him and persuading him to come back to bed. But I was afraid to: I imagined that he was beginning to lose heart in our little venture and I didn't want to witness his listless apathy; I might be infected by it and then where would we be?

Tracing his fingers over the carved lid of the musical box, Peter said, 'And you don't mind that Michael and I go out together?'

After their outings in the van they had begun to visit a public house called *The Castle & Anchor*. Late in the evening Michael would return home to me with his clothes thick with the stink of cigarettes and beer and whiskey fumes on his breath, and it seemed as though he was containing some childish agitation; I put this down to the drink; he wasn't used to drinking.

'I don't mind that you and Michael go out,' I said. How dull I sounded, so resigned to the idea that a friendship should have come about between my husband and brother, so resigned in fact that Peter frowned at me.

'You shouldn't mind. You have the best of him, after all.'

He made Michael sound as though he was a thing that could be cut into pieces and doled out, a slice for me, a slice for him. Perhaps I should have told him this, made a joke of it, but that would have meant overcoming my wariness of him; Peter had always been a spiteful boy, always quick to sneak or take advantage of a perceived weakness. I thought back to the letters he had sent me during the war and knew that he could begin again his inquisitorial campaign against me whenever he cared to.

All at once he became bright. 'Listen. I've booked a table for lunch at The Grand. Call Michael—if we leave soon we won't be late.'

◆   ◆   ◆

I went upstairs and found Michael lying on our bed, staring at the ceiling. He turned to me as I closed the door softly. It seemed we both felt the need to be quiet because he whispered, 'What does he want?'

'To take us out to lunch. At the Grand Hotel.'

Michael closed his eyes. At last he said, 'Tell him . . .' He exhaled sharply. 'All right. I'll be down shortly.'

'We don't have to go, if you don't want to.'

He looked at me, holding my gaze as though he was on the brink of a confession. At last he said, 'Go downstairs, Eddie. Tell him I won't be a moment.'

◆   ◆   ◆

I hadn't been out with them alone before, there had always been my father to chaperone us. Without Donald's presence—the presence I suppose of an adult—it seemed to me that we barely knew how to conduct ourselves. In the Grand's restaurant as we ate consommé followed by roast beef followed by spotted dick, Michael barely spoke, Peter spoke too much, too loudly, and I, well I was rather like one of those anxious women who laugh for no particular reason except that they are nervous and afraid of causing some slight that might shame them forever.

As the waiter served coffee at the end of the meal Peter said, 'Michael, would you light me a cigarette?'

Michael did as he was asked, lighting the cigarette between his own lips before handing it to my brother. Peter smiled at him then turned to me. 'He has very dry lips, your husband. That's good, isn't it? We wouldn't want a slobberer.'

Michael glanced at the waiter who had heard all this, of course, who was keeping his face straight except perhaps for a slight raising of an eyebrow. 'Peter,' Michael said, 'there is an ash tray to your right, just above your table mat.'

Peter nodded impatiently. 'The Major's being very bourgeois. They shouldn't care that I get ash on their table cloth.'

'It seems a shame, that's all.'

'Major, you are a bore.'

'Don't call me that, please.'

'I'm sorry, *Michael*. But you know I don't believe in Michael. I bet your mother only ever called you Micky or Mick—a true bog-trotter's name.'

'My mother called me Michael.'

'All right. If you like.' Peter turned to me. 'What do you call him? I suppose you have a range of ways in which to address him. What, for instance, do you call him when you are . . . in bed?'

I laughed, of course, nervously glancing from Peter to Michael. Michael was lighting a cigarette; his hands shook a little. Catching my eye, he said, 'That's enough, Peter. You're behaving badly.'

'But I'm allowed to behave badly!'

'No, you're not.'

'Oh, please, Michael. Please allow me to be bad! Edwina doesn't mind. Edwina, you don't mind if I ask you this one thing?'

I tried to keep my voice light and only sounded foolish. 'Depends what it is.'

'Edwina, when you and Michael are alone together do you talk about me?'

'Why should we?'

'Oh, no reason. I just wouldn't like to think that I'm forgotten, that's all.' He drew on his cigarette then felt around for the ash tray, allowing ash to spill on the white cloth. From the corner of my eye I could see how still Michael was, how watchful. At last Peter said, 'I'll pay for lunch, of course. My treat.'

◆   ◆   ◆

Later, when Michael and I were alone together in our peaceful little flat, Michael led me into the bedroom and undressed me and laid me down on the bed and said such things as *my love, my darling girl, I love you, I love you so*, and he undressed himself so quickly a button was torn from his shirt and I remember thinking how I would have to crawl under the bed to find it, to stitch it back on again because we couldn't afford to lose even such a small thing; I thought all this as Michael made love to me, even imagined taking down my sewing box and finding the right needle and thread; I imagined pricking my finger and saw the ruby bead of blood as Michael climaxed and called out. *Oh Christ,* he called, *Sweet Jesus*, and he looked so pained that I closed my eyes, ashamed of him.

◆   ◆   ◆

Ralph came to the house again today. He is painting his picture in earnest now, he is absorbed, content, and he thinks hardly at all about the war he fought in, worries less about actions he didn't take. In fact he barely thinks of anything other than colour and shape and shadow and light; he fixes on the way the pattern of horse chestnut leaves changes on the lawn as the Earth takes its turn around the sun. The leaves are stencils; they are no more than the gaps between them; he works quickly, as quickly as he has ever worked; something in Gaye's garden has made him fervent:

fervently content—such a state exists, believe me.

Gaye is not an adulteress today. Today she gives me no peace but trails around the house, unable to settle because Ralph is painting her garden and his energy is everywhere like noise. She goes from room to room and in each room she senses him, his indifference to her. She goes upstairs; her bed is already made, already this morning there is nothing more to do. Impulsively she takes a shoebox of photographs from the wardrobe, only to put it down again on the tidied bed. For a moment she stands over the box and then lifts away its lid. There, face upwards, its corners creased, a picture of David and Emily demands to be noticed. I stand beside her. I find I am holding my breath.

Emily is three. David has lifted her into his arms so that they might make quicker progress across the beach. Rain pock-marks the sand, heavy drops that are the storm's advance troops. The rain will drench them if they don't hurry but Emily wants to stay—weather is nothing to her. The sea is everything. She would be a sea creature if she could, living deep beneath the troubled surface where there is only stillness, a weightless, slow-motion world. Over her father's shoulder she holds her hand out to the sea that is becoming more distant as her father begins to run, and her hand furls and unfurls, a grasping sea anemone. Longing transforms her and her mother knows that she must capture this expression, is seized by the idea that somehow this look will help her to understand her daughter more profoundly than she already does.

Gaye lifts the camera and calls for David to stop. Her hands shake only a little, her finger is firm on the button; she hears the click and whirl of shutter and film, and imagines that this photographic evidence will be a turning point. From now on her relationship with Emily will be as it should be, as she imagined motherhood to be when she was pregnant and full of ideals. She laughs. The sand shifts beneath her feet as she runs in David's footsteps and when they reach their car, when they are all safely out of the storm, she kisses him, her new happiness incidentally spilling out over her husband.

David wonders why her eyes are so excited, why she looks so much like she did in the times before Emily, and he hooks a wet strand of her hair back from her face so that he might see her better. He knows nothing of Emily's longing, or of its expression that Gaye believes she has caught; he thinks how lovely his wife is and how they have not made love for so long, so long; such a long time he believes he will see changes in her, the reshaping of her body by the weeks and months they have wasted. 'I love you,' he says. The car rocks in the storm's blast and Emily cries out for the sea.

Gaye picks up the photograph and I exhale. She sinks down onto the bed, holding the photo in her lap. The picture is blurred; it has a ghostly quality, perhaps because of the rain, perhaps because David didn't stand quite still enough. Her daughter's face is a pale, sad round against the rain-splattered dark of David's shirt. The camera lied, or at least held back the whole truth; she circles that pale face with her finger, remembering her disappointment when she first tore the photo from the developer's envelope. This wasn't evidence, merely an image of a little girl in her father's arms.

But now for the first time she notices how David holds his hand above Emily's head, his fingers a curled, protective canopy, and how he looks straight at the camera—at her—with such acceptance. Before when she has studied this picture her eyes had only ever skimmed over him, concentrating her efforts on seeing only what she had hoped to see. Now she sees David, younger and almost unrecognisable. She had forgotten he could look like that.

He said, 'I love you,' and the car rocked in the blast of wind. She didn't hear her daughter's cry; there were certain noises she had become deaf to. She remembers only that David suddenly took her face between his hands and that his voice was quick and intense, surprised, as if he hadn't believed in his love until that moment.

I sit down on the bed. The shoebox between us is full of photos, almost all of David and Emily, although there is a picture of Gaye and David on their wedding day, a stray from the white, faux-leather album stored out of sight and mind. Bride and groom hold champagne glasses in a staged toast. Gaye will not look at this picture; after so many years she now finds herself embarrassed by her wedding day: her dress, which was too fussy, her hectic smile and her determination for everything to be wonderful, the speeches that were too short or too long, and her father's white-faced nervousness. Most of all she is embarrassed by David's awkwardness in the photographs: he is so stiff, his smile that of a man preparing bravely for bad news. No, she won't look at this photo, but rifles though the box in search of Emily, a true likeness. Her hands are quick, quicker as she begins to believe that the search is futile.

But if she looks hard enough she will see Emily, if she is calm and allows herself to remember properly; and so she takes a breath and picks out a picture randomly. There is Emily at a birthday party and there is a pink cake in the shape of a figure eight and the little girl beside her is blowing out the pink candles whilst Emily grins into the camera. What was that eight year old called? *Amelia:* Amelia who was Emily's best friend for a time, whose mother had asked Gaye why she hadn't had an amniocentesis test.

'It wasn't offered, I was too young,' Gaye replied. How matter of fact she had been—matching Amelia's mother's tone, although she had been astonished and her insides had loosened as though the woman had smacked her across the face. She could hardly speak after that; hardly join in with the happy birthday singing or the gossip with the other mothers. Out of her cowardly need not to make a scene her face had become a smiley mask and all she could think of was how quick her betrayal had been, how willing her concession that a choice could have been made.

That evening, when David came home and he had put Emily to bed and read her a story and asked her about the party, the cake and the presents and the games, his usual, gentle inquisition, he had come down to find her crying in the kitchen, her tears falling into the casserole she was preparing.

He stood behind her, putting his arms around her waist and holding her tightly. 'Emily had a good time today,' he said. And then, 'Don't be sad, my darling girl, not when I love you so much.'

Did he really say that? Why not—isn't that what husbands say to their weeping wives? And he was always kind: the other mothers at Amelia's party were so jealous of her being married to him—David, the thoughtful, beautiful man. Other husbands were plain and unthinking, ordinary in fact. But David might have stepped out of a Hollywood film, one made for women who haven't quite got over their disappointments nor yet found ways to live with them, one where the lead man can say *I love you so much* and not fluff his inflection or burn with self-consciousness.

Whatever he said, she remembers that she allowed him to hold her so closely for only as long as she could bear—a few seconds at most. Then she freed herself and wiped her eyes with her fingers and said, 'I'm all right. All right. Don't fuss.'

Gaye takes another photo from the shoebox. This picture is of two-year-old Emily and David on a swing. She remembers this bright sunny day in the park close to her parents' house for no other reason than she has always had this photo to remind her of it. Emily is wearing a pinafore her mother made from navy corduroy—quite sombre but rather classy and expensive-looking teamed as it is with red jumper, tights and shoes. As if to keep with the mood of her outfit for once Emily isn't smiling but gazes seriously at the camera. David is distracted—Gaye can't remember what had caught his eye just as she took the photograph; nothing, perhaps, only a child calling out, or a bird taking off, a leaf caught up in a gust of wind. His face is in profile, his hair ruffled by that breeze, his hand going to smooth it down, his other hand pressed against Emily's body, holding her safe. In a moment he will stand up and lift Emily onto his shoulders and the three of them will walk back to her mother's house. She will hold David's hand because they held hands quite naturally in those days.

There are more pictures, many:

Here is Emily dressed as a lamb for the school nativity play, David adjusting her crepe-paper fleece.

Here is Emily, five, ecstatic in their bed on Christmas morning, David bleary-eyed beside her.

Here is David alone.

She looks at his picture for a long time; it was taken last year, not by her, she had long since given up her camera. They had been at a barbeque—a cousin of David had been celebrating a milestone birthday; neither of them had wanted to go, both of them feeling an effort should be made. That effort is etched deep into David's face; she hasn't noticed before but he has aged so. She puts the picture down and her hand goes to her face; she has aged too, of course she has.

The box of photos is put aside; the picture of Emily and David on the beach that rainy afternoon placed on top of the others. She should put it in a frame, perhaps, but where would she place it? Beside her bed, she thinks, and wonders if she is ready for such a step.

Going to the window she looks down onto the garden where Ralph is working. He is indifferent to her, but hasn't always been so—she remembers a time when they looked at each other speculatively. She used to imagine how her life might have been if she had met Ralph in that nightclub instead of David: her heart would have been harder, she thinks, she would have laughed more and cared less, such a bright and breezy life she would have had, married to David's bright and breezy brother, and all David's earnest intensity would have been unimaginable to the wife she might have been. Ralph's wife would have laughed, aghast at the idea of being married to such a quiet man as David, whose seriousness scared her, if truth be told, whose shy heart seemed too closely guarded.

Ralph senses that he is being watched and turns to look up at her. She lifts her hand in greeting and he smiles his wide, careless smile. He was Emily's favourite uncle by a very long mile, a more playful copy of her Daddy. For Emily to walk down the street holding the hands of these two men who looked so alike but were, in fact, so different, thrilled her because their difference was her secret, something no one could guess just by looking.

Gaye opens the window and calls down, 'Would you like some lunch?'

'I thought you'd never ask,' Ralph calls back, and Gaye grins, and feels like a girl again because for a moment it's easy to pretend that her life had taken a difference course. I am standing close, and I brush my fingers against her arm but she doesn't notice me, only feels a breeze from the open window. I will bide my time; she will acknowledge me soon enough.

CHAPTER 8

∾

I am in the churchyard where yesterday David and I encountered the mad boy with the broken glass in his pocket. I was hoping that the boy might be there so that I might be recognised again, but there is only the rusty spot of blood by the bench and that peculiar smell that those who are very sensitive leave behind. The priest is here, though, Father Purcell, the man David had so wanted to come to him without being asked, and I follow him into his church. His ghostly congregation fills every pew. These days most of the other dead wear modern dress: I have become a grand old dame of ghosts; the few of my contemporaries that remain I avoid—we know each other too well and even the very depths of depravity become boring given enough time.

I watch as the good priest Father Purcell prays, his fingers busy worrying his rosary; he hunches himself protectively around this work, making himself small, a little black knot of anxious life. He knows we dead are here, although some of us make more of an impression on him than others. Me, for instance, he knows very well that I am watching him. I have an urge to sit beside him to whisper something like *forgive me, Father*. Hah! I won't be forgiven, not by him, not by anyone.

I don't pray but think, as I occasionally do, about insanity, that perhaps sometimes it's infectious. My thought is that if we live with the insane their ways become normal to us, acceptable, we begin to behave in such ways ourselves. It's an ordinary enough idea I suppose.

But let's get on. I should say that my father died a few weeks after that lunch at the Grand Hotel, how a frail vessel burst inside his heart and his knees buckled and his expression was one of fleeting surprise, like that of a man felled by a sniper's bullet. So quick, so easy; no time to be afraid or to dread the process; Michael said we should all die such a death.

A policeman came to inform me. It was early evening; we had closed the shop and had retreated to bed, the relief of quick sex over with so that when the officer came we were only lying side by side, just our feet touching, the smoke from our cigarettes merging. We were peaceful and lazy as stopped clocks and it was at such times that I would find myself thanking God for my existence. When we heard the hammering on the shop door, when the policeman called out his sturdy hello, I felt as though God had thrown my thanks in my face.

The policeman—Sergeant Thomas—said, 'I'm sorry, Mrs Hardcastle.' He looked up as Michael handed me a cup of sweet tea, saying, 'It's a terrible shock for your wife.'

Tea was handed to the sergeant, too. Michael had become Major Hardcastle again, de-briefing those who had returned from their mission, his voice authoritative and solicitous at once. 'What's next, Sergeant?'

'We need one of you to identify the body, sir.'

'Of course. I'll do it,' Michael said.

I kept my head bowed over my tea cup, silent as a shy girl amongst strangers; I hardly knew whether I cared that my father was dead. Michael nudged my foot with his. 'Edwina, my dearest . . .' And Sergeant Thomas cleared his throat, colouring, charmed by this portrayal of manly sensitivity.

I stood up. 'I'll identify the body.'

Michael and the policeman exchanged looks, decided silently, together, that to avoid unnecessary argument or hysterics this should he allowed.

We went with Sergeant Thomas to the hospital morgue where a man turned down the sheet that covered my father's face, standing back wordlessly so that I could step forward and claim him as my own. I had half believed that my father had staged his death, knowing that I would go along with the deceit and confirm that a stranger's corpse was his. But this was Donald, my father who had not escaped so audaciously, and I nodded at the mortuary assistant and the man drew up the sheet again. It seemed proper that there was no exchange of words, that the business should be so cold and quick and decisive. I walked out of that freezing room where each breath hung suspended and Michael and the sergeant followed me, temporarily awed by my new status.

It was only then that I remembered Peter.

'My brother—'

Sergeant Thomas placed a hand on my arm as if to calm me. 'It's all right—a neighbour is with him.'

'Then we must go to him,' Michael said. He turned to me. More quietly he repeated, 'We must, Edwina. For pity's sake.'

◆   ◆   ◆

I feel sometimes that if only I tried hard enough I could re-visit moments in my life and do things differently. I could be a time traveller, if only I truly concentrated, a warning voice to myself. Only then I wonder if I would have taken any notice of such a voice and conclude that I would not. All the same, I like to imagine that I would, that Michael and I would leave the mortuary, walk to the station and board the very next train bound for some distant place, and I would think of ways to distract him so that he might forget all about my brother. Perhaps, as I stood next to him on the platform and the train approached, I would take the opportunity to push him onto the tracks and it would be quick and painless and save so much grief. My life would take a different turn.

But Michael and I went from the morgue to my father's house, where a woman I didn't recognise sat in the kitchen, warily watching Peter, who sat in an armchair, smoking, a model of frustration and rage. She stood up quickly, her relief obvious. 'I'm so sorry for your loss,' she said, and looked at Peter so for a moment I thought she was talking about him. Then she looked at Michael, and her relief was even more obvious, here was a man who could take charge.

Michael stepped forward. 'Thank you, you've been most kind.'

The woman's hand fluttered to her chest. 'Not at all,' she said, and her cheeks flushed.

When Michael came back from showing her out, he went to Peter, squatting down in front of him. 'Peter, I'm so terribly sorry.'

Peter stubbed out his cigarette. 'I tripped over his body. Isn't that ridiculous?'

'Frightening, I think,' Michael said.

'Foolish.' Drawing breath he said quickly, 'So, what's to be done?'

'What would you like to be done?'

'I can't be left alone. I'm not ready to live alone.'

I said quickly, 'Perhaps if I came each morning and evening—'

'No! That's no good. You need to be here all the time! Both of you!'

'But there's the shop,' I tried to smile, as though by smiling and not betraying my dismay I could reason with him. I even laughed. 'We have the business to see to.'

'It's all right, Eddie.' Michael shook his head as though warning me to be quiet. 'We could live here, for a little while, until Peter feels he can cope.'

'There! I knew Michael would see sense.' Peter took his hand. 'Thank you, Michael. You won't regret your decision.'

Michael got to his feet, embarrassed, I'm sure, that Peter could make such a display in my presence. He glanced at me and his smile was that of a schoolboy who has been unexpectedly praised by a prefect. I felt less like his wife then than I had ever done and more like a sister in whom he had confided his most secret desire, someone who could share his excitement at that desire coming closer to its fulfilment.

◆   ◆   ◆

So, that was that. Michael and I had to give up the little flat we had made our own. Although I had never been much interested in the homely things girls are meant to be interested in I had wanted so much to make our first home warm and comfortable—a retreat to keep Michael safe. He should have a soft bed with clean sheets and blankets, an armchair that was his alone, always available, angled in front of a good coal fire. I gave him all this, along with thick curtains at the windows to cut out too much sunlight and noise, bright rugs at his feet to deaden his footfalls when he paced and paced because, for all this, I couldn't keep him from himself.

But as much for Michael, the little flat had been for me, my good occupation. I had cleaned and polished and bought daffodils in the spring to grace the mantelpiece, sweet-scented stocks in the summer, easy-going flowers that wouldn't worry him. I had brought one of the chiming clocks from downstairs but it ticked too loudly and its chimes made Michael look up too often from his book or newspaper. I couldn't have him disturbed, his concentration on things other than himself broken; I didn't want his mind to wander. I had wanted him to sit warm and comfortable in his armchair, in our snug little room, and have a go at being, if not sane, then safe at least.

So not only the flat, then: we had to give up the life we might have had together. I couldn't persuade Michael that we were not obliged to Peter or that we could walk away if we chose to, of course I couldn't.

During our last night in the flat, the night of my father's death, we lay side by side in bed, holding hands like children too in awe of the coming day to sleep. I remember that the moon was very bright and its light changed our little room so that I felt prematurely evicted from its safe familiarity. We had been silent for some time when Michael said, 'Perhaps we shouldn't have left him alone tonight.'

I wanted to protest that we had done enough. Hadn't Michael put him safely to bed, hadn't he reassured him that he would be there in the morning to see him safe again, and there every morning afterwards? I wanted to say that we deserved our last night alone together but Michael gave me no time; suddenly he was out of bed, pacing the room, pale and insubstantial in his crumpled pyjamas, in the cold, fragile light of the moon.

'If he gets up, if he stumbles, if he falls down the stairs . . .'

I sat up and held out my hand to him. 'He won't, he won't—'

'He's blind, helpless—'

'Not helpless—'

'He's blind.'

I tossed the bedclothes aside and went to him. 'He'll be fine.'

'He's my responsibility.'

I laughed although I could have wept in despair.

'He's my responsibility, Eddie. You must see that.'

'No, I don't. How can he be your responsibility? He could go into a home—'

'How could you be so wicked?'

Wicked. I stepped away from him; I remember my hands clenching into fists. He didn't notice, only turned away, pacing the room again.

'If anything happens to him ... How would I live with myself?' His eyes were quite frantic, as though an alarm was sounding and there was no way he could escape, and he gazed at me as if I might help. I thought how mad he looked, how really he should have been kept in the hospital and that he shouldn't have been allowed to marry me; he shouldn't have been allowed to ruin my life like this.

I thought all this but still I stayed calm, and perhaps I was numb from his attack on me because I felt nothing as I took his hand, as I soothed, 'Come back to bed now. Try to sleep. Sleep will help.'

He allowed me to lead him back to bed. I tucked the covers around him; I kissed his forehead as a mother might. I lay down beside him and held his hand and eventually he slept. I stared and stared at the ceiling, the light of the full moon making everything strange, and, as I often did, I pictured my husband and my brother in the cab of the van, bumping along together down the winding country lanes, happy as boys.

And as he drives Michael says, 'Peter, shall we stop and picnic beneath that lilac tree there?'

He has chosen the lilac for its scent, for its dense, rich perfume, but also because a little way from this tree a bird is singing. Michael doesn't know which species of bird; he is a city boy, after all. But this bird sang sometimes in France, when the guns stopped, such a rare sound, so true and clear on the spring air. The sky is blue as can be and cloudless and the sun is shining and Michael wants Peter to feel its warmth on his face, to smell the lilac and hear the nameless bird. He wants him to sit down on the grass beneath the tree and know that even the earth is warming; he might pick a blade of grass and place it between Peter's lips so that he will taste the spring.

So Michael stops the van on the grass verge beside the field where the lilac grows. He helps Peter down from the cab, drawing his arm through his as they set off. He says, 'Can you hear the birdsong, Peter?' He is self-conscious, not yet used to leading another man like this; also he is watching the ground, which is uneven and stony; he feels the weight of Peter's arm and knows that he will feel this weight even when they are sitting beneath the tree, side by side, not touching. He has an idea that once they have eaten their sandwiches and the pale, grainy slices of rice cake, Peter will lie down, his hands clasped behind his head, his eyes closed, making him appear ordinary, as if he could open his eyes and see him. He wonders what Peter would think of the sight of him and whether he would be disappointed. For a moment he is glad that Peter's blind; better to be what Peter imagines him to be than have the truth let him down.

Beneath the tree, Peter draws his arm from his. Still Michael feels the weight of it, where bone had rubbed against bone through jacket and shirt sleeve and skin. Peter reaches out, his hand closing around a blossom; all those tightly packed lilac flowers are crushed in his fist and the perfume released is heavy as heartache and the bird begins to sing again, one long sweet note.

Here I closed my eyes, screwing them up tight as though the moonlight was as blinding as the sun. Michael was asleep beside me and I was still holding his hand; I pulled away from him. For a little while I lay rigid and when he rolled over I all but leapt from the bed; I would not have him touching me, reaching out in his half sleep to pull me into his arms, murmuring all his soft, deceitful words. Once again I found myself getting up and going into the other room to wait until morning. I would not sleep; there were decisions to be made; I would need to plan carefully if I was to survive.

CHAPTER 9

~

I am sitting on Gaye and David's bed watching as she selects an outfit from her wardrobe. This afternoon she and David are going to a christening and she is concerned to wear only what is appropriate, although nowadays she's unsure of propriety. Her history is known to those who will be at this gathering and she imagines they will think of her as the bad fairy hovering over the crib. Choosing a dove grey chiffon dress she slips it in on and goes to the mirror, turning first this way then the other, spreading her fingers over her flat belly. The dress is cut on the bias and flatters her figure. If she told David how much it cost he would be shocked, but only momentarily, until he remembered just what they can now afford.

David is downstairs, already dressed in a charcoal grey suit and pale blue shirt. His cufflinks are engraved with their entwined initials, *G & D*—look quickly and the engraving appears to read *GOD*. On their wedding night he had pointed this out to her, laughing, and she had been embarrassed. The cufflinks were her wedding present to him and he had realised at once that his laughter hurt her feelings; he had made her feel absurd, as though she really didn't know him very well at all to give such a gauche gift.

He traces his thumb nail along the letters' curlicues, remembering how he tried to make his clumsiness up to her, probably with a kiss. He would have caught her hand and pulled her to him and kissed her; he would have said sorry, no doubt. 'Sorry. I love you,' starting how they meant to go on.

He goes into the hall and calls up the stairs and she appears in a grey dress, her hair styled, her face carefully made up. 'You look lovely,' he says, and she smiles at him. He knows they make a handsome couple, as though they have been given every advantage, every chance and made the very best of themselves. Together they are poised, gracious, polished; theirs is a glassy front against the world. He thinks of Luke, who asked him how he could live with such dishonesty.

Gaye walks down the stairs and puts on the coat David holds out to her. She is wearing the perfume she has worn since the day they met, *Youth Dew*, and it is heady, heavy and intense, she has always been too young for such a scent. He watches her as she pauses to check her reflection in the hall mirror, notices that she frowns only a little before rehearsing her smile.

I am undecided whether or not to follow them. Then, at the last moment, as David closes the door behind him, I slip out and follow Gaye into the car. We watch David pause on the drive as if he may have forgotten something, and we have time to consider him. He is so smart, so handsome; we think of him in bed with Luke and quickly turn away.

◆   ◆   ◆

This baby who is to be christened today is David's second cousin. It will be David's family assembled at the church, cousins, uncles and aunts he sees only on such occasions as this. Ralph sits alone, towards the back of the church, bored in advance of the small talk he will have to make. This talk will have nothing to do with him; his family will not mention his work, afraid of letting slip how little about art they know or care; Ralph doesn't mind, is relieved in fact; being bored is preferable to being embarrassed by feigned interest.

Yesterday he finished the painting of Gaye and David's garden. He shifts on the hard pew, opening and closing a hymn book, reading snatches of the hymns he sang at school. As he turns the flimsy pages he thinks about the painting; it's the best work he's ever done. It's also a failure because he can never quite interpret his own vision, he is constantly frustrated. His talent can go only as far as his muddled thinking will allow. He stretches and grasps after truth but still it evades him and he is left with only an approximation of an idea he had, an idea that may have been off-key but seemed imperative at the time, only to flit away from him all the same.

Ralph closes the hymn book. The service is about to begin. The congregation stands and he sees Gaye turn her head. She catches his eye and smiles and she is so lovely in the church's ancient light he wonders why he didn't warn her about David when he had the chance.

◆   ◆   ◆

He had the chance one evening in May 1985, a week before his brother's wedding. He was home on leave and Gaye had picked him up from Darlington Station. He made a joke about her car, said it was the colour of three-wheel invalid carriages and she had laughed because she was a bride-to-be and she was happy, manically so; this revved-up happiness made her seem less shy than he remembered and more like a girl he could take for himself in a could-have-her-if-I-wanted-her way. As she drove he found that his eyes were drawn to her; he had to admit that he was curious, of course he was. He tried to think of the best question to ask to satisfy his curiosity but all he came up with was, 'So—what d'you see in old Dave then?'

How idiotic he sounded, not even like himself—he was never so matey, so fake. Gaye took her eyes off the road for a moment to frown at him, and he forgot that they didn't know each other because it seemed that she was as surprised at his idiot fakery as he was. But she was only surprised at the question, not its tone. Also she wanted to answer him as truthfully as she could, it seemed important to her that he should understand how she felt about his brother. She slowed down for a red light.

'What do I see in David?' Again she glanced at him. 'Everything.'

He had to laugh her off, her sincerity was enough to make him squirm; he wanted his revenge on her for making him feel so much like a cunt. So he laughed and said, 'Are you sure you see *everything*?'

She laughed too, uncertainly because the nastiness in his voice was disconcerting—she was a bride to be: no one should be nasty to a bride so close to her wedding. The lights changed to green and she moved off, crunching through the gears. He silently rehearsed the words he might use, how he might phrase his revenge that actually was no revenge at all because she would thank him in the long run. He rehearsed, *'If you saw everything you'd know that David is queer,'* and also, *'My brother's homosexual, I'm sorry.'* The *sorry* was a lousy touch; it made him draw breath at his own rottenness. She turned to him. Shyly she said, 'We thought we might all go out for a drink tonight, if you're not too tired.'

In church the godparents stand at the font, promising to renounce the devil and all his works. Ralph blinks at the very idea but the devil is quickly forgotten; his eye roves the church and alights on the stained glass window like a thunder-bug attracted to the yellow of the desert sand at Christ's feet; he squints and allows the colours to merge into kaleidoscopic abstraction.

◆   ◆   ◆

The priest, Father Anderson, would rather not mention the devil as he holds this strapping baby in his arms and gently, gently cups a shallow handful of holy water over her head. Anderson believes that mentioning the devil is inviting trouble, but he knows this is woolly-headed superstition; he knows he should be more intellectually rigorous, but still he crosses his fingers discretely as he says the words. He holds the child close; this baby is a gurgler—he has come to categorising each infant: criers, gurglers, twisters, those who are slightly too old or a little too young for what he considers to be the ideal age to be baptised. The parents and godparents are, like their baby, at a right and proper age; they are appropriately well dressed; for non-church goers they have an innate sense of how to behave during the service. He wishes the charade was over then immediately feels a failure: he should be spreading the love of Christ amongst them, not wishing them gone so that he might be alone to pray. I stand beside him, so close, making mischief. He draws away, stiff with the effort of ignoring me.

Bored, I allow myself to notice the other ghosts that wander up and down the aisle or stand and sit, stand and sit, in time with the living. Some of the dead I recognise but others are new and confused in their modern clothes. I play the usual game of wondering how long each of these new ones will stay. Not long, I think, on the whole; no one is so bad nowadays. I smooth down my Sunday best dress because I feel as though the newly dead are watching me for clues and I'm suddenly ashamed that I have been around for so long, although such a feeling is only vanity: these ghosts are too caught up in their predicament to care about me.

David watches Father Anderson closely: this is not the man he had hoped to open his heart to; he's discovered that the man who conducted Emily's memorial service, Father Purcell, has retired, and this is terribly disappointing because his replacement, this Anderson, is too self-conscious and eager to please. David needs someone with a rigid set of standards; he needs to be bound good and tight to morality and all the soft, decadent options taken away from him by a man who will be hard and stern and uncompromising, strict. David groans inwardly, despairing because all he can imagine now is this strong man—this ideal—fucking him. How can he be so weak in church—in *church* of all places. The air is too old, too dense, and he is suffocating. Mumbling *excuse me, excuse me,* he side-steps and stumbles into the aisle and out into the sunlight.

◆   ◆   ◆

David slumps against a tomb that is a table-like solid block of waist-height, weather-worn stone, the engraved names on its surface hardly legible any more, just like its escaped dead who surround David, alarmed. A young airman reaches out to him, a boy who is so faded that surely he has only a few days left at most. His hand brushes David's arm and although it is scarcely more than a shadow David is calmed; he breathes deeply and feels rather ridiculous—he has made a fool of himself for hardly any reason. After all, he has sabotaged himself far more effectively in the past and remained standing; he could almost laugh at his own hysteria if he didn't feel so humiliated by it. I sit on the tomb, my fingers picking at the lichen as I wait for whatever is to happen next.

Ralph appears next, of course. How could he contain that curiosity of his? He walks towards his brother and stops a few feet away. He says, 'All right?'

Ralph takes a step closer. 'Say if you'd prefer to be alone.' He lights a cigarette and I can't help feeling that this is a clever move, conveying as it does a certain nonchalance. To make himself even more convincing he should wander away a little and pretend to read the gravestones that slant sideways as the earth shrinks and gives in. But I'm underestimating Ralph—it seems he cares too much to behave so artfully. He really needs that cigarette to steady him. On a rush of smoky breath he says, 'David— you could come to me for a while—stay with me while you decide what to do.' Lamely, all too aware of his poor script, he adds, 'Give yourself some time, some space . . .'

'I'm fine, Ralph. Don't worry.'

Ralph sighs. 'David . . . you know you can be honest with me—'

A magpie is chattering from one of the gravestones until its mate appears and they fly off together. David has heard that magpies are jealous of their mates, that the male hardly lets the female out of his sight. Such an anxious, watchful life, David thinks, so constrained by fear and distorted by mistrust. And now Ralph wants him to be honest, just as Luke wanted him always to be honest, to confess what he truly felt in his heart and not be afraid of himself and to say—honestly—that he didn't love Gaye, because how *could* he love Gaye? Such love went against everything Luke believed in.

The christening party comes out and gathers in small groups that divide and realign as introductions are made and old alliances are re-established. There is much smiling and laughter and cheek kissing, so many confident voices competing. One of David's aunts grasps Gaye's hand and says, 'My dear, how well you look!' This old lady peers at Gaye, thinking that she would have rather died than suffer what Gaye suffered—at least she is sure she could not have appeared in public looking so unaffected. So, we are to consider then: is Gaye so enormously philosophical that she has come to terms with her loss, and if so does this mean she lacks some motherly instinct? It's all very well putting on a brave front but this woman would like to peep behind the mask, see Gaye's ravaged heart and soul and be satisfied that she is grieving properly. But perhaps, the aunt thinks, losing a child such as Emily is easier—one would not grieve so much for all she might have achieved: the glittering career, that distinguished husband, those sweet children. She looks past Gaye to her own grandchildren jumping up and down the church steps. There are degrees of mourning, she decides, and smiles at Gaye, content with her reasoning.

David thinks he should rescue Gaye from his aunt. But he himself is trapped by an uncle who wants him to feature in a photograph of cousins. David is the eldest of these and so the newly christened baby—her name is now officially Patience—is thrust into his arms. He is told to say *cheese.* His fingers become entangled in the crocheted mesh of the christening shawl, there seems to be metres and metres of this shawl, swaddling the baby so that all he can see is her face; he sees that she is teething because her cheeks are red and tight as drums and she is drooling. He imagines probing a finger around her gums, seeking out the budding tooth. This is what he used to do for Emily and she would clamp down hard, comforted. Now though his hands are caught in this fine web of wool; he has to look up and smile and not allow his expression to show anything but pleasure in this baby. '*Cheese,*' he says, along with his cousins, younger men and women who laugh and barely stop talking so that he knows how animated their faces will appear in this photograph besides his own.

His mother had said to him, 'You can have other children. There is no reason at all to suspect that your future children will not be normal.'

And his father had said, 'David, my boy . . . my dear boy . . .'

He holds Patience closer; bowing his head he kisses her cheek and catches her baby smell and is at once thrown back in time to a moment when he had held Emily like this and considered future children, when such children had even seemed feasible, even a natural progression. He remembers how brief that moment was, so blazing with an optimism too disloyal to be sustained. Here was Emily heavy and warm in his arms and those future babies were only his mother's idea, an idea that was as incomprehensible to him as Emily was to her.

Patience's mother comes and holds out her arms for her child. But he is entangled, his watch and those cufflinks caught in the shawl, and there are embarrassed smiles and laughter and jokey suggestions that he is welcome to keep her if he is so attached. Then the father comes and wordlessly frees his daughter, his face serious as though this is a joke too far and that David is guilty of an unmentionable transgression. This boy is angry; he is out of step with his partner's family: they are aliens, thrusting out their hands and *hellos!* their faces full of questions; he can see their opinions forming, setting. Wankers. David is the biggest wanker of them all. He catches David's eye as he bundles his baby into his arms. An understanding passes between them and David feels that quickening in his guts that is fear and lust and defiance and shame, each so hard on the heels of the other.

And then, to one side of him, David hears a man laugh, hears him say, 'My word what a well behaved baby! There are those that scream the place down! But this child, Patience—well named, I would say.' This man's voice still retains its Irish lilt, although he has lived in England for so long he can only, reluctantly, think of it as home, and David recognises this voice at once as that which gave Emily's eulogy. He turns, and the man is there squarely in front of him and his hand is steadying on David's arm as he says, 'David, my son. It's good to see you again.'

◆   ◆   ◆

They walk away from the christening party, to a quiet, more ancient place in the graveyard free of ghosts, a place the priest knows and has chosen most deliberately for this reason, although he is aware of me, will tolerate me if I behave. I stand a little way away from them because although I am afraid of this priest and what he might do to me, my curiosity has the upper hand.

The priest is Father Douglas Purcell, such a big, brawny man, a frontline fighter for God. To David he is larger than life, bigger even than he remembered—he would like to lean into him, to give in to his fear and grief, knowing he would be supported and that he wouldn't be allowed to fall. This is such a comforting thought that he realises he is on the edge of tears and is appalled because this weakness is pre-emptory, there are more polite stages to go through first. But he can't help himself; he closes his eyes and bows his head and tears splash onto the ground. The priest's arm goes around his shoulders.

After a while Father Purcell produces a handkerchief from his pocket, all clean and folded, pressed, and David laughs because he feels so foolish, so ashamed of himself for jumping the gun like this. The hanky smells of old-fashioned blue fabric softener and if he isn't stern with himself this scent of baby clothes will have him crying again.

'David,' Father Purcell says, 'would you come and see me?'

David nods—isn't this the invitation he has been seeking? Doesn't he believe that this man will make him behave? But he can't trust his voice, and can only force himself to meet the other man's eyes, to make that connection which he finds so difficult. Purcell's eyes are fragile blue; perhaps he needs glasses, David thinks, and then wonders if perhaps he can't see him clearly enough, dismayed by this thought because he needs to be seen by this man, to be uncovered. Then it occurs to him that perhaps Purcell doesn't need to read expressions because he can read his mind—since they met he has suspected he is a man of uncanny abilities. If Purcell can read his mind and not turn from him in despair then he is saved: there is a cure or the priest wouldn't waste his time.

Purcell smiles. 'We'll talk, yes? Now, I think your wife is waiting for you.'

They both turn, as I do, to where Gaye is watching a few feet away. She looks so anxious that David is filled with panic: how can he return to how things were when he has cried like this? He hardly knows if he can put one foot in front of the other or speak the most rudimentary words. He is broken, finally; he imagines falling to the ground, Purcell stepping over him to explain to Gaye that this is the end of it.

But Purcell only grasps his arm, saying firmly, 'You'll be fine. Fine. I promise.'

And he is being steered towards Gaye, and Father Purcell is saying something, his voice full of smiling warmth so that David finds the strength to take his wife's hand.

CHAPTER 10

~

Gaye sits at the breakfast table in her dressing gown and sips her coffee; in front of her there is a thank-you card illustrated with a willow pattern bowl and she stares at the tiny pigtailed men crossing the tiny humped bridges, thinking how much it reminds her of the sympathy cards they received after Emily's death. She couldn't bring herself to look at these cards too closely, was even unsure of whether to display them or not as she would if they had been to celebrate a birthday or anniversary. So she had left them in a neat pile on the dining room sideboard, still in their opened envelopes, having glanced at each one; the cards might have been relics of a long lost, unknown civilisation for all the sense the verses and signatures made to her.

Then after a few months had passed, she had found herself bundling the cards together and carrying them through into the kitchen where she had left a cup of coffee to cool, and she had sat down at the table to read them, deliberately, formally, taking each from its envelope slowly, studying the picture a moment before reading the message inside; she remembers feeling an odd kind of nervousness for the senders: what had they written? Had they made a good show of themselves? Were they more or less of the person she expected them to be? She allowed for clumsy phrasing, clichés, hurried words and quick signatures, knowing she would have been no better at this had the roles been reversed. The carefully worded letters that were sometimes within the cards touched her, she was grateful and surprised at such kindness; but there was also a part of her that felt ashamed; she could not have written such letters, perhaps would not have even thought to do so.

For a moment she had thought that this card that had arrived that morning was another of these, delayed in the post but finally finding her; now she imagines tearing it in two, but picks it up and reads its message again.

To David and Gaye—thank you both so much for the beautiful gift you gave to Patience for her christening. Lovely to see you both, with love, Anna and Christian and Patience.

So, she thinks, that odd boy who had all but snatched his baby from David's arms was *Christian*. Not married to Anna, David's aunt had told her—no, the relationship was not what one might call *steady*. Aunt Pamela had lowered her voice a little at this, glancing over to where Christian was standing, smoking, alone. 'But I'm told they share the parenting quite equally. He works in a bank, apparently.'

Gaye had kept out of the way of introductions; as usual on these family occasions she became a bystander. She had watched Christian watching; his sullenness seemed a symptom of his age, a gracelessness he would grow out of in time. He was just young enough to be her son and she felt shy of him. If he caught her eye, if he guessed that she was observing him, he would be contemptuous: middle-aged woman like her should keep their eyes to themselves or else risk getting their noses rubbed in their pathetic desires. All the same she dared herself to keep looking, resigned to a brief humiliation if he should catch her out. Christian reminded her of David when he was young; the two men shared that same closed expression, both of them tight as fists against the world.

While she had been looking at that boy, David had walked away with Father Purcell and he had cried.

This fact of David's crying is like a rotten tooth she can't resist probing, punishing herself with its painfulness, astonished that it can hurt so much. David had cried; she has to think about this in small bursts and not allow her pity to overwhelm her.

She thinks about her lover Noel, and whether David has somehow found her out. But she dismisses this thought—David would not cry because she was unfaithful. All the same she feels guilty, of course she does, and so, to cure herself of guilt she thinks of Luke and whether David cried because he misses him. No, David would not miss anyone so much, no one but Emily, of course. Because really she knows why her husband cried: because for some reason his grief has resurfaced, has become all at once unbearable again; it's this resurfacing she can't understand, its trigger, at least. Perhaps it was seeing that baby, holding that baby, the real life warm and weight and sound and smell of her in his arms; but it seems to her that David's grief had returned even before the invitation to the christening, that it was awoken by something else. Or perhaps, she thinks, it has no cause and it's just there, all the time, like a cancer in remission—there is no reason for its return other than the sheer bloodiness of it.

Gaye picks up the thank-you card and decides it will be ok to throw it away. After all, the card seems almost insulting in its impersonal tone. Their gift to Patience had not been *beautiful* but a cheque for fifty pounds. No doubt Anna wrote the same words on identical cards over and over and over, becoming to hate the sight of the Chinese men and bridges. Christian would've had nothing to do with this chore; Anna wouldn't have even bothered to mention it to him.

The card is torn in two and dropped in the kitchen bin. Gaye stares out of the window and thinks again of Noel, but more abstractly—of the things she must do this morning, it being a Noel day. She must shower and shave her legs and underarms of the stubble that has grown over the last few days. She must put on make-up and style her hair and choose the right earrings to wear. Most of all she must try and think of a way to tell Noel that their affair is over. All she can think of saying so far is, 'I feel bad about your children,' and yesterday this had seemed an impossible thing to say; his children should never be mentioned, she has an idea that he needs her to forget he had ever told her about them. Their names are Annabel and Nadia, five and seven years old and Annabel loves Barbie dolls and Nadia does not. He told her this months ago, when they were at the flirting stage. Did she *ever* flirt? Wasn't it simply that they exchanged only one, meaningful look?

Perhaps it will be only necessary to say, 'My husband cried.'

I follow her out into the garden, keeping a little distance, not wanting to disturb her because her thoughts today are interesting to me: she is thinking of planting more fruit trees. It's as though the planting of these trees will mark the ending of her relationship with Noel and the beginning of a new way of living with herself. She will be content, steady, faithful, and these characteristics will manifest themselves in gardening and jam making, as if she had stepped back in time fifty years, as if women could get away with such a life.

Together we gaze at the place where the trees should be. She doesn't see what I see, of course—the old trees still growing, heavy with fruit that only the wasps will taste. She doesn't see the shadows the branches make on the ground or hear the wood creaking or the wing beat of the long-dead birds. But after a little while she frowns and steps forward and it's as though she has heard a noise that is unmistakably human, that seems to come from right there, in front of her, where the trees used to be. She takes another step, only to stop, stock still as though she is playing a game of grandmother's footsteps; her skin bristles; she peers and peers into the empty space and I think that this is quite brave of her, given what she might see if she allowed herself to. What I see has become ordinary to me, although I used to avoid this place in the garden; over time even the most shocking tableaus can lose their horror.

After a little while of straining to hear, Gaye exhales the breath she has been holding. She looks around her and sees that the noise she heard could have come from next door, or from the road beyond the fence, carried on the air in that way that ventriloquists use to throw their voices. She reassures herself that all is well and quite ordinary and returns to her interrupted thoughts, how she believes she should look for a job. Lately she has been buying the local paper and reading and rereading the job pages. PAs are required, as are receptionists and call centre workers; she doesn't need the money. Years ago, before Emily, she too had worked in a bank like Christian. She thinks of this boy, how they have their awkwardness around David's and Anna's hearty, snobbish family in common; her own family had seemed odd, even subversive, compared to them.

Her father had been a butcher. Later in life he bought a large white, anonymous van and began transporting the bones and uneatable innards of all Teesside's butchered beasts—*beasts* is the word her father used—from slaughterhouse to glue factory. The van stank and hummed full to capacity as it was of huge, bulbous bones, some still fresh enough to glisten white and pink like just-shelled pearls. The flies were black and green and blue, iridescent, gourmets. In the summer the stink soaked into her bedroom, the same thick, ancient stink grave-robbers would recognise. The bones were a secret, an undeclared business that transformed the remains of sheep and cattle into rolls of soft, well-used bank notes. Gaye and her brothers and sisters knew not to mention the bones.

Gaye's brothers and sisters live around the perimeter of her life; she talks to them occasionally on the phone. Her family are careful with one another, they each have their favourites although none are declared; each is as tolerant of the others as genteel passengers on a crowded train that has stopped too long for no discernable reason. Each understands the need to get on without interferences or judgements. That they may be united by their shared inheritance hardly ever occurs to them. Gaye's brothers live in Australia, her sisters in the Home Counties; they have each made brand new lives, more meaningful connections. She is the youngest, the baby who stayed at home, close to her mother and father, defiantly not minding about the bones.

Her father joined the Territorial Army in 1939 and came home from the war in 1946 never to leave England again; he felt he had seen enough. In Jerusalem he traded Palm Sunday crosses; in Sicily he begged tinned peaches from the GIs' mess. South Africa, India, Egypt: each country they shipped him to was distilled into anecdotes he would tell his children. Palestine stayed with him longest—everywhere he turned a spot-the-difference God to be despised. The Palestinian sun was white, disinfecting the poverty, bleaching it clean, and the minarets and domes shimmered in the heat haze as though they were made of gold, a waste of riches. He thought of home and his mother, widowed in an earlier war, worrying over her garden that without him was becoming unmanageable, its extravagances encouraged by the English rain.

Gaye thinks about her father often. Most often she thinks of him in his garden with Emily and they are picking sweetpeas. 'White. Lilac. Purple.

Pink,' he says as each flower is cut and handed to his granddaughter, a chant that Emily takes up; she holds the pastel bouquet to her nose, breathing in so deeply the petals are sucked against her nostrils. *White, lilac, purple, pink.* Her father is used to Emily, as she is used to him; they are comfortable together, absorbed in cutting the flowers so that more will bloom and go on blooming until October; he does this for his wife and because the scent of sweetpeas reminds him of her. Four year old Emily holds the cut flowers because it's her job and she is good at it and the naming of the colours is another part of her usefulness.

Gaye watches Emily; she see how dark and shining her hair is and that her jeans are almost too short for her now, showing too much of her new, pink and white trainers the laces of which are trailing so that she will call out to her to be careful not to trip. In fact, she will go out into the garden now, stoop to tie Emily's laces herself, asking her father if he would like a cup of tea, and he will say yes because he always does. They will drink it on the lawn with a ginger cake that Gaye has made and Emily will sit on her grandfather's knee for a little while, until she becomes bored and wanders off to pace around the edge of the garden, the colour chant still on her lips. Gaye and her father will watch her when they have run out of things to say to one another; she will be the focus of their companionable silence, their contentment.

Inside the house the phone rings and drags Gaye back to the present. She hurries to answer. But when she picks up the receiver there is only silence. I watch her from the stairs; she puts the phone down gently, relieved that she didn't have to speak to anyone, not even a stranger in a call centre in Bangalore.

◆   ◆   ◆

I am with Gaye in her hotel room and she has told Noel that their affair is over. She said, 'I want to try to make my marriage work,' and she thought how unlikely her words were, as though a marriage was a machine that could be tinkered with, a sum of its nuts and bolts, gears and fan-belts to be replaced or oiled or screwed down tighter. That she should think of this analogy and not of Noel seemed to Gaye a symptom of her lack of heart and so she forced herself to take his hand; worrying at his fingers she said, 'I'm sorry. It's for the best.'

'Yes,' he said, 'I'm sure you're right,' and his voice gave away a little of his relief, even though there was some regret in his eyes, as though he could have gone on, that he hadn't quite had enough of her.

Now Noel is in the hotel room's tiny bathroom. She has heard the toilet flush and listened—because there was nothing else to do—as he washed his hands. He steps into the bedroom and closes the bathroom door behind him. He smiles sadly and she sees how young he is, how handsome, although she must not think of that, he isn't hers to objectify any more. Sitting on the bed, she stands up, her coat already over her arm, her fingers tight around her handbag. 'Goodbye, Noel.'

'Gaye,' he steps towards her. 'Gaye, you know if you ever need anyone to talk to you can call me, at work. If I can help . . .' Then he says unexpectedly, 'A friend sees a bereavement counsellor . . . She—this friend—lost her baby. Cot death. Perhaps—'

Gaye shakes her head. Although she supposes that he's entitled to say this now they are no longer intimate, she can't bear to hear him become just another someone that offers advice, it's too soon to feel such scorn for him. She wishes that she had left him while he slept, left a goodbye note tucked beneath his wallet on the bedside table. Her memory of him would not have been scarred like this.

'I must go,' she says. She kisses his cheek and feels that she should say 'Good luck,' or some such. But she catches his scent and knows how much she will miss him and all at once she is rushing away, along the hotel corridor, through the foyer, out to the sunny car park. She didn't think that she would cry; she thought that it would be easier than this. But here she is in her car, crying and rummaging in her bag for a handkerchief. I sit beside her—she is too caught up in herself to be even a little aware of me, and feel prim and judgemental but only because she's crying; I would have more sympathy if she had been honest with herself.

When she has collected herself a little she drives home. I follow her into the house and sit at her kitchen table as she makes tea and toast with which to comfort herself. She is wearing jeans and a yellow cashmere cardigan over a paler yellow vest. Noel hadn't seen her in jeans before; this outfit was a signal to him, she had hoped to make their parting easier with such subtleties. But these are the kind of subtleties that David would notice and she realises now are probably lost on most men. She realises that her actions and ideas are calibrated to David; she has become as odd as he is; his rawness and vulnerability are hers, too, and it seems wondrous to her now that she could have ever thought of leaving him, ever imagined that Noel might be anything more than a distraction even in those early exciting, breathless days of their affair, even in her wildest, most escapist fantasy.

The telephone rings and Gaye answers and again there is silence. She is about to hang up when all at once David is saying, 'It's me. I thought I'd come home,' he hesitates then says, 'for lunch. I thought we might have lunch together.'

◆   ◆   ◆

For days now David has been thinking about Father Purcell and their meeting which is scheduled for tomorrow. David thinks of what he might say to him, how he might explain himself, as he searches a child's teeth for signs of decay. The child's mother tells him that she doesn't allow sweets or sugary drinks and that three-times-a-day teeth-brushing is routine in her home. David wears a mask and latex gloves; he makes his eyes smile at the little girl whose legs and body are rigid, her fingers white-knuckled from clutching the arms of the chair despite her mother's too emphatic reassurances that he won't hurt her.

He presses a button and the chair brings the girl up to a sitting position. 'All done,' he says, and 'would you like to rinse around your mouth with my special pink water?' The mother looks relieved and is effusive with her thanks as he removes his mask and gloves and asks her to sign here and here and here, but David is absent, thinking of Father Purcell, who will, he believes, save him from the dark, drowning sea of longing and regret and guilt. Automatically, he holds out a sheet of cartoon stickers and asks the little girl if she would care to choose one. She takes her time and the mother goes on talking and David thinks how he will try not to be shy with the priest, and not avoid his eye as he is wont to do but will try—really try with all his heart—to be straight and honest and open and not hide all the things he is most ashamed of. This, he considers, is the only way to change.

When the child and her mother have gone he telephones Gaye, not expecting an answer knowing as he does that today is her day for seeing her lover; he telephones merely to confirm her absence so he can be surer of his position. Gaye's adultery is a small humiliation in the scheme of things, but must be part of his confession. But Gaye answers on the second ring, her voice uncertain; it's this uncertainty, this timidity, which stops him hanging up as he normally would. Instead he finds himself telling her that he's coming home.

◆   ◆   ◆

Gaye sets the kitchen table with cheeses and ham and a salad of tomatoes and basil, with bread and the butter that she took from the fridge after David's phone call. She guesses he won't have much time and so she wants this meal to be easy and quick so that he can get back to his patients with the minimum of fuss. She works around me, quick with irritation that is undermined by her anxiety: David never comes home for lunch. She drops the salt and throws a pinch over her shoulder into the devil's face.

Lunch is prepared and she waits at the window, watching out for his car, a black Mercedes, a soft-top. In that open-topped car he is a handsome, wealthy man, a success. He doesn't much care that other drivers automatically think *wanker*. Gaye remembers how Emily loved her father's cars, their smell and speed and shininess. David would take her to the show rooms and the men who sold Jaguars and BMWs and Audis would help her into the driver's seat, smiling while all the time unsure of this child's capacity not to soil or otherwise besmirch the pristine interiors. They tried to remember what they'd heard of Mongoloid children and realised all they knew was only that they weren't to be given that un-pc title—and what were they to be called nowadays? *Downs*. The Down's child made vroom vroom noises but was otherwise placid and rather serious as she clutched her father's hand.

David's car pulls into the drive and Gaye steps back from the window. For a second she expected to see Emily sitting in the passenger seat. There is only David, of course, his face blank because he doesn't know he is being watched. Quickly, before he can see her, she turns away from the window and goes back into the kitchen.

◆   ◆   ◆

David says, 'Thank you—that was delicious.'

'It was only cheese and bread.'

'All the same.'

He wants to say, 'Is your affair over, then? Because I sense a change. Or perhaps I'm not that perceptive, perhaps he was just too busy today?' He wonders what kind of a profession *he* has to be free on a weekday morning, to take x amount of time off to . . . To what? He can't name it; he struggles with the pictures in his head, those very few, unimaginative pictures that are like blurred stills from a French film. He can never see the man's face, or even make out his build or height; it occurs to him now that perhaps he would find himself attracted to him because surely Gaye would not waste her time on an ugly or uncharismatic man? But that seems to him to be a vile thought—so outside the bounds of normality, of what is right and proper for a cuckolded man to think. Rather he ought to want to smash the man's face in, to drive recklessly to his house—apartment?—and hammer on his door, bellowing abuse, making some blood-boiling scene. But what he feels is too cold for that, he can't summon the energy to do anything except wonder vaguely if his wife's lover was more than ordinary, someone he would pay more than a little attention to. Such wondering makes him realise just how much he needs Father Purcell.

But he is here, unexpectedly eating lunch with his wife, Gaye; he had enough energy to leave the surgery, get into his car and drive home. There must have been something behind these actions, something more than curiosity; he remembers that as he put down the phone he had felt nervous, as though he was about to do something that would have implications he couldn't imagine.

Now, sitting across from his wife he thinks that perhaps he could bring himself to mention next week. Next week, Thursday, would have been Emily's birthday. For the last few days he has been thinking that perhaps they should mark the day in some way, wondering if Gaye could bear to, whether he could even bring himself to mention the day to her. He's been wondering if they could go to the seaside, to that stretch of beach that Emily loved best. But he thinks that this might be out of the question, an impossible place to even consider let alone visit. But then he remembers that the seaside seemed to him to be the place where he was closest to his daughter, where rocks could be turned over to reveal tiny crabs, where there were devil's toenails, ancient, collectable: look, he would say, look Emily, look! See the ships, see the gulls! See the sea. The sea: look Emily, look. All at once it occurs to him that perhaps he should have simply allowed Emily to play, to dig holes in the sand for the sea to fill, to go backwards and forwards with a sloshing bucket of salt water for the castle's moat. But he wrote her name in the sand with a fishing net's cane: *E is for Emily and what comes next . . . ?* Did he ever give her any peace?

I watch David closely; when he thinks about his daughter like this he becomes unreadable, his thoughts obscure and muddled, panicked, because if he tries to begin to think clearly, logically, he imagines he will be overwhelmed by guilt. And so he over-loads his memory with other images of himself as a father; he points outs the scuttling crabs and the tankers on the horizon and yes, yes, you can have an ice-cream, yes, a ninety-nine, later, later, when the castle has been built, the moat filled most efficiently by the in-coming tide. Yes, I will carry you on my shoulders, yes, I shall hold onto you tightly. You're heavy, though, heavy, almost too big, your knees at the level of my chin smell of salt water and are crusted with sand and the hairs on your legs are fine and blonde against your newly tanned skin. Your fingers tangle in my hair; you'll make me bald; you'll make me old before my time. You'll eat the ice cream too slowly so that it melts down your hand and wrist and arm, so messy, the chocolate flake long gone, only a small melt stain on your chest, a tiny taste for later, salty so that it will remind you of the sea.

'David,' Gaye says, and her voice is panicked, as though she has found him curled up tight on the floor. She reaches across the table and touches his hand, only to draw back when he meets her gaze.

'Next week,' he says.

Gaye nods. 'Yes, I was thinking of it, too.'

'We should do something, together.'

'Yes.'

But what, she thinks, should they do together? She imagines lifting down that box of photographs from the wardrobe and taking out each picture one by one to be placed chronologically in an album. Their memories would differ to a greater or lesser degree and they could discuss the accuracy of their own recollections. The pictures could be shuffled and re-shuffled, arranged and rearranged on the album's pages until they settled on an agreed order. Together they would make a sensible progression of Emily's life. She wonders if she should suggest this, or whether he would see it as a tidying away.

David stands up. 'I'd best get back.' After a moment's hesitation he kisses her head. He wonders if he should stay and imagines leading her upstairs to bed, if it would be possible to revive their life together. Tomorrow, he thinks, I'll try tomorrow.

CHAPTER 11

~

I sit alone in my empty attic and I try not to listen to Gaye moving about in her room below. There are times when all I want is to be alone—to have the house back as it was: empty, silent and free of the living and their excesses; at times like this my resentment is such I wonder how Gaye cannot feel it, and I despair of her, her stubborn insensitivity.

Gaye is folding clothes into a charity bag, thinning out her wardrobe of dresses and skirts, blouses and trousers, the clothes that belong to the Noel era of her life, outfits chosen for their understated-sexiness: dour, dark, she realises how unimaginative she is. There is one particular dress, navy with a sweet-heart neckline and a thin belt, that she wore the first time she met Noel for lunch, when an affair was just a shivering idea. This dress she holds up against her, wondering if she should keep it, then realising that it's the guiltiest of her Noel garments, bought to make an impression. The dress didn't suit her, but then nothing suits her, she should wear head to toe black and nothing else.

Gaye is listening to the wireless, Radio Four, a play. Through the floorboards it seems to me that she has company, that there is an articulate, animated conversation going on—so unlike Gaye. Gaye is silent, of course; the house is silent apart from those broadcast voices talking out a story that is only half-listened to between dresses, between memories that are more or less guilt-ridden.

She met Noel at a friend of a friend's hen party. The bride-to-be wore a veil and 'L' plates because she was young and very happy and it's all right to wear such things when you're in that blessed state. Gaye's friend, Sarah, a nurse—as were all the women in the party except Gaye—had said that they would stay for only one or two drinks and then she and Gaye would leave the youngsters to their drinking and dancing and go somewhere quieter. Her friend had promised Gaye this, part of her gentle coaxing to encourage her to leave the house for the evening—something Gaye hadn't done for months. 'Listen,' Sarah had said, 'if you feel it's all too much I'll take you home. But who knows? You might enjoy yourself.' Gaye doubted this and her doubt must have shown on her face because Sarah added, 'All right—you might not enjoy it but at least it will be a change of scene.'

Sarah had known Gaye since they were seven years old and had sat next to each other in primary school. Sarah had been there with Gaye in that night club when David bowed to her on the dance floor. She had been Gaye's bridesmaid and after the wedding disco Sarah and Ralph had fucked enthusiastically in Ralph's car, such happy sex with no regrets afterwards because this was 1985 and sex was what one did, and besides, all dirty diseases had been cured or were not yet invented in Thorp. Sarah thought of Ralph as the best fun she had ever had. For all these years she has kept him secret from Gaye for the sake of their friendship, but also from a sense of propriety, even though, despite appearances, she doubted that he really could be David's brother.

So Sarah picked Gaye up from the house one summer evening and it was the first time Gaye had been out for many months and she looked pale and too thin so that Sarah had begun to regret her careful coaxing and to think that actually it was too soon for Gaye to do this, that she should stay at home, safe with her grief. But it had been such a long time since Emily; but then, Sarah thought, how long was long enough? and she made her voice bright as she said, 'We'll have a good time—you'll see.'

And Noel had said, 'I'm so sorry—did I stand on your foot?'

The pub had been crowded. Drinkers even packed the pub's garden because this was one of those rare, warm summer nights in England when even darkness doesn't bring a chill. Gaye was in the garden, beneath the canopy of a sycamore tree, and she had been separated from Sarah and the girl with the 'L' plates who had lost her veil a few pubs ago. She had been watching Noel, who was with a group of large, noisy men who laughed a lot and gave out such an air of authority and confidence that a space had cleared around them, a few, resentful steps. And then Noel had moved away from the group to go to the bar and he had caught her watching and smiled. When he reappeared with a tray full of pints of beer the few steps that had been cleared around his group had been filled for want of space and he had to step past Gaye, so close to her, so close that she could smell his deodorant and aftershave and the salty sexy warmth of his tanned arms.

And he hadn't stepped on her foot, and knew that he hadn't, but she was so beautiful, so frail and lovely that he would have said anything and this was the first thing he thought of: 'I'm so sorry—did I stand on your foot?'

She had said, 'No, I'm fine, really,' and had heard his friends laugh and say that he was a clumsy bastard as they took their pints from the tray, thus freeing Noel of his burden. He turned his back on them and said, 'Noel England—hello.'

'Noel, hello.'

He laughed; it seemed the only reaction to her reticence. He laughed and thought, *Christ, she's lovely* but all the same managed, 'And you—what's your name?'

'Gaye.'

'Gaye. Can I tell you something at once, Gaye? Get it out of the way?' He leaned a little closer, his voice became quieter, his breath warm on her neck. 'I'm a policeman. We're all policemen. Is that something you'd care about?'

'Of course not.'

'Good. Good girl.' He was staring at her, leaning still closer, he couldn't help it, and because he had drank a little too much he reached out and hooked a strand of her hair back behind her ear. 'Some people mind, you know? They get one speeding ticket and think we're all bastards.'

Gaye stepped back from him; his breath was beery and he licked his full lips in a way that made it seem as though he was about to devour her; she saw how white and straight his teeth were and thought of David but only for a moment, and so angrily that she couldn't stop herself from saying, 'All men are bastards.'

He laughed, delighted, imagining—correctly, from her too emphatic tone—that this was the first time she had ever said such a thing. 'Yes, you're right. So it doesn't matter what job I do?'

'No. Not at all.'

Lightly he said, 'You're married.'

'Yes.'

'Is he a bastard or the exception that proves the rule?'

'He's queer.'

Now why did she say this? As Gaye folds a dress for the charity shop bag, as the radio play finishes and the three o'clock pips sound, she closes her eyes in dismay. This is a harsh memory, one that has grown and grown out of all proportion to the hurt it caused, which anyway was only to her, her sense of her own loyalty. Noel had only drawn back a little, had sucked a sharp breath between those predatory teeth. And then, leaning in close again he had said, 'I could have him arrested, if you like?'

'It's not illegal anymore.'

'No, but there are other crimes—we could think of something.'

She'd met his gaze squarely for the first time. 'I shouldn't have told you. No one else knows.'

Noel pressed a finger to his lips. 'I won't breathe a word.'

This was not the true-to-life Noel but Noel a little worse for drink and full of the bravado that came with an evening spent with his colleagues. Also, earlier that evening he had argued with his wife—he saw too much of these men, all the hours of over-time, all the weekends, the evenings drinking—he should spend more time with his family, would if he wasn't so selfish. That last accusation—he seethed from its unjustness. He wasn't selfish, only ambitious. His career was the challenge of his life, absorbing, complex: he was up against the world, his past achievements—his wife should recognise how important his struggle was. But three drinks into the evening he had decided that yes, he was selfish. Four drinks, being told not to be so fucking stupid, he returned to his seething. And then he caught Gaye watching him—oh, he was sure she *was* watching him—and he stopped thinking about his wife altogether, about anything but Gaye.

Noel and Gaye sat down side by side on the bench that ran around the base of the sycamore tree, his thigh just light against hers. The garden was full of the noise of drinkers, the smell of cigarette smoke and—for Gaye, at least—the scent of lavender which grew beside the tree and through the slats of the bench. She had broken off a stem and crushed it between her fingers as Noel entertained her. This is how she thinks of that brief hour now, that he was out to raise a smile from her, a laugh if he could, so that she might lower her guard, look up from the crushed flower in her hand and respond. And she did laugh eventually, at some half-cruel remark he made about a group of middle-aged men eyeing up some teenage girls. 'There,' he said, and took her hand. 'You know, I hate the smell of lavender.'

She tossed the ravaged, oily flower heads to the ground. 'Yes,' she said, 'so do I.'

◆   ◆   ◆

They kissed later that night, like teenagers, snogging in the alley that ran along the back of the pub and beside the River Tees. She allowed him to put his hand on her breast, between her blouse and her bra and he had groaned, pressing her back gently against the alley wall so that she could feel his erection through their clothes. But then he stepped away and wiped her mouth lightly with his fingers as though she was his child and he was brushing away biscuit crumbs. 'Look at that face,' he said, 'beautiful.'

She would smell of him, Gaye thought, and when she climbed into bed beside David she would be afraid of giving her infidelity away, but all the same she put her arms around Noel and pulled him close to her, wanting to feel again that hard ridge of flesh against her, to know she was indisputably desired. He kissed her again, but as an adult man, one who was sobering, becoming a little wary of her and ashamed of his less sober self. He had never gone so far before: adultery was not truly in his nature. But look at that face, he thought, and brushed his fingers against her cheek. *Look at that face then say you don't want her.*

'I'd like to see you again,' she said.

He nodded. 'All right.'

'I know you're married.'

'Yes.'

'So that's all right.'

So that was all right, because she didn't want a man who might want something from her, a man who didn't have all he needed at home. There would be no talk, no remembering, no regrets or jealousies. There would be only sex, as sensual or as rough, as frantic or as slow as the mood dictated with no regard for history or custom or obligation. She wanted only to be his luxury, and for him to be hers in return.

◆　　◆　　◆

There are other voices on the wireless now, all at once silenced. I hear Gaye go downstairs with her weighty bag stuffed full of adulteresses' clothes. A high heel pokes through and kicks against her leg but she rushes the bag out to her car and locks it in the boot. She hopes that the women in the charity shop will not be the types who speculate on their benefactors' motivations. She has turned over a new leaf and she wants that to be the end of her guilt.

CHAPTER 12

~

My own guilt comes and goes; it is like the sea before a tsunami, receding far, far out to the horizon so that one is shocked at how one can lose sight of it. It leaves behind a calm flatness, a different prospect. But you know how black the sky is, how much of a warning, you know that the sea will surge back with such force and power and you will be drowned. I go with it now, allow my guilt to rush over me; I've realised I can only retreat further and further into myself, that eventually I will resurface. And if then there is less left of me I've come to believe that it's for the best: I like to believe I am being worn away, slow and sure as rocks on a beach.

Lately I try to comfort myself, to think away from my guilt by remembering the good I did—in France, for instance. In France there was a boy called Arthur Duckworth, a corporal with the Durham Light Infantry. The ambulance man who brought Corporal Duckworth to the dressing station knew of my reputation, visualised it as a filthy stain on my apron, it made his nostrils flare, his lip curl. 'Christ,' he said. 'You—still here.' His disgust made him ugly and he frightened Arthur even more than he was already frightened, which was unforgivable I thought. I was doing good, after all, although I was less certain of this at the time, and more likely to make excuses for myself. So I followed this ambulance man out to where the ambulances were parked—idle now after the morning's rush—to where he was in the throws of lighting a cigarette, shaking out the match, tossing it down, nonchalant in the restless way that angry frightened men are. He looked up at me from the spent match and he fancied himself as Peter or John or James eyeing up Judas, not yet wanting to be saintly.

I stepped towards him, hating how timid I was. I had an idea of saying *it's not me—you're wrong to blame me. It's God, I think . . .*

I was doing God's work—I had considered this excuse before, in case anyone should ask. I didn't believe it—it was a naughty child's whine, I was just making excuses, casting blame anywhere, everywhere but at me. The ambulance man—his name was Harry—looked me up and down and didn't know what to make of my timidity, my hands clutching and unclutching my filthy apron. He sneered, although sneering seemed inappropriate to us both.

He said, 'Haven't you got work to do?'

I had. There was Corporal Duckworth whose pallor couldn't be ignored, who called out to me as they all did. Why keep him waiting only to justify myself to this man? All the same I said, 'I haven't done anything wrong.' My voice was too faint, I was so frail and transparent he could have punched a hole right through me. He flared smoke through his nostrils; he closed his eyes and laughed bleakly, a parody of long-suffering sensibility, a fool. He didn't understand anything, no one did.

I went back and sat by Arthur Duckworth's bed. By then I had stopped talking to them or holding their hands; I just sat. Arthur opened his eyes and looked at me and wasn't frightened. He said, 'It's a shame, isn't it nurse?' And then he died.

You're wondering if it was a gift or a curse or simply a trick—a knack I had, perhaps. Or you're thinking that I put a pillow over their faces, held it and held it until their noses and mouths made an imprint in all that softness, a mould in which to cast their death masks. But I only sat by their beds and waited and I was allowed to: I was a kindness the doctors wanted nothing to do with.

I only sat by their beds and waited and no one could blame me because I didn't do anything.

The night of my father' death, that last night in our little rooms above the shop when I couldn't sleep, when I couldn't bear to lie beside Michael because it seemed I knew every thought that was in his head, that I could eavesdrop on his dreams, that night I had begun to plan how I might take my life back into my own hands. I had realised then that I had married in haste, that I need not have married at all but only used Michael as a man might have used me, to satisfy lust, an itch that had been neglected for far too long. Now that itch had been attended to I realised that all I had achieved was an end to my freedom, that I had become no more than a nurse, a cook and a skivvy and now not for only one man, but two— because what had I become other than Michael and Peter's housekeeper, their unpaid shop assistant?

The morning after my father's death Michael hardly noticed that I had not slept in our bed. He woke early and dressed and was only pleased that I was already up, ready to go to Peter. His anxiety and haste to be off showed on his face, the relief when we reached my father's house and found Peter safe so obvious that I wondered if he had ever made any attempt to hide his true feelings from me.

As soon as he saw Peter dressed and waiting for us in the kitchen, Michael laughed and said, 'There you are! Safe and sound. If you'd waited for me I would have helped you!'

'I don't need so much help.' Peter looked towards me. 'Edwina. Are you glad to be home?'

'Of course she is! That flat is so poky—there's hardly room to breathe there. We'll be much happier here.'

'Lots of room for all of us, eh Edwina?' Peter sighed as though wearied by Michael's happy enthusiasm, by my sullen silence, as though he knew that this was the next stage of the game, perhaps the dullest part when he had to defend his advantage. But he only allowed himself this indulgence for a moment; his voice became business-like. 'Shall we have some breakfast? Then I think we should plan the funeral.'

I set about preparing bacon and eggs and Michael and Peter went out into the garden because it was a beautiful morning and because they wanted to be away from me, alone together.

As I worked, as their voices came to me through the open window, I thought of Michael and Peter beneath that lilac tree, peaceful side by side, picking at the raggedy tufts of grass as the sun climbed the sky and the scent of lilac made them remember a sunny day in France when the guns were quiet and they had enough time to exhale, to feel their hearts beat easily, to think about what they might do with their lives in the peaceful, half-believed-in future. This silent sharing of memories means they have a telepathic awareness of each other; they don't need to touch, but all the same Peter's hand moves towards Michael's, a finger brushes against a finger. One of them sighs, I can't tell which, but it is such a sigh that comes from longing and regret and there is no peace in it, none at all.

CHAPTER 13

~

Looking back, I suppose it is true to say that I had been around the sick all my life. Even when I was a child those of my father's patients who were able to would come to the house where Donald practiced his brand of kindly medicine and I would watch them from the stairs, unseen, assessing the extent of their sickness. I had an eye even then; no death ever surprised me as they occasionally surprised and dismayed my father.

I began my nursing in Thorp Infirmary where the matron took a shine to me because I was meek and willing and thorough, and because I was Doctor Johnson's daughter. My father set her heart fluttering like a girl's, and so I could do little wrong in her eyes. Soon enough I moved on from only emptying bed pans and rolling bandages; I was a quick learner and my lack of squeamishness, my steady nerves, impressed the doctors who began to take me to the station to meet the wounded off the trains. The soldiers were laid on stretchers on the platform to wait for our ambulances: these were the Blighty wounded, those who wouldn't be going back, and some of them considered themselves lucky, those who had the strength. I went from stretcher to stretcher, crouching down to light a cigarette or raise a man up so that he might take a sip of tea. The station filled with the lousy-sweet smell of them and the quiet, humble noise they made: *thank you nurse, thank you nurse, thank you nurse.*

I arrived in France thinking I could only do good, knowing how much I was needed.

There was so much of everything, at first, so many men and so many ways of their being maimed. I believed I would be overwhelmed by their suffering, that I would lose my ability to stand up straight to pain and not flinch or be too pitying and that death would become sickening to me and not the easy presence I was accustomed to.

But the relentlessness parade of wounded helped me, there were so many, so many that within a few days each man became the same man with the same way of needing—those men who would survive. Only those who would not live were individuals, each one unique in my memory. Those men anchored me and made me more steadfast in my work: I never missed a day, often working through the night when the ambulances came and came until I believed that the whole army was lost and that there were no men left in England, in Scotland, Wales or Ireland.

I wonder why I wasn't scared: what was to become of me, after all, if there were no men left? But I only went on and never thought about myself or the future; besides, I had no control other than the control I had over myself. I could conduct death, but I couldn't stop its course.

But here I am in the present now—the house that was once mine belongs to Gaye and David and I am dead. I wander from room to room, up and down stairs, out into the garden. Wandering—isn't this what ghosts are supposed to do? As I am the only ghost that haunts this house I should try to live up to expectations, shouldn't I? Today Gaye is not in any mood to even begin to recognise me and only the cat takes any notice, it arches and spits, its fur standing on end along its spine. This morning it stalked a mouse to death; I have no sympathy for puss.

There are other ghosts around. This is an old place; the houses along this road have been here more years than I can remember. Next door there is a man who will not acknowledge me although I raise my hand in greeting whenever I see him, afraid to speak in case he's easily startled. I find that some of them are scared of the living *and* the dead, scared all the time; also, many seem to be searching for those they once knew. I suppose their question is *why am I here and not them?* They can't acknowledge that they were any worse than their contemporaries.

My dead neighbour wears an evening suit and his bow tie is undone, his collar stud removed; anger emanates from him like heat from a fever. Perhaps I knew him when I was a child because my father had a suit just like his and the style dates him, although I don't remember his face. He is faded hardly at all and so I wonder what keeps him here, sin or guilt: there can be one without the other.

Sometimes I find myself staring at my hands, holding each one up to the light to see if I am becoming any less. A little, perhaps, perhaps just a little. I feel that I'm quite robust: my guilt preserves me and it's as bright and vivacious as ever.

My guilt takes me back and I am in bed beside Michael and listening to his breathy snores. He always appeared so young in bed; he made me feel as though I had lived a thousand lives, that I must guide him in everything and be stronger than I thought I could be. He cried out from his dreams and rolled onto his side, pulling the covers from me and leaving me exposed, my nightdress bunched around my waist because a few minutes earlier we had made love. In the next room something fell to the floor, a soft thud like that a shoe or a book would make, and this was followed by the kind of silence that came with intent listening: Peter listened out for the noise of our bedsprings, for every sigh and groan, his jealousy almost palpable, keeping me from sleep, and, as I often did when I couldn't sleep, I travelled in time, to relive this or that death so that I might understand and, by understanding, absolve myself of blame.

There was Lieutenant John Sparrow and he was so handsome and clever except that he had lost his sight and his hands. He asked me what was left to him. 'Music,' I said, and he laughed and asked, 'What else?'

I could have said the taste of ice cream and the scent of lily of the valley and conversation with a girl who thinks you are brave and wonderful and can't believe that she will ever care about never feeling your hand on her breast. I could have said all this on a rush of breath, blushing because what I say is so ordinary and useless—*count your blessings, name them one by one . . .* Or I could have been brisk—as most of my colleagues were: *come, come, Lieutenant, no self pity now! You are, after all, alive!* He didn't want to live. He wanted me to wait with him and try not to persuade him to stay, and so I did, and it was too late as I pulled the sheet over his face to remember kisses, but all at once I was desperate to undo my work so that I might remind him, pressing my mouth to his so that my kiss might bring him back. But he was gone, the speed of his leaving a testament to how much he wanted to go. Even the promise of kisses wouldn't have been enough, even the feel of my lips that anyway were too hot and parched, too reminiscent of hopelessness. He was too tired, *and really*, he asked me, *what is the point?*

Michael turned over in his sleep, tugging again at the covers that I tugged back, impatient with him. He had broken my concentration; I'd been only half-way to reassuring myself that Lieutenant Sparrow couldn't have been saved and now I would have to go back to the beginning, when I first saw him sitting up in bed, the bandaged, narrow stumps of his arms resting so lightly in his lap. He had turned his sightless eyes towards me. 'Oh,' he said, and his voice was soft with relief, 'thank God you're not just a bloody rumour.'

The ward was full of sun—he could sense the light, feel its warmth, and all the windows were open so that the perfume of the purple lilacs that had all at once began to bloom was heavy, gas-like, and almost over-came those other smells that I would not bring to his attention, my own not least of them. Sweat darkened my uniform beneath my arms; my hair had remained unwashed for days such was our busyness. And I was bleeding, the clumsy pad between my legs chaffing at the soft insides of my thighs. This was blood that had had only one purpose—to prepare for a child and, when found to be redundant, to seep away, clean because it hadn't been flogged around my body. This cleanest blood of all became tainted by air, by my sweat and mucus, and began to stink. I hoped he wouldn't sniff me out.

So, it was May and the ward was full of sun; my shoes squeaked on the clean, clean floor, catching and almost tripping me because I could barely lift my feet such was my weariness. You can picture the tidy row of beds beneath the tall windows, a shaft of light falling on each stoical man, smell the lilac and the other green smells of spring. And you can imagine Lieutenant Sparrow's mutilated limbs and his bandages which are rather grey in the bright light and if you draw close to him you can feel his feverish heat and hear his too-fast breathing and know that he is afraid. But not afraid of me, I don't think so. He smiles when he hears my footsteps and turns his face towards mine; he says, 'You're tired. I wish you could lie down besides me.' And I imagine that we could leave together and that they would find us face to face, our noses almost touching because the bed is narrow and I would have put my arm across his hip to stop myself from falling and they would see how peaceful it had been.

But I had no will to die, not then; yet I'd no will to go on; I lived one moment to the next, trying to be still, to not think too much.

In bed beside me Michael stirred and briefly opened his eyes; he blinked as though surprised I was still there. 'Eddie,' he murmured. 'My sweet girl.'

He called me *sweetheart* and *lovely* and *my own true love* and he drew me close to him so that his body curved around mine like a shell, and he cupped my breast and sighed into my hair. 'I love you, Eddie.'

Such a liar he was. He lied and lied and hardly knew when to stop, or where the truth began. Only I knew the truth, the bitter, swearing-on-the-bible whole of it.

In the houses that Michael and Peter visited on their travels no one could imagine Michael lying and cheating because he looked so much the officer—even in his civilian clothes—the kind of straight-backed, clear-sighted young man—proud enough yet wise enough—who gazed out from recruitment posters—*He's doing his bit—are you?* The women of the house fell in love with him, the men respected the authoritative yet respectful way he had of speaking, even as he told them their grandmother's sideboard was all but worthless, that sadly no one cared for such furniture nowadays and it hurt him to offer so little. Occasionally, if business had been poor, he would limp, making sure he was seen pausing to catch his breath, a pained expression discretely contorting his face. He had lived through every yard and minute of the war from Gallipoli to Arras depending on the regiment badges of the young man whose photograph was kept on the mantelpiece. 'Perhaps you knew my son,' a mother would ask, and only then did Michael feel a twinge of shame. But only a twinge; in time he began to believe that he *had* fought everywhere he said he had; the war took up such a space in his head it seemed impossible that he had spent it confined within a few muddy square miles of France.

For his part, Peter would hold on to Michael's arm, his stick tapping out a shy, yet somehow ostentatious pathway, his blind eyes hidden behind dark glasses. Michael would introduce him: 'This is my partner, Mr Johnson,' and Peter would nod and in a voice that was a clever foil to Michael's in its quiet hesitancy would say, 'How do you do? I do hope you don't mind me tagging along like this—'

Here Michael would interrupt, 'Mr Johnson is an expert on this period of furniture,' (or that make of clock, or this school of artists) 'would you mind very much if I describe your dresser,' (or oil painting or vase) 'to him?'

No one could refuse them, these two gallant young men who had suffered so much. And after Michael had gone to so much trouble describing an object in such detail, after Peter had ran his hands over it and had obviously put so much thought into his final affirmation of his partner's valuation, few felt it seemly to argue. The van was loaded up; cash courteously accepted. Only when they were driving away, safely out of earshot, did Michael and Peter allow themselves to laugh.

I imagine them laughing; I imagine Michael banging the steering wheel with the heel of his hand, laughing with relief, and Peter grinning, beginning to sing, 'The bells of hell go ting-a-ling-a-ling . . .'

'For you—'

'But not for me!'

Taking his eyes from the road Michael smiles at him and says softly, 'For me the angels sing—'

'A-ling-a-ling!'

Michael stops the van. 'Peter, tell me you're a fraud. Really, I know it—you can see.'

'As well as you can, old man.' He returns the smile he can hear in Michael's voice; he takes off the dark glasses and his eyes are obviously ruined but all the same he holds onto the pretence, holds Michael's gaze steadily, holds him in the palm of his hand. Peter knows as well I do what a liar Michael is; he knows all the secrets of all our hearts.

He knows I drowned our mother.

Peter turns away and puts on the dark glasses again. 'I can smell the lilac,' he says. 'Shall we step out?'

Michael stops the van on the verge and they walk arm in arm across the field towards the lilac tree. They sit beneath its shade and Michael is content just to be there, beside Peter in peace and privacy, and he thinks that perhaps something will happen between them that will advance their friendship or perhaps not. Either way he is content not to rush or risk a wrong move, and so he lies back and closes his eyes; he might even sleep.

Peter, for his part, remembers his jealousy from the night before, when he had lain sleepless in bed, listening to the noises Michael and I made. He is jealous still, even though hours have passed and they have been alone long enough for Michael to have forgotten I exist. Peter's jealousy makes him say, 'There's something I've been meaning to tell you.'

Michael guesses at what Peter is about to say and smiles. 'Tell me, then.'

Peter is silent for a while; this is a big step, after all; what he has to say will change everything and may even turn Michael against him; Michael may not believe him—he has considered this. His silence goes on and Michael sits up, anxious now. He reaches out and touches Peter's back.

'Peter?'

Peter turns to him. 'Do you love Edwina?'

'I thought we'd agreed never to talk about her—'

'I know we did. But I don't think I can keep silent for much longer.'

'Silent about what?'

'I'm afraid you won't believe me.'

Michael laughs, anxious and exasperated at once. 'What won't I believe?'

Quietly, as though he believes it would be better if he wasn't heard, he says, 'She's a monster.'

'A monster?' Michael lets out a long breath. 'So, you heard those rumours too?'

'Rumours?' Peter is puzzled now and rather thrown off course; he frowns at Michael. 'What rumours?'

'The dark angel rumours . . .' He hesitates then decides to go on, best, after all, that everything is out in the open between them. 'The rumour was that she could sit by a man's bed and give him permission to die, to let go if he wanted to—if he didn't feel strong enough to stay . . .' Michael laughs a little, a desperate, frightened noise. 'I don't think that makes her a monster, though, not if they wanted to die . . .' He trails off because he can see Peter's expression, the look of a man who doesn't believe in anything that can't be proven. Tentatively he says, 'I'm not sure I believe it. And Eddie won't talk about it—but that was her reputation—that if you allowed her to sit quietly by your bed . . .'

Peter is astonished. 'Then why did you marry her?'

Michael is unable to answer him; he feels that the truth would be too hurtful to them both. But Peter is waiting for an answer, glaring at him as though he has something to be angry about. At last Michael says, 'Let's not talk about her.'

But Peter hasn't forgotten about what he had decided to tell Michael; in fact, after what Michael has just told him, it seems imperative that he should be told now, while the idea of Edwina's monstrousness is still in the air between them. Evenly he says, 'She murdered our mother.'

Now Michael is astonished; he thinks that perhaps Peter is mad, the kind of madness born of the feelings they have for each other. Perhaps he would say anything at all to turn him against his wife. He decides to say nothing; his silence will speak for the absurdity of what Peter has said. Clambering to his feet he says, 'Come on, we should go home.'

'Back to her? That murderess?'

Michael reaches for his hand to help him to his feet but Peter jerks away from his touch. 'Why should we go back there? We don't need to. We could get in the van and keep driving. We have all we need if we are together.'

So, Michael thinks, this is what I have been waiting for. He had thought that he would be excited at such words, charged with purpose. Instead, surprisingly, he feels uncertain, he thinks *be careful what you wish for*, a thought that springs up from that part of him that is sensible and kind, which would not dream of hatching plans. He looks up at the lilac tree, so heavy with blossom, so intensely perfumed. Some of the flowers are becoming ragged, brown with decay; soon the tree will be ugly for another year. He wishes that time could move on quickly, that year gone in an instant; he often wishes this, wishes his life away in leaps and bounds. Sometimes he wishes he was dead; he tries to ignore such wishes, but always he looks at his wife as though she is the ready-loaded rifle locked in the glass case.

Peter is directing his sightless eyes towards him, he seems keenly aware of his silence; it seems cruel to remain standing there, saying nothing. Kneeling down beside him, Michael presses his hand against Peter's cheek. 'How can I leave her?'

'How can you not?'

Michael thinks of his wife; he remembers the pity he felt for her when he first saw her in the asylum; he thought how plain she was, like a small, brown bird, so timid and alert to the furtive, fearful whispering, the sly looks of patients and staff as she passed by. He had wanted to protect her, but also to interrogate her—he would be gentle, careful—but he believed he would get to the heart of her and discover the truth, and by doing so he believed he would be absolved—no longer responsible for all the unnecessary deaths. After all, if those men had given in meekly to a girl like Edwina—who he guessed was neither monster nor angel, just a frightened girl who had a reputation for allowing that the other nurses did not—if they had wanted to die then he didn't have to feel their deaths so acutely; he could almost shrug off their dying.

So, he sought her out and took her into his confidence so that she might return the compliment. But she wouldn't allow him into her heart, only her body—her appetite for the sex act surprised and sometimes alarmed him, and sometimes made him feel that she deserved her reputation for otherness. But even after they were married he found that he was no nearer the truth; he thought that he didn't ask the right questions; he knew that the sex got in the way of the questions, left him witless, gasping for breath let alone coherent thought. He was thwarted by sex and quite in its thrall. A sense of shame crept over him and made him turn away from Peter, to say too airily, 'Listen, old man—'

'*Old man*? Who the hell are you pretending to be now?'

'No one—'

'*No one*—exactly! Just a product of my imagination—mine and Edwina's—I think we invented you.'

'Don't talk rot.'

'Because you're perfect—don't you see?' All at once Peter is scrambling to his feet. He catches hold of Michael's hand and pulls him toward him. 'You're a chameleon. Aren't you confused?'

Michael hangs his head; that he can't look Peter in the eye makes him more ashamed. 'Yes.'

'Don't be. *Don't be*! Decide. Come away with me. No more confusion.'

It would be simple, Michael thinks, to climb in the van and drive away. But the image he has is of himself alone, speeding along the country lanes until Thorp is far behind him; Thorp, Peter, Edwina. He would be free to start again, on a fresh, blank page and Peter would be right, there would be no more confusion, only liberation and a sense that anything was possible, even fatherhood. He can't imagine being a father to Edwina's child, can't imagine ever feeling entirely comfortable around such a creature.

But then he remembers Eddie and why he married her, remembers that he hasn't quite got to the bottom of her mystery and that he must, if he is to find any peace at all. He draws breath, holds it for a moment: when he exhales he will be himself again, the self he has chosen to be for now: sensible, loyal, the man who will find out the truth come what may. At last he says, 'Peter, I think I need a little more time.'

Peter snorts. He squeezes Michael's hand tightly, cruelly; there will be a bruise he hopes. He lets him go, a gesture that feels as though he is throwing something away. 'All right. You can have some time. I'll wait.'

'I'm sorry.'

'No need to be. I'll win. I always do.'

◆　　◆　　◆

I am dead, and I haunt the house of a man and woman whose marriage is unhappy, so unhappy that it seems to hold them together, this mutual, profound unhappiness. Sometimes I almost believe that it's their unhappiness that keeps me as well preserved as I am—not just my guilt alone, I'm beginning to believe that my guilt isn't so powerful. After all, others have done far worse and don't stay as long. It's unfair, I think, and so I find that lately I have been going to Gaye and David's room at night, watching them sleep, hoping that one or the other might wake and see me and know that they are no longer welcome.

CHAPTER 14

~

Ralph's painting of Gaye and David's garden is finished. It leans against his living room wall and he has covered it with a sheet to keep the dust away, but also to stop him from looking at it. There is something in the picture that disturbs him, something not quite right. I am in the picture, of course, somehow he has captured me, an ugly smudge beneath the chestnut trees. No one will notice me except Ralph, and even he can't truly grasp that I am there. He thinks only that he has made a mistake. He fears he is losing his touch, although this morning a London gallery rang him; they would like to show a small exhibition of his work, sure that this will be profitable for all concerned. Ralph agreed, absently, thinking of Gaye's garden painting and how he would like never to see it again.

Decisively he takes the still covered picture out to his car. He will take it to Gaye now—no need to stand on ceremony, after all. He will leave it with her in the most casual way possible, although he'll look away when she uncovers it and pretend a modest lack of interest in her reaction. He won't ask her if she can see the ghost, not that he's sure it *is* a ghost. No. He has simply made a mistake. Mistake is not quite the right word, but this is how he thinks of himself when he looks at the painting—mistaken. He has gone wrong, somewhere; his confidence is shaken.

Driving to Gaye's house, he thinks about the memorial for the Falkland War veterans he is still unsure of attending. Last night he rang Mark Walker, his former comrade, a man whose wounds seemed impossible to survive. But Mark is now quite fit and lives a life rather like his own, solitary, comfortable, urbane—Ralph smiles at this word that has slipped into his head: all at once he sees himself in a silk dressing gown and paisley cravat and he is smoking a Turkish cigarette in a long holder. This image is wrong—here he is, mistaken again. He should see himself as Picasso, muscular, paint-splattered, his sleeves rolled up, so intent on his work, no props except his own genius. But Ralph is just himself, someone who will be caught out, or a least not remembered past his death. 'I have no illusions,' he says aloud at traffic lights that have turned to red at his approach. For a moment, before the lights turn back to green, he truly believes this; for a moment he thinks of himself as pragmatic and not disappointed at all.

On the telephone last night Mark Walker had said, 'My father died. His death has helped me to come to terms with the past.' He had laughed self-consciously. 'I suppose I can walk into the Abbey a little more confidently now that things are rather more in perspective.'

Walker is a novelist. He writes books that women read but are never-the-less lauded in the Sunday broadsheets. On those very rare occasions Ralph goes into a bookshop, Mark Walker's novels are stacked high and sometimes there is a picture of him, unsmiling, sexy, appealing to women Ralph is certain. He and Walker have both achieved a certain fame; perhaps their names will feature in footnotes when the history of the war is once again re-written. The war. Their telephone conversation ended without any decisions reached about its commemoration, although it seemed to Ralph that Walker wanted him to say that he wouldn't go, that he would rather forget, thus giving him the excuse he needed to stay away.

But we are not supposed to forget, but to learn from our mistakes.

I watch Ralph park his car, take the picture from the back seat and walk up the drive to the house. Gaye is in the garden, she won't hear his knock; I imagine going to the door and saying *come in, come in! How nice to see you—it's such a beautiful day isn't it? Gaye's in the garden, come through, come through!* The living are so busy, so full of air and gestures, I feel weary even thinking about such palaver. All the same, I go out into the garden where Gaye is kneeling at a flower bed planting out snapdragon seedlings. To test her I say, 'He's here. Ralph. He has your painting under his arm.'

Gaye stands up. The knees of her gardening trousers are muddy, her hands quite filthy with half-moons of dirt under her finger nails, and she wipes her brow with her forearm, a curiously masculine gesture. Her hair straggles from her loose pony-tail and her cheeks are flushed. I understand at once that she is too absorbed by her work to sense me, so utterly unaware that she hasn't realised that Ralph has walked around the side of the house and is watching her. She looks picturesque, not haunted at all. Turning suddenly, her hand flies to her mouth—he has startled her, for a second she thought he was David, come to bring some terrible news, forgetting for a second that there is no more bad news left in the world.

Ralph steps towards her. 'Sorry, I didn't mean to startle you.'

He thinks how young she looks without her make-up, with her hair tied up so artlessly. He shifts the painting from one arm to the other, aware that the garden has subtly changed since he was last here; the ghost has gone; all he sees is sunshine, and Gaye, illuminated so that she looks like a girl of twenty.

She leads him into the house. I follow and watch as Ralph unveils the painting, as Gaye cocks her head to one side, frowning. He laughs self-consciously and feels he is too old to make such a noise, but today he feels young and even more unsure. Despite himself he asks her what she's thinking.

'It's wonderful,' she says, and turns to him, her face serious so that he knows she is telling the truth.

The painting is hung on the wall above the fireplace in the sitting room, it has pride of place. I stare and stare at it and touch the dark, ugly smudge that is me. Gaye and Ralph talk and their voices go through me and I can't make any sense of them. Michael and Peter are in the garden in this picture, I can see them if only I look hard enough.

I look hard. There is Michael and he is mowing the lawn, and there is Peter and he is sitting in a deckchair, his blind eyes following the racket the mower makes. Both are steeped in the scent of cut grass, both are wearing easy clothes, slacks and soft, collarless shirts, their sleeves rolled up so that their forearms are becoming tanned, their skin prickling with the transformation. They shout above the noise, their voices bouncing across the newly striped lawn; a bottle of beer dangles from Peter's lazy fingers, another bottle stands ready in the shade of his chair. Michael will be thirsty soon enough, such hot work that Peter imagines his face reddened, sweat patches blooming beneath his arms. He imagines the knot of muscles in his arms, those long fingers stained green from grass cuttings; he imagines that Michael will stop soon and tip the beer bottle to his mouth so that its contents glug swiftly down, his Adam's apple bobbing greedily. Peter smiles to himself and shades his eyes that can make out light when light is as bright as this. He shades his eyes and imagines shouting, *'I can see you!'* because the picture in his head is so real, he has worked on its composition too long for it not to be. He's discovered that he doesn't need to touch Michael to make him solid flesh, that particular trick of the blind is quite redundant when it comes to Michael.

Michael sits down beside the deckchair. He is breathing heavily because he isn't quite fit, still frail in fact, if only he would admit this to himself. He is breathing heavily, quickly, and Peter reaches out and ruffles his hair, unable to resist.

I look hard. There is nothing to see, really. They are two young men, friends, brothers-in-law, partners, and young enough for high jinks and easiness. There is nothing to see and so I step out of the shadow of the plum trees and they turn towards me as though they had caught my scent.

I remember that Michael smiled at me. 'Eddie, come and sit with us.'

'Yes, Edwina,' Peter's voice was less enthusiastic, 'come and sit down—don't skulk about in the shadows.'

'I have work to do,' I said and I could hear the coldness in my voice and I knew that Michael believed that I was turning into a nag, the kind of wife he hadn't bargained for. He pretended to be dismayed, although I knew that he only wanted rid of me so that he could be alone with Peter. He thought I was a fool, one that couldn't see through his act.

◆   ◆   ◆

Time passes; Ralph and Gaye have gone and outside the garden is in darkness and the seedlings Gaye planted wilt into the ground. The slugs come out, the snails and the beetles; nothing survives them. I step closer to the painting. I'm still there, but alone now, as before. Gaye hasn't noticed me; if she does she will turn the picture to the wall.

CHAPTER 15

～

David is writing in his diary. It is early evening; he has shaken off the tiredness of the day and he writes quickly because the memories keep coming, it's difficult to keep up. There's a particular memory he wants to unravel, prompted by recent events, of Emily's christening.

He remembers how he hadn't wanted her to be christened—God didn't exist in those days—but he hadn't voiced his opposition because to do so might be taken as a rejection. All other babies in their circle were christened—all wore their white gown and heirloom shawl; all received silver tokens—lockets, bracelets, money boxes, all were indulged and doted on for the day; all were photographed. A christening was a public display, after all, a kind of coming out party: *this is our child—isn't she wonderful? Aren't we rather wonderful for producing her?* At Emily's party there would be cake and champagne and everyone on their best behaviour, guarding their thoughts with broad smiles and off-the-peg inanities lest they give their true feelings away.

David writes *Emily was already over a year old at her christening, a heavy baby, not yet walking; she had a heart murmur, but we were told that actually her symptoms were mild considering her handicap. The doctor sought to reassure us—saying that some Downs children grow up to live semi-independent lives. I was determined that she would—that I would do everything possible to make her life ordinary. I was at times wildly optimistic—she would go to college, find a job, marry, have children—and terribly despairing. I saw myself as a very old man, still holding Emily's hand. I found myself looking at adults with Emily's condition and sometimes following them, from a little distance, like a spy, unable to approach them directly, honestly—how could I? I was shy of them, and besides—what would I say? That I have a child like you and will it be all right—are you happy—does the world treat you kindly?—as though everyone like Emily is the same, all sharing the exact same experiences. But I was looking for clues, pointers, I wanted to know just what to expect.*

I turned to books, to the cold facts about chromosomes as well as the testimonies of parents. And then I would put this or that book down and go and stand over her crib and watch her and watch her and sometimes lift her out and carry her into the garden and I would give her a running commentary on the flowers and trees and birds and there is Mr Simpson with his dog and the dog is called Henry and he is a spaniel woof woof. Talking all the time, making up stories, giving out facts—everything can have a fact pinned to it—the sun, a dandelion, a Ford Transit van. And the toys I bought, the picture books—all had a purpose: to beat the odds.

David puts down his pen. He can only write like this in short bursts before his mind begins to wander and becomes tangled in regrets and self-recriminations and justifications. He is very hard on himself; actually he believes he was the very worst father that ever lived. But then, he also thinks that he is the worst husband. He even made a poor adulterer. Luke said once . . . Ah, no, we mustn't think of Luke. Yesterday he saw Luke in his car with another man; they were stopped at traffic lights and he was walking down the street and had to look away quickly and dodge into a shop doorway; he must have appeared odd, like a cartoon secret agent so exaggerated was his reaction. It took some time for his heart rate to slow, time spent staring into the shop window—a chemist's careful display of Radox bottles. Eventually he had to get out of the way for a young girl with her baby in a pushchair. The girl scowled and the baby whined and he had held the shop door open for her, apologising. Luke was with another man; he could have been a friend or a colleague. David knew he was his lover.

David goes outside and sits down on the summerhouse steps. I sit beside him and together we contemplate Gaye's garden that his brother has painted and so seems even less like anywhere that has anything to do with him. He remembers how he cut the plum trees down—how ancient they were—how gnarled and twisted—and wonders now why he had gone to so much trouble, except that he was full of rage and the powerful vibrations of the chain saw were an expression of this rage, reinforcing it: he had never felt so dangerous or so powerful; he thinks of that rage now as a no-holds-barred tantrum. Afterwards, panting, the bitter scent of sap and crushed green leaves seemed like an admonishment. The splintered branches quivered on the grass in a tangled heap, a monster's nest, and all he could do was clear it away, his rage seeping out of him as he worked. He remembers forming a plan as he dragged the wood into a tidier heap: he would write to Luke and explain himself and everything would be all right in some way that he couldn't yet think of but would, eventually, if he thought rigorously enough for long enough, become clear. It was just a question of becoming a slightly different person, one who could think in straight lines and move forward. Come the right time and there would be nothing to it.

The tree stumps are all that remain of that day. David stares at them—they are like wooden stepping stones across the lawn—this is how he would have described them to Emily. Everything has its story, its set of facts half-remembered, half false. At her christening he had held her in the crook of his arm so that she faced outwards and he had pointed at the bright stained glass depicting Christ as the Good Shepherd. The lamb at His feet had a smiling expression—do lambs smile—does any animal smile—or do they look so pleased with themselves only when they are in the presence of God? 'There's a lamb,' he explained, 'and there is Jesus, who some people called the Good Shepherd because he risked the flock to find the one sheep that was lost.' Did he really say all that? Was there no one else to hear him? If there was, he can't remember them. The memory he has—and he knows it's quite wrong—was that he was alone with Emily and that she gazed at the high window with her dark, unblinking eyes and was heavy and peaceful in his arms, her white dress dazzling against the dark of his suit.

That boy at that other christening—his cousin's partner, Christian, he had worn a similarly dark suit, and his daughter, Patience, had been quiet and peaceful just as Emily had been, as though babies sensed goodness in the church's stones. And Patience had been wrapped in a lacy shawl that caught in his cufflinks and her father had glared at him, angry for some reason best known to him, although he had made more of the boy's anger at the time. He had imagined the boy was homosexual—*bi-sexual*—like him—the worst king of *sexual* to be for its dishonesty, its panicky, indecisive flapping. He had imagined this for no good reason other than the fact that Christian had a rough-edged handsomeness, because he was tough looking and well built, wishful, wistful imagining set off by that particular challenging look in the boy's eye. Then he thinks of Father Purcell, who had saved him from such thoughts with his timely intervention, who had seemed to see into his heart—no, his guts because surely that's where such longing begins, nothing to do with romance—and had not been so offended as to walk away.

Gaye comes outside, wiping her hands on a cloth. She calls, 'Supper's ready—would you like to eat out here?' She's smiling, trying too hard. David clambers to his feet. He wants to reassure her, to say something like *I'm going to change*. But if she asks him how he will change he knows he won't be able to say; he's not sure even if he believes in this idea—it's too much of an abstraction, too heartfelt. Intellectually he's certain he will always be himself, always the hard core David, petrified by loss. So he says nothing, only that the evening's growing chilly and they should eat inside.

◆   ◆   ◆

Supper is cold ham and salad, pickled beetroot that stains everything it touches—the whites of the hard boiled eggs become pale maroon, the new potatoes too in their yellow slicks of melted butter. The table with its brightly patterned oil cloth is covered with jars of this, little bowls of that, all to tempt David's appetite. Gaye is afraid that he is becoming too thin. He has always been thin, skinny—she remembers how his hip seemed to give a little when she pressed her own wider hip against his, as though he was made of something more malleable than bone. They had been standing side by side for a photograph and had known each other only a few days, but for some reason her mother had posed them in the garden beside her father's humming van. That smell of bones, of the inedible—David had been too polite to mention it. Her father called him *son* and couldn't take him seriously, he was too young, too skinny, too malleable; it seemed unlikely that he had even begun to shave.

(You're thinking that this isn't the David I described earlier—not this skinny boy! Hadn't I described a tall, broad, dark man, one who shaved often, his testosterone working overtime? You must allow me my tall tales; and I have queer fancies. But he *is* handsome. Beautiful, if you like).

Gaye and David eat in easy silence—they have been married a long time after all and they are terribly used to each other. Because it's second nature to Gaye, she takes note of what David eats, pleased if he seems to be enjoying his meal. She knows how most women would think this small pleasure was beneath them, she knows how old fashioned she is. When David sets his knife and fork down neatly and quietly on his cleared plate she asks, 'Would you like some more?'

He shakes his head. 'Next week,' he says, 'Emily's birthday. Have you thought anymore about what we should do?'

The photographs of Emily are still in their shoebox, although she has bought an album to arrange them in. Taking the album from its cellophane wrapping she had realised that arranging the photos on its pages was a job for one person only, more than one and it would be an awkward business with too many hands and elbows and eyes. And where and how would they sit? And what would happen if they disagreed on a date, or a place? None of the photographs were inscribed. Then she remembers the trees she has been thinking of planting in the garden and all at once it seems so obvious what should commemorate her daughter's birthday.

'I thought we could plant a tree,' she says. 'Perhaps two. Plum trees—a species that bears lots of fruit.'

She watches his expression wanting him to agree because now she has thought of this she needs it to become reality. It's something they can do together and she imagines the two of them working closely, in companionable silence. But now she is full of doubt—don't they need to talk?—yet the idea of this silence appeals to her and she tells herself that there will be a telepathic understanding between them; whenever they have worked together it has always been so. She remembers their first house and how together they decorated its small rooms. Emily's room was last; she had been pregnant and over the morning sickness that had made the smell of paint unbearable, the semen-like stink of wallpaper paste even worse. David had chosen a frieze of bunny rabbits in bright colours to run around the walls, a bunny rabbit mobile to match. The rabbits wore waistcoats, not one of them in pink or blue—they didn't know if their baby was a boy or a girl because in those days there seemed to be a law against giving such a secret away to parents. Months later, as she nursed Emily, Gaye would count the bunnies and try to commit to memory their coloured waistcoat sequence. Such a mindless task helped to keep her thoughts contained.

David is thinking of the trees he destroyed and how, by planting others, he might make amends. Meeting Gaye's gaze he sees how much she wants to do this; her hopefulness has made her quite beautiful and although he has been thinking so recently about that boy, Christian, or perhaps because of those thoughts, he reaches across the table and takes her hand. 'I think we should go to bed.'

◆   ◆   ◆

Their bed is made so neatly—Gaye is always so neat—their bedroom as tidy as that of any five star hotel's. They undress as though it's bedtime and nothing unusual is taking place at all, except David is a little quicker and discards his clothes carelessly on the floor and Gaye is shy—which is ridiculous, she knows. Her husband smells strongly of his desire for her, such a dark, male scent, and he has pulled back the white cotton covered duvet and lain down on the exposed white sheet and his erection rises from its fuzz of dark hair; his belly is concave, his chest rising and falling as though he has been running, and he has covered his face with his arm, his fingers curling loosely around the bars of the bedstead. When she lies down beside him he turns on his side to face her, although she wanted him as he was; stretched out like that his body was vulnerable, he had seemed brought down to her, her equal.

Her breathing matches his, becoming steadier as they lie there without touching. The evening light is soft and outside in the garden birds sing and over the fence their neighbours' children call to one another. Inside the house is as silent as ever, cool and sweet smelling because Gaye has kept the windows open during this spell of warm weather. The bed shifts beneath her as David moves onto his back. Taking her hand he lifts it to his lips.

I won't watch this. Imagine only that they make love tenderly but not without the well-practised moves and responses of their long marriage, although his orgasm has a different register of intensity and her climax sends her away for a little while to where there are no memories and no thoughts of anyone at all. He slept afterwards and she laid on her back, seeping into the sheets, not sleeping; she has never slept as easily as him. Her memories creep back; she blocks a few, follows a few down their dead ends. Sleep will surprise her eventually.

CHAPTER 16

∼

Gaye is sitting on the edge of her seat because she has just seen her brother-in-law on television. There was Ralph, walking up the steps of Westminster Abbey to attend the Falklands War Memorial Service. Gaye, her hand over her mouth as if to contain her surprise, peers at the TV screen in the hope of seeing him again. The cameras scan the Abbey's interior but they concentrate on those famous faces whose careful expressions the viewers will be most interested in. Ralph is not famous enough; nor is his erstwhile comrade, the novelist Mark Walker, who stands beside him, so Gaye is disappointed, although it's a disappointment that is tempered by her surprise. As the first hymn rings out from the television, she slumps back in her chair. She wonders if she should call David in case his brother should make another appearance, but already it's too late, the programme has cut to the next item: a reporter is talking rapidly outside the Old Bailey. Besides, David is in his study—he wouldn't want to be disturbed. Besides, doesn't he dislike his brother? Hasn't he failed to get over his childhood jealousies?

She thinks of Ralph as he was at her wedding, how he got drunk and asked her, 'Sure you're not going to regret this?'

Even drunk he was handsome, even with his mouth twisted with cruelty. She remembers that he had taken off his tie and unbuttoned his collar and that he leaned towards her, too close so that she could smell his beer-breath. 'Listen,' he said, and swayed a little. 'Listen . . .' But what ever he wanted her to listen to he seemed to think better of; she saw the exaggerated frowns and lip-pursing of a drunk's second thoughts play out across his face, saw him raise a finger to his mouth, briefly pressing it to his lips before pointing unsteadily at her. 'Mum's the word, eh?'

Gaye stands up and turns off the television. She wonders if Ralph will be home by now and imagines telephoning him, saying '*I saw you on tv!*' But her excitement would be wholly inappropriate after the solemnity of the occasion, and although she guesses he would indulge her she knows how silly she would sound to him. Instead she should phone him and ask, soberly, how he is, how much he has been affected by the music and the sermons. Her heart beating too quickly, she finds herself dialling his number and listening to the ring tone which seems too insistent, too intrusive. Only his answering machine picks up. Gaye sets the phone down softly without leaving a message.

She goes into the kitchen and boils the kettle, takes a tea bag from the caddy and thinks of going to David in his study to ask if he would like a hot drink before bed. She imagines David lifting his gaze from his laptop screen and frowning as though processing her question just as his computer might before considering his reply. 'No,' he would say eventually, and then, 'thank you.'

The light in his study would be dim, his desk tidy, the walls around him quite bare. She isn't sure what he does in there night after night, although she has an idea, nasty suspicions which she tries to talk herself out of. He is working, she tells herself, researching, keeping himself up to date with the world of dentistry. But her imagination conjures downloaded images of naked men, oiled, muscular torsos and buttocks and thighs and ever-ready erections.

She pours the boiling water onto the teabag in her mug. The bag floats to the surface and she pushes it down again with a teaspoon, stirring and stirring. The naked men reside at the back of her mind; she only rarely allows them to be imagined—they are altogether too animated, too over-bearing, they take up so much space and are so tightly packed she can almost smell them. Their penises spring against their abdomens, tensile, even comic if she could bring herself to look hard enough to laugh. She should look harder, she believes, and imagine less; perhaps she *should* laugh because there is something quite childish about their naked poses and sometimes it's best just to laugh at naughty children.

Gaye carries her tea into the living room; the news has finished and a film has begun. She turns off the television and goes to the window; the curtains are still open and she sees her reflection in the dark glass; she is too thin because grief has made her so; luckily, this skin-and-bone look is fashionable. She has high cheekbones and big, wide-apart eyes, and it seems that grief has fashioned these, too. Her complexion is clear and her teeth are good, of course, and Luke Harding said he had expected her to be beautiful as some boys are beautiful: fey, delicate, exquisite.

Luke Harding said, 'Thank you for meeting me.' He shook her hand and his grip was strong. Had she expected a limp-wristed man? A camp, waspish dandy? She had expected to blush when she met him—and she did—because she had never met a gay man before.

'Please, sit down,' Luke said, and indicated a chair he'd pulled out from the pub table. He had chosen this pub because it was out of the way, found along a winding country road, a place where those with too much time on their hands drove for a lunch of scampi and chips or a two-for-one supper deal. There were hunting prints on the wall and horse brasses and pewter tankards engraved and hung above the bar. On the next table two pensioner couples frowned at their menus. Beside the glass of white wine Luke had already bought her was a single pea. Delicately, Luke picked it up and dropped it in the ash tray.

He was handsome, rather strikingly so, even the barmaid looked twice. His good looks made her feel even more nervous, even intimidated, he had such poise, such confidence and what did she have except her red-hot blushes? She gulped at her wine and her hands shook and her lipstick left an unsightly imprint on her glass, and she was aware of how ripe she smelt: too bloodily fecund, like her mother.

How did he begin to explain himself? She can't remember. She thinks he said something like: 'He's been meaning to tell you for months, promising me that he will tell you,' and 'I just think it's right that you should know. He needs to be honest with both of us . . .' He mentioned love, she thinks, his love for David, David's love for him, David's love for her (which wasn't comparable, how could it be?) And then his poise slipped and he said,

'You've hardly spoken. Tell me what you're thinking.'

Staring at her dark garden beyond her reflection, Gaye remembers how vulnerable Luke Harding looked and suddenly desperate so that he became transparent: she could see right through to his greed and neediness. She had stood up, the wine unfinished. Taking her car keys from her bag she said, 'I should go. Thank you for the drink.'

He stood up too, too quickly so that he almost knocked the wine glass over. 'What will you do?'

And it came to her then, and made her feel powerful: she would do nothing. She would pretend that this meeting had never taken place; that he had never called her to invite her here; she would pretend that this man was nothing other than David's way of throwing himself away from grief and pain, far beyond the normal reaches of his life with her, an expedition into unexplored territory where nothing mattered except the next step away from the agonising known.

She had driven home calmly, knowing she was strong enough to keep her new knowledge to herself, her jealousy closely guarded, and this guarding would make her stronger still and allow her to keep other feelings to herself; her heart would harden, she knew, but this seemed to her to be a good thing: she would be reinforced, contained and self-reliant and nothing could hurt her ever again.

Gaye sips her tea. She travels swiftly in time from that car journey to this afternoon at the garden centre where she had gone to buy the trees she intended to plant with David. The trees were intended, she supposed, to give their grief a place to settle, but as she walked the gravel path where the trees were roped together like chain gang prisoners, she wondered whether such a place would help. How much comfort could she expect, anyway, how much did she deserve? Her mission seemed all at once pointless, and her despair was such that she had to stop, the gravel sharp through her too-thin soles; she tried to make sense of the Latin names on the trees' labels with the only words she knew of the language: God at my Right, the words so unlikely she knew she must be wrong.

But then a man had stepped towards her, cautiously as though he was afraid of scaring her away. He had helped her and he had been so knowledgeable that all at once her despair seemed a mean and ignorant thing and she had wanted to give information in return, had almost confessed to him the reason for the trees' purchase. But then he would start on an explanation of this or that variety, its merits and disadvantages, and her reasons for being there began to recede, their painful edges softened by his quiet enthusiasm. At last he had laughed a little, said, 'I'm boring you—you must be wishing you'd never asked.'

He was wearing a plaid shirt, its sleeves rolled up to reveal muscular, sinuous forearms; he was short and stocky and balding and he reminded her of her father and so she astonished herself by saying, 'The trees are a memorial for my daughter.'

How could she have said this so plainly? She had crossed a boundary and at once became panicked. But he had only nodded as though he was told such intimacies everyday. 'A tree makes the best memorial,' he said, 'a living, growing thing that can help us find solace.'

Amazingly she blundered on. 'I don't believe in God.'

He had touched her arm. 'I'll choose the best trees and help you plant them. They'll bear fruit in no time, just you wait and see.'

Gaye hears David come downstairs and turns away from her reflection. He is there, in the doorway, about to say something when she cuts in, 'Ralph was on TV just now, walking into Westminster Abbey for the Falklands Service.'

'Really?' He raises his eyebrows. 'I felt sure he wouldn't go.' Stepping towards her he says, 'I'm going to bed, are you?'

The naked men are all around him—occasionally they gather like this when weariness with herself causes cracks in her defences. It is late, and her tea has grown cold and there is nothing else for it except to say, 'Yes, I'm coming up now, I just need to turn off the lights.'

She thinks how much she loved him when she was eighteen, when she found his face quite astonishing. His face made up for the odd times when he made her cringe with some remark, some awkwardness born of their incompatibility. Wasn't he too clever for her, after all? Wouldn't she have been better suited to his brother, who was more ordinarily handsome? But Ralph's face didn't compel her as David's did. She had been known to stare and stare at David in the undercover dimness of a night club or a cinema, where the silvered restless light flitted across his face and made him even more extraordinary.

For his part David thinks how much he wants her to forgive him—not to say *I forgive you* out loud—they are too far beyond that, those words would only be a re-opening of wounds—but to demonstrate her forgiveness with gestures, with expressions, with small kindnesses. *Christ!* He truly amazes himself with such self pity; his ego must know no bounds to want so much! Small kindnesses indeed! He tries not to wonder if he has always been such an arsehole.

Gaye catches his eye, she is puzzled that he is still standing there in the doorway, so still, so expectant-looking as though he has just asked her a question and is waiting for a reply. Perhaps he did speak and she didn't hear. About to ask him, he turns away. Gaye switches off the lamps and follows him upstairs.

I am left in darkness.

For a while I stare out into the garden before taking myself off on my tour of the house. Later I will stand over Gaye and David's bed while they sleep. Later still I will go into the garden as the sun rises above the neighbour's house and think about what I have learnt so far.

And what have I learnt? Only that the minutes and the hours and the days pass and it feels as though I count every second: *one Mississippi two Mississippi* just as I was taught to count in school: accurately marking time. I observe Gaye and David and much as I would like them to leave I pretend that I'm their confidante and sometimes that I'm an anthropologist, quite detached and merely intrigued by their antics. I pretend all the time that I am not in love with David because my love for him makes me feel silly, it's best dismissed as a crush. But he *so* resembles Michael, and so I suppose I can be allowed my infatuation, rooted as it is in authentic feeling.

CHAPTER 17

~

David sits in The Castle & Anchor's lounge, away from the bar where football is on the TV. He has been there ten minutes and has already drunk most of his pint of beer. It's not that Father Purcell is late—rather that David is early.

Apart from him the lounge bar is empty and unwelcoming with its worn vinyl floor, its scuffed tables and chairs, its posters advertising last month's quiz curling from the dirty-cream wall. Opposite him on a window sill there is a stuffed seagull in a glass case. The window lets in a grey, rain-soaked light and looks out on wheelie bins in the pub's yard; the bird contemplates these bins with a speculative glint in its dark eye. It's the way the sunlight catches the glass that makes the gull seem so alive, along with the skill of the taxidermist who has gone to the extra trouble of scattering sea shells at the bird's webbed feet, an artless arrangement on the white sand. David gazes at the case; the bird is a Herring Gull, a scavenger, an opportunist: enclosed in glass it nevertheless gives the impression that its imprisonment is nothing, it could be free at any time. David thinks of Emily, how they would study the bird together, how her up-close curiosity would leave her palm print on the glass. *Look, Emily, look*. He closes his eyes and hears the loud, laughing cry of the gull.

I can't go on blaming myself, he thinks. But this is an idle thought and so meaningless it might just as well be the words of a song he can't stop singing. Aloud he says, 'I blame myself,' and this helps because it leaves him nowhere to go, there is nothing left to worry at, yet even this stern comfort feels undeserved.

I sit beside him. I pretend that I am drinking a port and lemon and that the barmaid with her two blackened eyes and her too thin arms is as alive as David, and not like me or the men leaning against the bar in their filthy working clothes who are still so shocked by the industrial carelessness that brought about their deaths. How could the roof collapse, after all? Wasn't death so unlikely as to happen only to other people? I avoid their eyes; their outraged surprise makes me want to laugh.

The priest comes in. David gets to his feet, relieved, fearful—these emotions showing on his face so clearly; he is afraid of what he might do to sabotage himself. But he is aware of the living, breathing barman who hovers in the doorway between public and lounge bars and who is anxious to get back to the game. So he takes a measure of control and says, 'Father, hello. What can I get you to drink?' He reaches in his trouser pocket for his wallet. 'What would you like?'

◆   ◆   ◆

I would like, the priest thinks, for this man not to care so much but to go home to his wife and not mix with these ghosts. He should lay down the burden of his grief . . . Oh, how glib he has become, but he feels there is some truth here; pain like David's should not be held so close, so tightly that a man becomes calcified around its pitiful form.

But Father Purcell hides his exasperation with a smile and says, 'Whiskey, I think, with just a little water, thank you,' and his smile is warm and smiling like this causes him to remember the sympathy he feels for David and forget the arthritic pain that makes him less of what he used to be: a forbearing man, even kind. Easy to be kind around David, his gentleness demands to be reflected.

Purcell sits opposite the place David has just vacated. He nods at me curtly and I nod back—I think he realises I won't be moved on as the other dead have been vanquished at the sight of him, less sure of themselves and how they should behave around such a man. I am determined to be brave and I fold my hands in my lap and sit up straight, feet together, and I am as dignified as can be. The priest snorts and looks away; we are all like children to him, playing our silly games.

David returns with the drinks, sits downs and says, 'I think Liverpool may have scored.'

'Good for them.'

There is a silence in which David, of course, feels too solid, his back too straight and stiff so that he despairs of being able to behave naturally, and these feelings, mixed with his terrible need to be liked, are a combination that robs him of his voice. Beyond the priest's shoulder the Herring Gull is watching him, unblinking, contemptuous, and he bows his head and turns and turns his drink on the beer mat which warns him not to drink and drive. Father Purcell takes out a pipe, tobacco pouch and matches and begins the pipe-smoker's ritual. A match is struck, held to the pipe's bowl, and the ready-rubbed, golden flake takes the flame as the priest sucks, concentrating. The silence becomes right and proper then—such a process does not take well to small talk—and David is grateful and becomes calmer, breathing in the sweet smoke as he allows the stiffness in his spine to relax a little.

He clears his throat but this preparation to speak comes to nothing—what can he say, after all? Purcell catches his eye, and, lowering the pipe from his mouth says, 'This pub used to be surrounded by back-to-back terraces—all demolished for the new road. Now here it is, an isolated island, so cut off it remains as it was—no invasion of slot machines or karaoke, just the same, ageing faces who keep the place ticking along like a slow clock. And I can walk here—it's good for me to walk, my doctor says, and it's half-way to the church, a good stopping off point. It's bleak, though, I have to not mind its bleakness.'

'It's old-fashioned,' David says redundantly, and thinks that it's old-fashioned in the worst sense with none of the picturesque charm of sawdust floors and spittoons and coal fires. The 1970s made the pub's surfaces wipe-clean yet there is a sticky plasticised feel to the place and suddenly he does mind its bleakness and the sad incongruity of the seabird in the glass case. But he minds only for a moment because surroundings don't matter at all and if he was in the priest's church with its purple and green stained glass and carved and polished wood, its gentle-faced statues of the saints, he would feel just as he feels now—congested with words. He sips his drink and his beer is too thin and lively like a hyper-active fifteen-year-old and the beer mat warns him not to drink, not to drive and has no right to preach so in such a place as this.

Suddenly, as if his voice knows it must take him unawares if it is to be heard, he says, 'I blame myself for Emily's death. Gaye blames me too, I'm sure.'

He meets the priest's gaze challengingly. The man is sucking on his pipe and frowning as though afraid it is about to extinguish itself, and he meets David's gaze as though he is merely a distraction to the task of keeping the pipe alive. Then the pipe seems to be drawing satisfactorily and the priest takes on a look of contentment and all this unsettles David; it's as though he hasn't been heard and he can't repeat himself now, he is too self-conscious, although he is angry: this is not how the man was supposed to behave, not as he imagined his behaviour at all.

Father Purcell allows David's anger—it's good for him to be discomforted; the boy is too much inside himself—the guilt which he complained of—and which he himself had guessed at—has been indulged for far too long. He takes his pipe from his mouth and contemplates it; a good pipe, expensive, a retirement gift that was thought by those who purchased it to be an inspired choice, and so it was, in a way. His old pipe had become too worn, rather disgusting he had to agree, but this new one takes some getting used to and makes him feel like a novice again. I am old, he thinks, and the pursuit of some challenges seems not so worthwhile.

At last David manages, 'Father . . . ?'

Purcell looks at him, cool and direct. Evenly he says, 'Tell me what happened the day Emily died, David. From the beginning.'

◆   ◆   ◆

'We were staying in a cottage,' David begins, and he wants to add that it was mid-August, cool and breezy on that stretch of Northumberland coast, the sea grey and wintery and sullen—but mercurial, too, he knew that within a few minutes its surface might sparkle with sun. But he doesn't know how much information the priest needs or desires, or how much time he has to tell him everything, from the beginning. He draws back a little and tries to be precise.

'We were staying in a cottage right by the sea. From the garden gate you could be on the beach within a few minutes—we'd—I'd—chosen the place for this very reason because Emily loved the sea . . .' Here he trails off, clears his throat, makes his voice behave. 'She loved the sea and we—I—thought that she deserved a treat . . . The atmosphere at home between Gaye and myself had become so strained—and she was disturbed, upset...' He laughs shortly, turns his glass around, lifts it and puts it down again half-way to his lips. 'Emily asked me if I was going to leave home—like her friend's Dad.

'Anyway . . . Anyway, we booked this weekend away—it was a cancellation, we actually thought how lucky we were. And we packed too quickly and forgot Tog, a pink bear . . . She'd never slept a night without him. I should have turned back for Tog, but I was cross with her, cross that she'd forgotten . . .'

He takes a breath and checks the priest's expression which remains the same. 'Gaye hardly spoke in the car—except to say it was my decision to turn back or not. But we were half way there. And Gaye sat in the passenger seat beside me so rigidly, keeping herself so tightly together, so distant . . . I'm not blaming her . . . Not at all. She was angry and she had every right to be . . . *angry*. No, I thought at the time that she was angry but now I don't know . . . Disgusted, I think . . . Oh, Christ . . . I'm sorry . . .'

'Go on, David, I'm listening.'

'Gaye had found out I had been looking at gay pornography.'

There, he has said it, he is out; still the priest is unmoved. He's heard worse no doubt in the confessional, perhaps this is even an anti-climax. Quickly he adds, 'I'd been to a gay bar, too. Just to look . . . Sorry, I don't want to lie to you . . . I had ideas . . . Hopes, I suppose . . .' These are not the right words and he honestly, truly doesn't want to lie but the truth is harder to grasp than he had thought, he can hardly remember what he was thinking as he set out for that club, except that he probably wasn't dressed properly, that he would be smirked at and made to feel like a ridiculous, dirty old man; or else he would be beaten or humiliated in some way he could only think around the edges of, half thrilled, half appalled. He hadn't been thinking about Gaye, certainly not about Emily, he couldn't imagine any consequences other than the immediate—gratifying or painful or both. All he had wanted was to venture out, to test himself. With more truth than he had imagined himself capable of he says, 'I wanted some excitement.'

'And Gaye found out about that, too?'

'Oh,' David laughs bitterly, 'I was seen. I hadn't realised how malicious some people can be. And then she went on my computer, looked at the sites I'd bookmarked—the *favourites* . . .' He closes his eyes, remembering how he had tried to laugh off her accusations. 'It was so stupid, so bloody stupid and careless, hard to believe how idiotically careless I was.'

He sees that the priest, without him noticing, has finished his whiskey. Nodding at his empty glass David says, 'Can I get you another?'

'No, thank you. My round, anyway, in a while.'

David rightly takes this as his cue to go on. He sighs. 'So, we could hardly talk to each other after the initial row—which wasn't even a row, more like . . . more like an interrogation . . .' How relentless she was, he remembers: *did you sleep with another man? Did you? Did you? Is that what you want? Is it? Is it?* She asked him if he had always felt like this and how he could find her attractive when really all he wanted was . . . She couldn't find the words for what she supposed he wanted and had begun to cry instead and he had wanted to hold her but hadn't dared to. Besides, he had felt so filthy, as though he had exposed himself in each and every one of those dirty images his wife had scrolled through.

After a moment he says, 'We could hardly speak to each other. For a while we could hardly stay in the same room together. But then things became a tiny bit better and I suggested some time away—for Emily's sake. Only things hadn't got any better—imagining they had been just my wishful thinking. As soon as we arrived at the cottage, which was so small—its ceilings so low—I knew that I'd made a mistake, we could hardly breathe at home, never mind this claustrophobic place. And Tog Bear had been left behind because of the rush of it all . . . Emily was so sad about that.'

On a long breath he goes on, 'It all seemed like such a waste of time—so pointless because of forgetting that bear! Except it was nothing to do with that, of course, only felt like it, but anyway I shouted at Emily and made her cry and I had never done that in my life before . . .'

The priest strikes a match—his pipe has gone out—but his expression shows that he is listening still, with the same inscrutability as before. David waits until the pipe is lit then says, 'I was a good father. I think I was. I tried to be, I really tried . . . Then I think that *really trying* marks you out—if you can't be spontaneous, natural . . . then perhaps you're no good at all.'

He stops here, wanting Purcell to say that he is wrong, that he shouldn't talk such nonsense, but the priest says nothing, only gives him time to consider his words and decide for himself. He thinks of Emily, the spontaneity they had together, such ordinary times he has forgotten just because of their ordinariness, all the songs and the jokes and the messing about and the time she had insisted that she search his hair for nits just as Gaye had searched her hair with the fine-toothed, metal comb. 'I'll squash them,' Emily said, blood-thirsty as any child, disappointed when none were discovered. He remembers the heat of her fingers, massaging his scalp after she had tossed the comb away, her laboured breath warm on his neck as she concentrated. Nitty Nora, Head Explorer, he called her, and she had laughed delightedly, never having heard the expression before, insisting that this should be her name from now on.

His silence goes on, he is lost in this remembering and doesn't care that Father Purcell is waiting for him to continue. But Purcell's patience is well practised; he can sit in another's quiet like this for a very long time. His glass is empty, though, as is David's, and the priest goes to the bar and waits patiently for the right moment to come in the football game when the barman can tear his eyes from the screen.

Later, when David is at home, in bed, Gaye asleep beside him, he thinks how little he told Father Purcell, how much there is still to tell—to confess. He had truly believed he could tell everything in one sitting. And then what, he thinks, staring into the darkness of their bedroom, would there be any relief? At the moment he has hope—he will see Father Purcell again and go on with his story and at the end the good priest will know what to say to make him well again. Because he does feel that he is sick and that there may be a cure; it's not a matter of time, as he was led to believe. Time has been no help at all; he travels through time, back and forth, back and forth, re-visiting pivotal moments, and all the *if onlys* remain agonisingly tantalising.

The if onlys reach far, far back, even to the moment of his conception. Apparently there are hormones secreted in the womb that make a male foetus grow up to be a man who loves other men. He's not sure he believes this, but would like to whole-heartedly, because then he wouldn't be to blame, the fault would not be his but simply a flaw in the workings of biology. If not for this flaw he would be normal (and he thinks of *normal* as completely heterosexual), Emily would be asleep in the next room, and he would be sleeping, too, free of guilt.

He turns over on his side and is face to face with Gaye who may or may not be faking sleep. Carefully he places his hand on her hip and she moves closer to him, murmuring, and he kisses her mouth as she draws him closer. She opens her eyes and says his name so softly, she hasn't spoken his name in such a way for years and it's a shock to him, as though they had parted long ago and accidentally met; how different she is, how well she has aged so that she is more beautiful than he remembered, and he thought he had remembered so well, forgetting that memory is a liar. He is nervous and when he says her name his voice trembles a little; she kisses him and strokes his hair and whispers *all right now, all right.*

CHAPTER 18

~

Like David, I travel through time; it's what we dead do well. I visit 1916, when a pale round moon hung above that field hospital in France and the clouds fled across its face and only I was motionless, trying to keep myself contained as the wounded cried out to me across the battlefields and the good doctors and nurses fought to save those who were rescued. I smoked a cigarette, although I was too tired to breathe properly, too tired even to sit down; I had lost count of the number of eyes I had closed that night. With each death I felt more weakened; I had begun to wonder if I would die, too.

Dr Marshall came out and his apron was bloody and his face was as ashen as the moon and he took my cigarette and drew on it heavily before handing it back to me. 'Five minutes,' he said, 'then back to the fray.'

In the distance we could see a convoy of ambulances making its way towards us. The guns grumbled on and we had five minutes in which to do nothing but smoke a cigarette and watch the ambulance headlights cut through the darkness as though they were searching for something lost in the road. The vehicles came nearer and nearer inexorably; I began to believe I could smell their passengers already, such a combination of stenches: blood and excrement and mud and cordite, and that I could hear their groans and curses and prayers. And when I touched them they would be warm like any living, breathing man and they would call out to me and clutch at my hand and some of them would recognise me at once and some would not and some would recoil from me and some would laugh, astonished, as though they had been given indisputable proof of fairies or unicorns or god or the devil.

I tossed my cigarette away and when the wind finally extinguished its glow I turned to go back inside. But Doctor Marshall caught my elbow, saying, 'Wait. Help me with these new casualties. No doubt you can save me some time.'

◆   ◆   ◆

It's possible that Peter was there that night because it was during that battle, in the middle years of the war, that he came to be blinded. Remembering, it seems to me that I sensed him there amongst the rows and rows of stretchered men, and that I took pains to avoid the places where my sense of him was strongest. A few days earlier I'd received one of his letters and it was as full as ever of his accusations so that whenever I stopped to think I saw my mother in her bath. Smaller details would come back to me as though I was studying a photograph I had barely looked at before: the mole on her thigh, the dark, shocking hair between her legs, the surprise in her eyes as if she hadn't expected God, or his absence, or me, or whatever it was she had seen during that rush towards the light. I saw her lively hair floating about her; I heard Peter pounding up the stairs, calling 'Mummy, Mummy,' laughing because he doesn't know. I heard the door fly open and bang against the bathroom wall and I remember that I had shut the door. I had shut the door. This may be significant, but it's the middle of the war and I'm too busy to think about such small details. I have so many men to see to; and now I have Peter to avoid, which is very difficult because he's calling out to me, as many of them do, but I can't help him, I'm too afraid of what he might say; he has always been a spiteful boy.

I leave 1916 and I'm in our little shop that is full of clocks in the throws of speeding up or slowing down or of making time chime out as if we need reminding of its passing. There are no customers; people pass our window quickly, although I have arranged a display of a pretty china tea set and two sad-faced pug dogs which gaze at each other across the cups and saucers. I have a feeling that these ornaments are old-fashioned and that no one will want them; I'm beginning to lose faith in myself and my decisions, my way of thinking. I can't stop thinking about Michael and Peter, the two of them together; they are always together; I am always thinking about them together.

I took one of the pug dogs and placed it on a table in a dark corner of the shop. I picked it up again, turned it over and read its maker's mark. I allowed it to fall from my hand and it smashed into three jagged pieces at my feet. Part of me wanted to cry over this, over the waste, but also over the silly, sentimental feeling I had about the grief the other pug would feel. My nerves had felt very raw for some time, my emotions too close to the surface so that they were bruised easily. But I stopped myself from crying; I went to the window, lifted out the other pug and threw it at the wall.

That morning Peter and Michael had gone out earlier than they normally did. They told me a tale about having to visit a farm way out on the moors, an isolated place where the farmer had thrown a rope over a rafter in his barn and kicked the stool out from under his feet. His sister had found him, Peter told me, and she had walked quite calmly out into the yard to ask one of their labourers to help her cut her brother down. Peter had laughed. 'Would you be so cool, Eddie?'

'No doubt her coolness was only shock,' Michael had said. He slipped his arm around my waist, pulling me close to him and kissing my cheek. 'We'll be late,' he'd kissed me again, a goodbye kiss. 'Don't wait up.'

I fetched a dustpan and brush and began to sweep up the pieces of broken china; the clocks chimed midday and I imagined Peter and Michael making their way along the moor road towards the isolated farmhouse they had invented, a square, low building surrounded by its tumble-down outbuildings, its windows blankly reflecting the noon sun so that it appears that there is no one left alive, not even the cool sister or her faithful helpers; as they drive closer they can see that brambles have grown thickly all around, casting their shoots out further into the once tended vegetable garden. Michael and Peter will have to hack their way through these barbed shoots to the front door that has blown open in the winter gales and swollen in the spring rain so that it's stuck permanently ajar.

Peter and Michael can only go in one at a time, sideways, breathing in, squeezing through. Inside the furniture, the paintings and the bric-a-brac they have come to plunder are all shrouded but spoilt never-the-less by the relentless weather. Only the china survives: the best plates, the never-used soup tureens and meat servers. Michael glances towards the stairs: perhaps in one of the bedrooms lies Sleeping Beauty—the brambles suggest this. He turns to Peter and smiles. 'So, here we are.'

Peter nods. He can hear the smile in Michael's voice but is still uncertain, he may still lose him, despite his sometime confidence, and so he is as cool as the farmer's sister and says only, 'The place stinks of damp.'

'I'll light a fire.'

'Do you think it's haunted?'

'By the farmer?' Michael is crouching at the fireplace; it has been swept clean, only a few dead leaves have blown into the grate, a few sooty spots where drops of rain have found their way down the chimney. He realises that there is nothing with which to light a fire, no paper or sticks, logs or coal. Perhaps upstairs the rooms will be dryer; perhaps blankets have been left, a mattress that has escaped the damp. Peter has come to stand over him and he glances up; sometimes he forgets that Peter is blind, but not today, he feels too shy of him today, just as he felt the day they met. He stands up and they are the same height, there is a physical equality about them that pleases Michael, although he knows that in every other aspect Peter is his superior, a knowledge that makes him feel shyer still. He laughs a little to try to overcome this feeling. 'There are no such things as ghosts.'

'No?'

'Because if there were—'

'They'd never give us any peace?'

'Yes. Exactly that.' Michael laughs again, making light of this understanding because it's so important.

Peter glances away as though he has heard someone squeeze through the door. Turning back to him he reaches out and touches Michael's arm, no more than a reassuring brush of his fingers against his sleeve. 'I believe in ghosts. Can't you sense them?'

'No. Don't talk like that.'

'Scared?'

'Yes, if you like.'

Peter smiles. He brushes his fingers against Michael's cheek. 'Shall we go upstairs and never mind the ghosts? Lead the way.'

Taking his hand, Michael leads him up the narrow staircase that creaks underfoot; the banister is loose and rattles beneath his hand; he says, 'Careful now, just three more steps. Duck your head, the ceiling is quite low at the tops of the stairs.' He grips Peter's hand more tightly, suddenly afraid of him falling against that rickety banister. On the small landing he hesitates, not knowing which of the three doors to open, afraid of what he might find. Peter is very close behind him, nudging him. 'It's very dark,' Peter says, and for the first time Michael realises that Peter's world isn't entirely blacked out. He turns to him clumsily in the small space so that it's as though they are performing some odd little dance.

'There are three doors,' he says quietly, 'left, right and straight ahead. You choose.'

'Which one might the farmer be behind?'

'No jokes, now, please.'

'All right.' But Peter can sense the man—his jealous misery at least. Not that he minds, he has never had much sympathy; quite brightly he says, 'Straight ahead, I think.'

Peter's instincts are right. Behind this door lies the largest of the little bedrooms; its window is closed tight so that it is dry at least and there are even curtains hanging, made threadbare by the sun and filthy with dust and cobwebs but curtains nevertheless—a touch of homely comfort. There is also a bed, a brass frame and a striped, stained mattress that sags in the middle, a trough for two bodies to roll into. A chamber pot is half hidden beneath the bed and on either side are rag rugs that appear to be made from strips of torn plaid shirts. A wardrobe stands in one corner, its doors hanging open, empty but for a single coat hanger. All the farmer's most intimate possessions have been ruthlessly cleared away as though someone wished to expunge completely every trace of him. Perhaps, Michael thinks, the farmer did this himself before that final, ultimate act of clearing away. He crosses the room to the window and looks out across the ragged land towards the hills that hem this place in. He is far from anywhere, so far from civilisation that nothing he does here will have any consequences. He has stepped outside of his real life; he has been let off. He turns to Peter, wondering if he feels the same, hoping that something in his expression might give him away.

But Peter's face is as inscrutable as ever; he only smiles at Michael and asks, 'So describe—is it what we hoped for?'

'Yes.'

'But you sound disappointed.'

'No.' Bravely he says, 'Afraid, perhaps.'

'Perhaps you haven't had enough time.' Peter's tries to keep his voice light, but it's a poor attempt at concealing his feelings because Michael can hear his bitterness and he goes to him, taking his hand, worrying his fingers.

'The room has been stripped bare, but there is a bed, a wardrobe, two rugs—'

'A mattress?'

'Yes. But no pillows, nor blankets.'

'Not exactly the Ritz, then?'

How nervous he sounds now—Michael is surprised. Peter had always been so certain, from the moment they met. But now they are so close, so close to what was always inevitable it seems that he is afraid too, that he also doubts himself, and so Michael says, 'We can go home, if you wish.'

'You're the commanding officer, Major.'

'I don't want to disappoint you.'

Michael is still worrying at his hand and Peter draws away. Using his stick he walks towards the bed, tapping the stick against it several times, making the brass ring out dully. 'How much would we get for it?'

'Not much.'

Peter turns to him. 'If we lie down, perhaps.'

'Yes,' says Michael, 'perhaps if we lie down.'

◆   ◆   ◆

Enough of this. I screw up my eyes and when I open them again I am sitting in Gaye's kitchen and Ralph is here. He is telling her about a woman he met during an exhibition of his paintings. She is called Debra and already he has taken her out to dinner. This much he tells Gaye, only thinking how Debra's smile was so warm and encouraging, how she leaned towards him in the candlelight and touched his hand for the briefest moment; Gaye thinks that Ralph looks as though he is in love and she tells herself that she isn't jealous. She says how nice it would be if he and Debra came to supper then laughs and says that of course, she would quite understand if he wanted to keep Debra to himself for a while. 'David and I might scare her off,' she says. This is the wrong note to strike, and there follows a silence that neither knows how to break. If only Ralph was sensitive, if only Gaye would allow herself to acknowledge me, I might rattle my chains and distract them—I feel it's the very least I could do.

But Gaye's cat comes in and this is distraction enough, hissing as she does in my direction. Ralph laughs gratefully. 'You really should get this house exorcised, you know.'

'Nonsense,' Gaye says. Nonsense. But she feels chilled and she glances in my direction. I smile at her wryly behind Ralph's back, as though I am the welcome guest and he the one we both wish would leave. To my surprise, Gaye takes a step towards me, only to stop. Almost imperceptibly, she shakes her head; I have made her sad; this is progress, I suppose.

Gaye turns away from me; too lightly she says, 'Listen, why don't we have our coffee in the garden—it's such a lovely day.'

They go outside but I can't be bothered to follow them. Instead I go upstairs to my attic and try not to remember.

CHAPTER 19

~

Ralph is driving Debra to Gaye and David's house; they are to have supper together, just as Gaye suggested. From time to time Ralph glances at Debra, who is gazing out of the car window contentedly, listening to the music playing on the car radio, even at times singing a few bars. She sings, '*Dancing Queen, young and sweet,*' and then laughs, turning to him. 'I used to think they were singing *young and Swede* because they were Swedish. I used to *sing* young and Swede! It made perfect sense to me.'

Debra was seventeen at the time, and beautiful, but not sweet—her temper could destroy whole countries if she gave it full reign. Such passion and joy, such anger and the deepest, darkest despair, Debra's emotions waxed and waned with the moon and exhausted her and made her believe that she wasn't quite right, that she was a step away from other girls. During this time she wrote long, intriguing letters to a squat and handsome, bone-headed Royal Marine called Mickey, hoping that he would love her; he did, in his lustful, misunderstanding way.

Ralph turns the car into Gaye's tree-lined street. He says brightly, 'Here we are!' as though Debra is a shy child he needs to encourage. But it's Ralph who is nervous, anxious that the evening goes well whilst believing that it won't. Gaye and David's sadness might be too overwhelming for Debra's light-heartedness to withstand and he wonders why he consented to this visit, only to remember how much he wants to show off Debra. He parks outside the house, pulls on the handbrake and turns off the engine. The Abba girls stop singing about being seventeen and into the quiet he says, 'Here we are.' He turns to her and repeats, 'Here we are.'

Debra touches his arm. 'We'll have a lovely time.'

He laughs. 'Yes.'

'*Yes!*'

He wants to tell her he loves her, but knows how wrong that would be; it's too early in their relationship, also it may smack too much of panicked gratitude: she has made him feel hopeful again, a feeling he has to contain for now or else risk scaring her away with his edgy enthusiasm.

◆   ◆   ◆

I watch Ralph and his new love walk up the path, notice how she waits for him to close the gate, how she smiles so he might feel easier. She is wearing a blue and white floral dress and a white crocheted cardigan and this outfit shows off her plump and lovely figure, her lightly tanned arms and legs and bosom. Her hair is dyed chestnut and is cut in a flattering bob and she is carefully made up, her fingernails and toenails painted the same pretty pink. Of course she believes she is fat—don't all women who are not Gaye?—but she pulled on tummy-flattening knickers and stood sideways on to the mirror in her bedroom, holding in her stomach to remind herself that she's not so big, not so bad. She is proud of her breasts and of her face in some lights. She doesn't quite believe in Ralph. He is too handsome, too successful, so for now she is pretending to be someone else, a woman who is breezily careless: in this she is more or less successful—her intimates would hardly recognise her.

Ralph closes the gate as quietly as he can because he doesn't want to announce their arrival too soon—he has an idea that the option of running away is still a real one. So he hesitates once the gate is secure, and shifts the bottle of wine he chose so carefully from one hand to the other. Debra is carrying a bouquet of flowers—yellow roses and white chrysanthemums and some greenery he can't name—and she is smiling at him as though this is quite a lark and that he is silly to look so anxious. I step outside to greet them, to test Debra. She gazes at me and her smile slips away, her hand closing more tightly around the bunched stems of the flowers. 'Oh,' she says softly, 'oh.' I pick up where her smile left off—it's always gratifying to be recognised.

Not recognising her distress Ralph takes her hand and leads her to the front door, ringing the bell before stepping inside the house and calling, 'Hello. David? Gaye?' He laughs a little because for a moment the house seems deserted. But then David appears from the sitting room and he is smiling and introductions are made and he leads them into the kitchen where Gaye is stirring a sauce and pretending to be absorbed in this task until the very last minute.

The wine is opened and poured. Debra, Ralph and David sit at the kitchen table whilst Gaye stirs and I sit opposite Debra and try to catch her eye. She is quite pale with shock: I'm like the recurrence of a disease she thought she was cured of because lately we dead have not been quite so numerous and she had begun to believe that she was free. 'Sorry,' I say to her, and she looks away, as if by ignoring me I'll disappear. *Old houses*, she thinks, *I should have known better*, and she forces herself to glance in my direction to guess at what I might be about.

She believes there will be more of us—a whole family of the dead: mother, father, child and baby, too, like a set of dolls in a dolls' house. And mother is in the kitchen and father in his study, and baby in her pram beneath the tree: a model family, arranged with a little girl's sense of proper respectability. Becoming resigned to my presence, all the same she dreads going anywhere else in this house. We ghosts are temperamental and prone to terrible re-enactments. Although I myself have never gone in for such theatrics Debra has witnessed the worst type and so she is wary of us; she feels her heart can't go on surviving these fairground shocks.

Ralph for his part has noticed the change in Debra's mood and believes it is down to David's shyness and Gaye's brittle, smiling chatter. It's as if, he thinks, his brother and sister-in-law have never had a guest in their home and he is embarrassed by their gaucheness. Also it seems to Ralph that David has taken a few steps back inside his grief and this in itself is excruciating to Ralph, who believes there should be a time limit on such raw, unruly emotion. *Conform*, he wants to tell his brother, *for God's sake be normal!* He remembers how long Emily has been dead and feels justified in his anger.

Gaye says cheerily, 'Would you like to see the rest of the house, Debra?'

Of course, Debra can't refuse—what would she say? Besides, over the last few minutes she has become resigned to face whatever there is to be faced. She stands up; taking her glass of wine she follows Gaye out into the hall.

◆   ◆   ◆

Gaye likes to show visitors around the house; it is the part of a visit that she has a script for, the part when she feels not so much herself but rather like a tour guide, relating the history of each room's restoration. Here is where the builder discovered damp; here is where we re-installed the fireplace; here is where we found the body beneath the floorboards. Gaye usually laughs at this point, making fun of herself, but this evening she feels it's a joke she can't tell—Debra doesn't seem interested enough, there is a coldness about her as though she would rather be back with the men. Gaye has seen the way she is with Ralph, so attentive, so quick to laugh at his jokes and encourage his anecdotes, and feels contemptuous.

We trail from room to room; Gaye has lost heart and Debra is all too aware of me; her resigned bravery belonged in the kitchen—now she wants only to escape. With each door Gaye opens Debra expects to see some horror—although she knows there is only horror for the first moment and that shock quickly transforms into pathos. Pathos is worse; pity is so dogged and can't be turned away from so easily; she will want to do something yet there will be nothing to do. Exorcists, she's learnt, are useless—even those exorcists who believe as they should.

At Gaye and David's bedroom door, Debra hesitates. This used to be Peter's room and all at once I want to hang back too, although I know he's not there, that the space is filled only with my own memories, my anxious going over and over of events. My agitation has seeped into this room's walls, floor and ceiling more than anywhere else in this house. I realise I am wringing my hands. Debra glances at me, dismayed.

'Gaye,' she says softly, 'are you happy here?'

Gaye laughs, embarrassed. 'Yes!'

'It's just—' But Debra can't go on; Gaye is stubbornly oblivious to me today, too taken up with what her visitor will think of her, and so how could Debra possibly talk about hauntings and ghosts? Instead she says, 'I'd love to see your garden before the light fades.'

Gaye is relieved. 'Of course,' she says. 'Of course.'

Oh the garden! The garden will make Debra's hair stand on end but I can't stop them walking down the stairs, into the dining room and through the French doors. Nor can I follow them because I am afraid of Debra's fear. I am stranded on the landing outside Peter's room. I squat beside his door and cover my face with my hands.

CHAPTER 20

~

In the garden Debra eyes the stepping stones of plum tree stumps. She stands just outside the French windows and smiles unhappily at Gaye. 'It's lovely,' she says. 'Your garden—lovely.'

'I try to keep it tidy.'

'Yes,' Debra nods, thinking how everything in this house is so neat; she imagines opening any drawer or cupboard and finding its contents folded, stacked, a picture of orderliness. Debra, whose own home is chaotic in comparison, knows that this show-home order is not for her benefit but is a chronic state created by Gaye to keep her misery at bay. Who can think above the noise of a vacuum cleaner? Who cannot lose themselves in endless, mindless housework if they concentrate hard enough on the arrangement of furniture, the plumping of cushions, the polishing of glass? And out here in the garden, you could almost feel as if you were at least doing some good feeding the earth, nurturing the flowers and trees and grass.

Debra is a tax inspector, a career she chose specifically because it seemed so far removed from the concerns of the dead, except, she learnt, the dead worry about money just as much as the living. (More so, I find, it's one of the preoccupations that hold us back most). Since her divorce, since her children left home for university and careers of their own, her work has become less important and she wonders if perhaps she should do something more . . . *artistic*, something more in keeping with how she truly sees herself. This way of seeing herself is rooted in her ability to see us, the dead; she knows how it marks her out, how special it makes her, or so she believes. All the same, she felt her search for her artistic side should begin more conventionally and so she went to that art gallery, where Ralph's paintings were being exhibited because she'd been hoping to be inspired but in the end had only bought a birthday card that was a reproduction of Ralph's *Parrot*. Ralph had watched her buy the card and was achingly attracted by her look of wistful disappointment.

But Debra is not conventionally artistic; she can't paint or draw or write poetry and she feels that the other arts—those she can immediately think of—pottery, embroidery, sculpture, are somehow too obscure or fiddly or smack too much of dreary evening classes in shabby colleges. In the end she knows that all she can lay claim to is her ability to communicate with the dead and sometimes she wonders if she should pursue this as her creative outlet, set herself up in an artfully lamp-lit room and place an advertisement in the local paper: *Lost a loved one? Let me help!* She knows how lucrative this would be, but has to remind herself that the dead are a curse and being creative is somehow about lying and being released from the every day ho-hum. Her encounters with us are too ordinary, much too bleakly real to take her out of herself.

Now, in Gaye's garden that was once mine, she sees me weeping. She sees me with my face all swollen from this dreadful keening: the me that appeared in Ralph's painting, the tableau me, the me suspended in time that draws me and holds me here. Debra is compelled to look, her curiosity overcoming her fear, which is in turn overcome by pity. 'Oh dear,' she says softly. 'Oh dear.'

'Is there something wrong?' Gaye asks.

'No!' Debra turns to her smiling too brightly as though she has been caught snooping; she reddens and Gaye is puzzled by her.

'I do like your dress,' Gaye says to be normal.

'Marks and Spencer.' Debra smiles as naturally as she can although pity drags at her heart and makes her wonder at the pointlessness of everything. She glances back towards the house, where the men are, Ralph with his charm and good looks, David who must surely know his house is so haunted because he is so disturbed. She would like to go home with Ralph, to ask him in so that she might reconnect with the ordinary business of life; her bed is made up with fresh linen, although she wondered as she shook out the pillows if this might be tempting fate. But Gaye has complimented her on her dress like a shy, friendless schoolgirl and Debra feels obliged to be kind, to stay, despite her fear of me and whatever else I have to reveal. I am at her elbow now, wanting to reassure her for Gaye's sake; she is reassured, I think; besides I have nothing more to show.

◆   ◆   ◆

Ralph and David, alone in the kitchen, drink the wine Ralph bought and talk about this and that—a little about the christening, a little about Ralph's next exhibition in the small, terribly exclusive London gallery. Then David says shyly, 'So, you went to the memorial service in the end?'

Ralph doesn't ask how David knows this, forgetting he hadn't told him of his decision to go, a decision which was taken at the very last minute and until that last minute he had talked himself into believing he wouldn't go, that going was the one thing he really did not want to do. What would be the good of remembering so formally when his informal memories take so much out of him? But in the end he found himself showering and polishing his shoes and dressing in his best suit and standing in front of the mirror for too long, thinking how middle-aged he was, how far removed from the boy who was so scared on that battleship. Not that he was so scared—Ralph's memory is as faulty, as prone to misfiring, as anyone's. Ralph was excited and nervous and sick with anxiety and the motion of the ship; proud (yes, truly—proud for a few seconds at least) and focused and afraid of getting it wrong; he didn't believe he would be killed—no one could have talked him into believing he would be killed or even wounded no matter what was said by grave-faced superior officers. All soldiers are immortal in their secret hearts—how else could they go on?

Ralph pours them both another glass of wine. 'What do you think of Debra?'

'She seems very nice,' David ventures, and it crosses his mind to ask Ralph why he is seeking his opinion, but to ask would only be provocative and impolite and for the purposes of this occasion they must be polite to each other as strangers are polite. David for instance must not say, 'You know what? I think she's too heavy—her breasts are too big—you know how I like women to look like boys.' He mustn't impersonate the clichéd idea that Ralph has of him and so make his brother ashamed and defensive and miserable, although that is often how Ralph would make him feel, especially when they were younger, before Emily. No, such revenge is out of its proper time and besides, lately it seems that Ralph has been making an effort to be kinder, although this evening he is edgier; there is more of his old, impatient self about him. David gazes at this man at his table and thinks that this woman, Debra, has brought out the spiteful, swaggering boy in his brother and that he must be careful if he isn't to be humiliated. But then he thinks, *fuck it.*

'David?' Ralph laughs uncomfortably because all at once David looks livid, as if he might smash his face in. 'Come on Dave—pull yourself together, eh?'

'What?' David laughs too, but aggressively, his eyes so darkly angry he could be possessed. '*Pull myself together?* How shall I pull myself together? Do you think it's so easy?'

'No.' Ralph's voice is sullen. 'But does it have to be so—'

'So what? Painful? Like every bone is broken and you don't want to breathe anymore but you do—although you know you don't deserve to because you're such a shit, such a perfect waste of space? Does it have to be like that? You have no idea what this has to be like—no one has, not even me—least of all me!'

Ralph can't bring himself to look at him; it's as though his brother has exposed himself, his cock and balls shrinking from their display. Helplessly he says, 'I thought you had made progress, that's all . . .'

'Progress! One step forward, three steps back like some hellish bloody dance! You know at that christening . . . at that christening . . .' But he can't say what he was about to say, that holding his cousin's baby had made him want to re-start his life, to make different choices, but that was impossible and he might as well be a child again, wishing to be like Ralph—like any other boy, anyone but him. He can't admit this to Ralph, not now when he has made such a show of himself that he is actually breathless and he has to wipe away the spittle from his mouth. At least he isn't crying, although his throat is sore from the suppression of tears. He hadn't meant to behave like this; he had hoped to be cooler. He laughs in despair—cool is such an adolescent word—and presses the heels of his hands hard into his eyes. 'Christ!' And then, allowing his hands to drop to the table, says, 'I'm sorry.'

There's not much to be sorry about only a flash so hot and bright it couldn't be sustained, the kind of flare up only brothers could have: no build up, no arguments, no explanations necessary. But an apology does have to be made and accepted because this is how David and Ralph behave with each other, both unable to bear to dig too deeply into past grievances.

So Ralph has to reply, 'No, I was thoughtless.' But then he does something more—he reaches across the table and covers David's hand with his own. 'I wish you would talk to someone—'

David draws his hand away, although the memory of his brother's touch remains and makes his skin crawl. Father Purcell can't be discussed in case he is made to seem less of a saviour; Ralph never did have any faith. Forcing himself to smile he says, 'Listen, I am making progress, I think. I think so.'

'Are you?'

'Yes! Yes, I think I am . . .' Reluctantly, but feeling that it is necessary in order to placate Ralph who does, after all, look so concerned, he adds, 'I am talking to someone.'

'A professional?'

'Yes. A professional.'

'Then good. That's good. I'm pleased, David, relieved. Does Gaye know?'

That Ralph should need to ask this makes him feel ashamed. Even though he knows that Ralph will see through his lie he says, 'Yes, she knows.'

'Perhaps she should see someone too.'

'Gaye?' David laughs, astonished. 'Gaye's fine!' He thinks of the affair she had—he is almost certain it is over now—and how it seemed to help her a little, albeit the kind of help that gave only temporary relief and was dangerous in the long run. She gave up her lover because she didn't need him anymore—her grief more manageable than it was, and because she was aware of the damage she was doing to her self-respect. This is what David truly believes.

And then Gaye and Debra come in and David gets to his feet, smiling too much, talking too much which of course isn't like him, and which makes everyone feel as though the world has sped up. Gaye tries to still him with her eyes but he won't look at her so directly as to make this work. He knows that if he were to stop smiling and talking he would have to stop altogether, curl himself up on the floor, and that would be shameful and he would let Gaye down. Most of all he doesn't want to let Gaye down, doesn't want to vandalise the small amount of progress they have made lately. So he becomes this other, bombastic man, and half-way through the meal he catches Debra's eye and sees that she knows all about him.

CHAPTER 21

～

I loved Michael; I think I may not have made this clear enough and I want to be very clear: I loved him, his body, every inch of him. He was quite perfect, physically, his naked body was a marvel to me and I would lie beside him on our bed just looking at him or stroking his chest, his belly, his manhood rising greedily towards my hand ignored for a while. He would keep his eyes closed, his warm and generous mouth closed, his fine straight nose flaring a little as he breathed in and out, deep breaths to steady him and hold him back. Beneath the dark hair of his chest, his skin was very pale, his nipples hard pink buds encircled by golden areola. He smelt of thick honey and tasted of sweet salt—that first taste of ice cream from the salted-ice churn—and he was slim and his feet were long and narrow and bony, his toes straight and blunt. His knees were rounded like a child's and his thighs were well muscled because he had ridden a horse in the army—something all the officers were taught to do, something he thought ridiculous and secretly dashing.

Those well-honed thighs were scarred; the left had a hollow the size of a penny where shrapnel had cut deep. He would joke how lucky he had been as I soothed the hollow with my thumb, because an inch or so higher, an inch or so . . . I'd press my free hand to his lips when he started on this luck of his; I didn't want to know. The right thigh had a raised white scar, ordinary, ragged; this wound had been more dangerous, although he didn't realise it: he might have bled to death.

Sometimes I wanted to wrap his nakedness in the sheets and blankets, keep him warm and safe, bound tight like a newborn. Other times I didn't care that he grew so cold that his skin bristled, I wanted only to explore him, rolling him over onto his front, tracing my finger down his spine, between his sharp shoulder blades, along the dark line between his buttocks which he would tighten as though he was rising from his horse's saddle. And then there was that secret place, behind his testicles where the touch of my finger would make his breathing quick and sharp, and moving higher I would push my fingers inside him and he would cry out, ashamed of the rush of feeling.

Afterwards he would be rough with me and I think I preferred this roughness and selfish speed to his usual tenderness, and I would try to make my body harder and tighter, less yielding. That I was skinny and bony and strong helped in this. Afterwards he wouldn't hold me as he normally did, but we would share a cigarette and he would talk a little in a brusque, mannish way I found endearing.

He was nineteen when he joined the army, when the war was still fresh as a daisy. He signed on the line without first mentioning his plan to Uncle, that man who had found him on Kings Cross station, whom he knew would try to dissuade him. 'So you have been a fool,' Uncle told him. His odd, off-key phrasing, its tone, was Uncle-like, and it seemed to Michael to underline his foolishness, because already he was regretting his action. He should have allowed Uncle to talk him out of the army; he should have had a few more months—perhaps a year or so—of peace. But no, he had decided he should be independent of Uncle—time to step out: this was how he saw himself—like a child who had been protected for too long and had become soft. If only there had not been a war to run away to, but rather a girl or the promise of some new world across an ocean, an escape just as traditional but less dangerous.

But there was a war and at first he was a private soldier. And oh he was so *good* at this! He became corporal, then sergeant, then, as the officers were killed and killed, a Second Lieutenant, Lieutenant, Captain, Major, going off to learn how to be these men, changing his accent, his way of standing, sitting, of eating, of talking without saying very much at all. Michael was a good mimic—he rode that army horse of his like a prince; if you were not from the born and bred officer class you would hardly

know him for what he truly was: a guttersnipe—what the born and bred
called him behind his back.

Michael wouldn't have cared what his fellow officers called him. Michael
only loved his men and it was a painful, sentimental love he could have
spared himself but chose not to because he imagined coldness would
distance himself from them in a way that wouldn't be helpful. For instance,
say a man was wounded on patrol; say you dragged him back and tumbled
him into the trench and tore his bloody tunic, his shirt and vest aside and
saw that he would not live—that you could almost take his heart between
your hands. Could you be cold then? Michael thought not. So he knew
the names of wives and babies and football teams supported. He knew
the village pubs and greens and the factories and the streets and whether
God would be a comfort or a worry. And he knew when to be quiet and
use that body of his, that warmth and strength, his hand pressing against
a wound as if he could stop a soul escaping, contrary to experience.

Michael loved his men; he had got into the habit of loving them so that
it was easy to love almost anyone at all, or believe he did, at least, and Peter
knew this, of course, and knew where his weakness lay.

Sometimes, when I am feeling particularly alone, I visit that isolated farm
where the farmer hanged himself. The farm and its outbuildings are quite
busy with the dead: men and women in the modern, utilitarian clothes
worn for leisure nowadays, walkers, I think, lost and disorientated even
with their weather-proofed maps hung around their necks. Then there is
the farmer himself, of course, and his sister and the man she had planned
to run away with—these last two are quite the happiest ghosts, although
they ignore me and pretend successfully that they are as alive as they ever
were. The farmer and I eye each other, he is suspicious but becoming less
so. He recognises me, the similarity of our respective situations. I think
one day he may even speak; at the moment we have reached a courteous,
nodding acquaintance which is satisfying enough.

I visit the farm in the early summer mostly. There is a meadow a little
way from the house where I sit by a swift stream and imagine the mild
warmth of the May sun on my face. I tilt my head back and close my eyes
and the scent of lilac is strong at first and then more elusive as the breeze

becomes less. With my eyes closed I can listen more carefully; if I am patient (and I am) I will hear Peter say,

'We should bring a picnic here.'

Michael laughs. 'We have a picnic!' He takes from his jacket pockets the sandwiches they have brought from home, cheese and pickle and ham. There are also two apples and a bar of Five Boy chocolate which he plans to break scrupulously in half, fair shares. Smiling, Michael says, 'But you mean a proper picnic—with a basket and a tartan rug and bottles of beer to cool in the stream.'

'Why not?'

Michael sits down on the grass; he begins to take off his shoes and socks so that he can dangle his feet in the water. Glancing up at Peter he says, 'Sit down. Should I describe the view? There are the Cleveland Hills—in the background, of course. Foreground is a field with sheep. Inevitable sheep.'

'I can hear them.' He sits down beside Michael. 'What else?'

'Nothing very much.' Michael's feet are bare now and he dips them in the stream, swirling the water, feeling the silkiness of the vivid green weeds that flatten against the current he creates. He thinks how pale his feet look beneath the distorting water, white as bone and clumsy against the fine fronds. He is altogether too pale.

He takes off his jacket, folding it carefully beside him, and rolls up his shirt sleeves because his arms are too white, too, and he would like to see them brown again. He doesn't mind this slow burning, rather he wishes the sun would penetrate to his bones and give him strength because lately he has felt weak, as though Peter sapped the small reserves of strength he had managed to build up. Closing his eyes he smiles and thinks *I am a sun-worshiper, I will serve no other God but this*; but his smile lingers uneasily, he is reminded that he hasn't smiled so thoughtlessly for days now, perhaps even weeks, since the two of them first came to this place. But he won't think about smiling, or venture into the territory that lies behind such musings—that wasteland of doubt and anxiety where it's so easy to become lost; he will stay in the present moment of warm sun; he will concentrate on the hard earth beneath him and watch the sun sparkle on the water through his closed eyes.

But Peter interrupts him. 'Michael?'

'I'm still here.'

'Of course. I only wondered what you were thinking to make you so quiet.'

He even wants to know his thoughts, even though he knows everything about him: about his childhood; about his war; about Uncle. But his thoughts are poor things and wouldn't stand up to scrutiny, and so Michael lies and says, 'I was thinking about one time in France when we had been sent back behind the lines to rest.' Although he hasn't remembered this scene for some years, at once he can picture it so clearly he might just as well be there. There, a few yards away, his men play football; he has decided that he will listen carefully to their shouts, to hear if he can make out distinct voices, an exercise he can set his mind to.

There is Thompson shouting foul.

There is Turner cursing, laughing.

There are Atkinson and Pearce, wheezing and breathless, older.

There is Lieutenant Harris, encouraging.

Michael believes Harris should be given a medal that doesn't yet exist but should be created and awarded for . . .Michael opens his eyes, squinting against the light. What makes Harris so uniquely deserving? He is his rock, he supposes, but there's something more, something that he knows has to do with superstition but feels more mystic: Lieutenant Paul Harris possesses an awe-inspiring stoicism; if he only stands close to Harris, as close as can be, he can accept anything. He is not so scared when Harris is around, and it's not only to do with the boy's calmness; his dignity rubs off on him, he is brave by association. Michael knows he is the worst coward imaginable but Harris is his prompt, reminding him how to behave.

And now the football has rolled against his feet and Harris stands over him. 'Sorry sir,' he says, 'I didn't mean to wake you.' The boy is very handsome; the men believe he is queer. He is twenty and writes long letters home that Michael can't bear to censor. I'm not in love, he tells himself, and the very idea surprises him and makes him blush: *love* had never occurred to him before.

Second Lieutenant Paul Harris is wounded and is sent home and Michael feels as though he has been disarmed. Defenceless, he imagines writing to Harris, *'Would you send me a lock of your hair?'*

'Michael?'

Michael is brought back to the present where he is trying to grasp the weeds with his toes but this is all but impossible because his feet are numbed by the water. Beside him he is aware of Peter waiting; it seems that Peter is holding his breath in his anxiety for him to answer, and Michael imagines that his silence might even kill him. He watches his feet, how they are becoming blue with cold, and he thinks of Harris and wonders if he survived. When Peter breathes out Michael says, 'I can't leave Eddie.'

'I don't want you to.'

'We can go on as we are.'

'Of course we can.'

Michael lifts his feet from the stream and lays back, his arm across his eyes. In a little while he knows he will feel Peter's head rest against his chest; he knows he will stroke his brother-in-law's hair as if he was a child to be soothed to sleep. It would seem that this is his role in life, to comfort other men in one way or another. He doesn't mind, not really, not since Uncle.

'So you have been a fool,' Uncle had told him, and then, 'you've broken my heart.'

'But I'll come back!' He laughed because Uncle looked so sad, a kind of comic sadness that went nicely with his musical-hall sentiment. He kissed Uncle's cheek. 'I'll be back in no time!' But already he regretted enlisting even though he was wearing his smart new uniform—how stiff it was! How it made him stand so straight so that he might be someone else entirely, a man who didn't kiss the cheeks of other men or was able to break their hearts with his foolishness. Timidly he said, 'I'll be back in no time.'

Men don't die from broken hearts. They don't. Michael knows this deep within his own heart—a damaged heart that has nontheless kept beating. But still he believes that he killed Uncle, he confessed as much to Peter, how he should have stayed and not put such a strain on Uncle's poor heart.

And now Peter knows all about him and Uncle; he has laid himself quite bare, although he doesn't know about Lieutenant Harris, there are some men he won't betray. He strokes Peter's hair, comforting him. In a little while they will sit up and eat their sandwiches and share the chocolate, saving the apples for later. They will go inside the farmhouse, that they have made their own and then, after he has comforted Peter in the very best way he knows how, they will drive home and he will kiss his wife and take her to bed because this is how he makes up for everything.

I sit beside the stream; the evening is drawing to a close and I should go because I don't like to be out here in the dark. I go home to Gaye and David; I have work to do.

~

Gaye isn't at home but is out shopping for new clothes that will be more suitable for the woman she intends to be. But this is a difficult task because what does a penitent wear these days? And she doesn't want to look too old—too dowdy, nor too young—she isn't young, not outwardly, at least, only in her heart and sometimes in the way she thinks, although lately she has had a feeling of time running out, she has begun counting years, doing sums, and twenty years seem like ten seem like five.

In the changing room mirror the clothes she eventually chooses look wrong on her; it would seem that for all her careful selection she can't escape from the very essence of herself: the black jeans and the ballerina-type cardigan in jade cashmere, the paler green vest top, make her appear chic but dull; and the purpose is, after all, for David to see a change, to know that she has decided to be different. She turns sideways to the mirror, then turns her back and peers over her shoulder. The jeans fit well (they are shockingly expensive) and make her appear as though she has a womanly backside. She turns to face the mirror; the cardigan with its fussy, complicated way of tying also lends her a little more bulk; the colour is good on her, possibly, simply, because it's not black—she is trying to move away from the idea that she should wear only black. This jade green, although not exactly bright, is perhaps after all a good enough signal of change, the jeans too, fitted as they are. She will buy this outfit, she decides, and is relieved because she has reached a decision and can go home.

She begins to undress and dress again in her old clothes: a long linen skirt, a woven leather belt and a tee-shirt that has lost its shape over this summer. (This is a look she experimented with; a failed experiment, she thinks because it is too unstructured, too sloppy and lies about how reticent she is.) As she carries the new clothes to the till, all at once she thinks of Debra and her lovely white and blue dress, and how she showed off her figure and her tanned limbs so unselfconsciously and sexily, how Ralph could not keep his eyes off her. How Ralph's eyes had strayed often to Debra's breasts, how David had glanced away, embarrassed when he noticed his brother's ogling. David had caught her eye and smiled wryly, there had been a moment of their old comradeship then. She had felt her heart soften towards him although he was behaving so badly, like an arch, ironic version of himself, causing such an uncomfortable atmosphere. Debra must have wondered at his oddness but there was no doubt she knew about Emily because later, as she left with Ralph, Debra had hugged him and said softly, 'Good night, David, sleep well,' as though sleep was a panacea he desperately needed.

Later, she had smelt Debra's perfume on him: *Paris*, that scent of roses so reminiscent of the time she was a young woman; such a sweet, pretty perfume she had forgotten about. And David had smelt of this, tantalisingly, so that she had been able to imagine him as someone else: an ordinary adulterer and it was a surprising image and distractingly outlandish.

When Ralph and Debra had left that evening, when she and David had both taken pains not to collide during the rituals of locking doors, climbing stairs, undressing and washing and teeth-brushing; when they were in bed and had turned off their bedside lamps, he reached for her hand. 'I'm sorry.' He had laughed bitterly, unable quite to discard the hyper-real David. 'Ralph won't forgive me, will he?'

'Yes he will,' she said, automatically placating.

'No he won't. And I don't care. He's told that woman everything—you could tell—we were a sideshow.'

She agreed, but silently, thinking that she should have tired harder to overcome this barrier that Ralph had set up before she and Debra had even met. She should have shown her Emily's photograph and said, 'This is my daughter, perhaps Ralph told you about her . . . ?' Instead she had behaved as though Emily had never existed, had decided—and this decision

had seemed absolutely the right one then—that it would be best to leave
such confidences for another time. Besides, she had thought that time
might never come, she might never see Debra again and then she would
have been too open and would have regretted giving so much away to a
stranger—why risk such humiliation? I'm frozen, she thought, so cold, no
wonder Debra hugged David and not me.

David's hand had closed tighter around hers, as though he sensed her
jealousy and understood it. 'At least you behaved well.'

At the till the shop assistant folds her new clothes in sheets of tissue
paper and places them in a sturdy paper bag with the shop's discretely
show-off logo on its side. Gaye holds her credit card ready in her hand
and thinks about Debra and if it ever would be possible to be her friend,
to one day be able to casually telephone her and say something along the
lines of *how was your day? Today I thought about Emily perhaps a little
less—perhaps more than yesterday but still . . . And I caught myself singing
to a song on the radio and it was a song that I once danced to with Noel
and it didn't hurt me quite so much and I hardly felt guilty at all because he
was so lovely and I thought Emily would forgive me, if I explained how kind
Noel was. She loved her Daddy, though, more than she loved me, I sometimes
think. Yes, perhaps you're right—not more, only differently.*

The shop assistant takes Gaye's credit card and absently Gaye keys in her
pin number, smiles at the assistant and says 'thank you.' She is still thinking
of Debra and their imaginary friendship. Then the thought occurs to her
that perhaps Ralph will marry Debra and then they would be sisters of a
kind and she would have excuses to telephone her. And perhaps Debra
would want to hear about Ralph's past, those funny, slightly embarrassing
anecdotes that new lovers are so charmed by.

She could tell her about the time Ralph came home from a trip to Japan.
He had bought Emily a silk fan decorated with water lilies and storks; she
could tell Debra about how he had taught Emily to open the fan with a
flirtatious flick of her wrist, and how he had made up Emily's eyes with
mascara and eyeliner—his own eyes, too, so that they both looked like
characters from the Mikado, especially Ralph, with a quickly plaited black
wool moustache. She could tell her how David had returned home from

work and had said, '*What on earth are you doing?*'

Although David had laughed; he had been charmed, although he wouldn't allow Emily to make-up his eyes. He had sat Emily on his knee and the house became calm, Emily content with her head on his chest, sucking her thumb absently, and the closed fan dangling from her fingers. He stroked her hair and her eyes lids stuttered between sleep and wakefulness, unable quite to let go of her curiosity as David asked Ralph about his trip and said finally, 'Mascara brings out the colour of your eyes, Ralph. As for the moustache . . .' And David had smiled teasingly at his brother over Emily's head.

Silly what you remember Gaye thinks—those incidental memories that stick most faithfully for some detail or other, detail she may even have invented or that has become distorted over time for all she knows. She is almost certain that later that evening Ralph took them all out for supper in the pizza restaurant that was Emily's favourite place at the time.

Walking through the shop towards the exit, Gaye remembers the pizza restaurant conversation:

'We should order raw fish,' Ralph says.

'Ugh,' says Emily, and at once she lowers the fan she has been toying with. '*No one* eats that!'

'Yes,' says Ralph, 'they eat it in Japan.'

'That's not true,' Emily says with great disdain: she is the lady with the fan—knowing and sophisticated. In the shop, in the restaurant, Gaye smiles to herself.

'Yes,' says David. He puts down his menu—he always orders lasagne, anyway—and repeats, 'yes. In Japan raw fish *is* eaten and it's called sushi. And it's served with a special kind of rice all wrapped up prettily in seaweed,' he frowns—she can see he is thinking *is this true?* But then he recovers and goes on, 'The fish has to be very fresh—straight from the sea—so that all it tastes of is the sea. Ozone,' he says, almost to himself, liking this word. Then he smiles at Emily. 'We'll try it, one day.'

'Never,' says Emily.

Never.

A man opens the shop door for her. 'There you go, love.' This man smiles as though she isn't quite right in the head and she realises that she has been standing at this door as though it is a puzzle to her. But she was only wondering where the Japanese fan was, whether it was lost in one day's frenzy of sorting.

David had come to her that day. He had sat on Emily's bed, Emily's clothes all strewn around him, and clasped his hands between his knees, his body hunched as though his head was too heavy, too burdened. He had tried looking up and smiling to make his voice less accusing as he said, 'What are you doing?'

'Can't you see?'

Tog Bear lay a few inches from his feet and he picked it up and turned it over and over as though looking for a way inside. He found the bear's washing instructions, faded and unreadable, and squinted, stretching the little tag of silky nylon out that he might read it all the same. 'It's too soon,' he said, as though these were the instructions, and he looked up at her. 'It's too soon.'

She remembers that she had been kneeling on the floor, rushing through the contents of a drawer, and that she stopped dead because he was right: it was too soon for this; she had realised it herself when the task had become not a neat sorting into charity bags but a frenzied hunting, the thing that was hunted evasive and quick to escape her clumsiness—or else had been destroyed by it. She had looked around her, the mess she had made, and then looked down and saw that her hands were full of Emily's underwear and there was a sneezy, gritty smell of old-fashioned bath cubes that a great-aunt had once given her. The cubes lay unwrapped and crumbling their corners in the bottom of the drawer and she would never use them and it seemed such a waste that all the trouble of making these things should come to nothing. The world was ruined by such waste and the pain of its pointlessness hurt her terribly and it was too soon, too soon and what on earth had she been thinking of? She was kneeling and she doubled up so that her head almost touched the floor and the scent of *My Fair Lady* bath cubes became stronger, eye-stinging, as she felt David's hand on her back.

'Gaye,' he said, 'Oh Gaye . . .'

'Will you leave me?'

'No! No—no . . .'

He drew her up so that they sat on the bed, his arm around her shoulders, closer than they had been for days, for weeks perhaps—memory plays such tricks. And then they laid down on Emily's bed, her head on his chest so that he could stroke her hair just as he had stroked Emily's hair the day of the fan and he had murmured 'I won't leave you, I won't leave you,' and she remembers that his heart sounded too quick and loud beneath her ear, racing away from her even as his words made her think that he would stay.

He would stay and that man he had been seeking in that gay club, in the gay chat rooms on the internet, that kind, manly, figment-of-imagination man would be told 'My heart is broken and I'm no use to anyone.' And this would be true, for a while, until Luke came, real and predatory and scheming, and made David think that it wasn't too soon anymore.

Gaye walks along the High Street to the multi-storey car park. She puts her ticket into the machine which tells her that there is nothing to pay—she has been quick and it feels as though the machine is congratulating her on this efficiency. She takes her keys from her handbag and presses the button that has her car blinking its lights in an impersonation of pleasure at her return.

◆　　◆　　◆

At home, I follow Gaye upstairs to her bedroom where she puts her new clothes away in the wardrobe, not taking them from the bag or removing the tags or the receipt curled on top of the cardigan. She might still change her mind and return them to the shop—the shop doesn't mind when you do this kind of thing—the assistants only smile and don't care about the lies they are told about the fit or the colour. They won't care that her husband—who was trying so hard not to fail her—doesn't notice what she wears.

Her husband is seeing someone else.

It's ironic, really: she has given up Noel and now David is the one who has become caught up in the secrets and the preoccupations and complications of an affair.

She is uncertain whether his affair is revenge—although he's not vengeful; it would be the kind of revenge that came not from his own principles but from an idea of what others do in such circumstances, the dishonest kind of revenge she took, after all. No, she tells herself, her adultery had nothing to do with Noel, with the idea she had that he was so attentive and flattering, so handsome and charming, exciting and funny or because he had a way of talking, of driving, of walking, of holding his knife and fork, that was so unlike David's way of doing these things. Such novelty was beguiling but could have been resisted. And it wasn't because Noel was adept at sex—treating the different moves and positions as though they were part of a gymnastic routine, as though he was practising this routine for an Olympic medal (gold—silver at least), because she found this kind of sex faintly embarrassing in its ridiculousness. No—the reason for her adultery was she had wanted revenge for Luke. She realised this after she had met Noel; it was as though she had turned into someone else, the kind of woman whose anger was such that it could be acted on coldly and with her eyes open for the right man, one who would be a tool and nothing more.

Oh, but this is wrong too—she loved Noel. But it's not so wrong that revenge can be discounted; because she loved Noel but he was also brash and full of his own importance sometimes, and he had sex with her which made him a bad man really, one she would have shied away from if it hadn't been for Luke.

She gives her husband's adultery a name: Luke; a face: sly, superior—at the same time needy and so lustful—really he hardly knows what to do with this face of his—can hardly control his expression except to express how much she is in the way. She credits Luke with everything—even David's self-control and contriteness that had until lately made him seem as though he could he fully hers again.

But he is seeing someone else because the other night he came home and smelt so alien, of tobacco and drink, and behaved as if the old shame had returned.

~

CHAPTER 23

David is seeing the priest. This meeting, however, is to be at the priest's home, and not in that forlorn pub. The pub had been chosen by Father Purcell as a neutral place, David thinks, where Purcell could sound him out and perhaps make sure he was not too dangerous to be allowed into his home. He supposes precautions have to be made if you're to counsel someone, addresses kept private until you are sure of your ground. Yet the priest is still taking a risk, David believes: he could be insane, after all, for all Purcell knows. For all David knows of himself he might become the kind of man who won't let go of any lifeline thrown to him; he might be a stalker, at heart, obsessed and resentful and full of all the other, wild emotions that could lead to murder. In the dock he would plead misunderstanding: *I thought the priest could help me, that he could cure my pain, calm all the anger that comes from wishing for impossibilities. I over-estimated his powers and so misunderstood him as I misunderstand most people. Are they mad, your honour, or am I?*

David walks through the cemetery, a short cut towards the address he has been given. As a child, during the long summer holidays—that were even longer for him, being a boarding school boy—he would play in this cemetery, if his mooching could be called play. Victorian and semi-derelict, the graveyard was full of mature chestnut, oak and sycamore trees; of stone angels and tall plinths of black marble inscribed with gold lettering, bold and chunky and clear for all time. Most of the graves were neglected; a few sheltered urns of flowers—burnt-orange chrysanthemums nearly always—their stems thrust though a mesh of neat round holes into stagnant, foul-smelling water. He would read dates and morbidly calculate ages; anything over seventy was fine. And there was one grave that looked as though a cot had been sunk into the ground to surround the little coffin, only the top of its frame showing; for a while he believed that this *was* a cot—what better use for it, after all, now its true purpose was redundant?

Sometimes during his mooching there would be a real live funeral, although rarely as there were few plots left. He would watch from a carefully calculated distance, a solitary ten, eleven, twelve-year-old boy who must have appeared rather odd to the mourners if any of them noticed him, lonely or sinister, depending on their depth of grief or fellow-feeling.

He had taken a friend to the cemetery, once, a boy a few months younger than him, and his motives had been so conflicted, so stomach-churningly confused and frightened that he had behaved as though he was another boy entirely: talking too much, daring too much, scaring himself because he really wasn't sure how far this version of himself would go. Not far enough, in the end, or perhaps too far: a brushing of his hand against the other boy's thigh because some grass clung to his short trousers. Walking past the scene now as a grown man he remembers how his skin had prickled as he did this, his whole body alert, even his hair, his finger and toe nails. He remembers thinking how wrong he was, how absolutely wrong and filthy that he could feel so much so intensely, and how he realised he now had a secret he would have to keep for the rest of his life: cross his heart and hope to die he would never tell a living soul.

Father Purcell lives in a maisonette, an ugly, red brick building just beyond the cemetery gates. I stand beside David as he pauses to glance at his watch. Once again he is early, but only by a few minutes. He looks up at the windows of the second floor flat, draws breath and walks purposely across the road. I follow, moving quickly to keep up with him.

◆   ◆   ◆

The priest's flat is small and sparse, at odds with the man himself who takes up so much space in the cupboard-filled kitchen. The priest opens the cupboards for tea, for mugs, for sugar bowl and biscuits and plates, and David sees the few tins of baked beans, the sliced brown bread and those miniature boxes of cereal that he has only ever seen before in hotels, children's cereals: Frosties and Rice Crispies with their bright, cartoon packaging scaled down. The fridge is opened for milk, its yellow light showing up the frugality of corner-shop cheese and eggs and margarine. David wonders whether he would fare any better for himself if he lived alone and imagines that he too would live on toasted cheese; the flat is full of the smell of toast. On the wall, just inside the front door, there is a crucifix, Christ's lean body tautly suffering above a bowl of holy water; a picture of the Sacred Heart hangs above the gas fire in the sitting room; somehow David had not expected these outward signs of devotion, but had thought the priest more of an aesthetic.

They sit on old, high-backed armchairs either side of the fire, one of a nest of tables between them on which the tray of tea and biscuits is placed. The chairs look as though they're on loan from an old people's home, as though such utilitarian ugliness first needs to be tried-out before any decision on giving up independence is made. There is no other furniture, no television, only a transistor radio, but there are lots of books. Books crowd the room on ceiling-high shelves in the fireplace alcoves, are built up in over-flow stacks on the floor. David reads spines and the titles and authors mean nothing to him. On the floor by the priest's chair there is a bible with a worn soft cover, a ragged brown envelope tucked between its pages; when Father Purcell sits down his fingers brush against this bible, as though he is reassuring himself that it is there.

'So,' says the priest as he pours the tea, 'how are you, David?' He hands him a thick white mug with *Towbars-to-Go* printed around its side. 'I think,' he continues, 'that you look a little more rested.'

David considers this and realises that yes, he feels less tired and that last night he slept better, without dreaming, and so he nods and says, 'Perhaps it's to do with all this,' and he feels that the priest knows that *all this* means this talking he has decided to commit himself to.

He remembers where he left off the last time they met and begins.

◆   ◆   ◆

'I was a good father, I think, but how can that be quantified? Emily would wait at the window for me to come home, run out onto the drive to meet me; if she didn't do this I would feel neglected, disappointed, but relieved too, sometimes, because if she wasn't there it meant that she had a life somewhere else, other people to look out for. And it's true, she had many friends, children and adults, our neighbours were like surrogate grandparents . . .'

He remembers those neighbours, Frank and Isobel, retired GPs, who had always welcomed Emily into their home that was filled with the kind of once-cutting-edge things his parents owned and which dated them to the early 1960s when they were young and socialist and self-consciously modern. He remembers that Isobel even owned the same Denby tea service as his mother, its chunky, dung-brown plates seemingly indestructible. Bourbon Creams were served to Emily on these plates in Isobel's wallflower scented garden, and Isobel would potter and Frank would talk to him over the fence and he would wonder *why aren't they my parents? I would love them more.* He had felt like a child for thinking this, with all the acute sense of disloyalty a child has.

David realises that his mouth is dry and he sips his tea. He is avoiding the real purpose of this meeting—to talk about that last day with Emily. He knows—as he is sure the priest knows, too—that last time he ended with how he had been angry with Emily for forgetting Tog, the bear she slept with each night and could not imagine sleeping without.

He has a Technicolor memory of Tog, of arriving home without Emily to see him lying face up on the hall floor and it's as if the bear takes up the whole of his world, so startlingly pink, so foolishly grinning with all its soft face. In this memory he shrieks, a noise unlike any he had ever made in his life before, the kind of noise that would tear cloth or cause the heavens to open, the kind of noise God would hear. He is on his knees and covering his head with his arms in this memory which he is sure is false; these actions are only those he had wanted to take.

'David?' The priest prompts.

'We arrived at the cottage and we were fraught because of the forgotten bear . . . only not just because of that, only focusing on that. And the cottage was so small that I knew I couldn't stay inside so I said that we should all go for a walk on the beach, that it would be good to get some fresh air. Gaye said, "You go, you and Emily," she said she wanted to unpack, that we would be *under her feet . . .'* This is not a phrase Gaye would use, he knows, and it feels as though he is remembering a stranger, one who was robust and straight-talking, a stranger whose fierce, violent anger would have made a different outcome. Is he blaming Gaye, then, for not being that person? For being instead someone who held onto their anger and made a fetish of it? He blinks, and finds that he is meeting the priest's eye for the first time. 'Sorry,' he says, 'I just want to get it right.'

'I understand.'

David smiles painfully. 'The police weren't so patient. Or at least they tried to be, but somehow I had the impression . . . They were . . . *keen*, you know? Wanting to get on. Anyway . . . Anyway, I didn't argue with Gaye, I couldn't have stayed inside even if I'd wanted to. Besides, I knew that once Emily saw the sea she would forget about the bear, forget everything. Emily loved the sea . . .'

There is a silence that the priest doesn't want to encourage, there is a momentum here, and so he says, 'That part of the world is very beautiful.'

'Yes,' David agrees gratefully. Quickly he says, 'The beach there was fine, yellow sand and the tide was out, way out so there were lots of rock pools and it took us a while to reach the water's edge because Emily wanted to explore every pool . . .Anyway it was just us and the birds, not gulls but some kind of wading bird I hadn't seen before. We followed their foot prints and Emily asked me what they were but I said I didn't know and how we would have to buy a book on ornithology. We liked to name names, make discoveries,' he draws breath. 'I held her hand, she wanted to run to the sea but I held her hand.'

He trails off, distracted because he is thinking about whether he does blame Gaye even a little; this insight is quite startling but he would need to be alone to explore it and for now he feels he must tell the story as straight as he can and not wander too far from the facts. These facts, he has decided, hold the answer, his absolution, if he is painstaking in their recollection.

From the shelf above the gas fire a clock chimes and David realises that he has been in the priest's home for half an hour and it crosses his mind that Father Purcell is bored with him, that perhaps there is something on the radio he would be listening to now, if he were alone, and wishes that he wasn't missing. David notices the priest's pipe beside the clock, his zipped tobacco pouch and matches, and finds himself saying, 'Do you want to smoke? I don't mind—not that you need my permission to smoke in your own home.'

The priest shakes his head. 'Go on, David, you were holding Emily's hand.'

'Yes, I was holding her hand . . .' He frowns, remembering how suddenly and blindingly the sun had come out, how the unnamed birds had taken off as one as though this brightness had startled them. The rush of birds had made him stop and the sand shifted beneath his feet and Emily had tugged at his hand, wrenching his arm; he had to say, '*Slow down, what's the hurry?*' He had been breathless, he remembers, with the exertion of keeping up with her but also with fear for his marriage, a pain in his chest as though his heart had been stitched up tight. In his mind's eye he watches himself bend double, his hands on his knees, his mouth taking great, gasping breaths of sea air. But in reality he only paused, glancing back to the little cottage on the edge of the beach where Gaye was, and he had wondered if he had broken her heart, just as his heart felt broken, and if the damage he had done could be mended.

In the priest's sitting room he exhales as though he has been holding his breath since that moment on the beach. He looks at the mantelpiece clock; it has a minute hand and a confident tick that he hadn't noticed until this moment and he tells himself he will speak only when this quick, jerking hand has travelled past the hour, a few seconds in which to compose himself. The ticking seems to grow louder, he is aware of Father Purcell sitting patiently as though time is nothing to him. The minute hand moves inexorably and then, 'Father, I'm so afraid I'll go to hell.'

I turn to the priest. David and I are both intent on him, David because he is desperate and frightened and I because I am curious: how will Purcell explain away hell when I am listening? It's all I can do to keep the smirk from my face and Purcell glances at me and then to the picture of the Bleeding Heart on his wall. At last he meets David's eye. 'David, God has forgiven you. You will find peace, I promise.'

'I don't deserve peace.'

'Why not?'

Because, David thinks, I let go of her hand. I looked back at the cottage and I saw Gaye coming towards me and I let go of Emily's hand.

He closes his eyes and presses the heels of his hands hard into them so that white lights spark and flash across the darkness and his tears are squashed to nothing and only his voice might betray him, his laugh which is harsh and foolish to his own ears. After all, he has been so melodramatic—*I'm so afraid I'll go to hell*! Jesus! And now here he is—covering his face like a child, unable to speak, although he had come here to unburden himself, had promised himself that he would, only not like this. He had thought he would be calm, he has always been calm, hysteria kept under close guard. Ashamed, he allows his hands to fall to his knees. He tries smiling and says, 'I'm sorry.'

'You have nothing to be sorry for.'

'I suppose you're used to people making fools of themselves.'

'You're not a fool.'

'No. Not normally.' After a moment he says, 'Should I go on?'

Purcell nods but I feel I can't listen—I'm not ready to hear this, not yet; I need to explain myself, to make my own confession.

CHAPTER 24

~

I leave David and his priest and go back to the house, to the plum trees that are only stumps in the ground now but were once so fruitful the wasps would become drunk on the plums we couldn't eat. I would bottle the plums and store them in the larder because I was a good wife; I tried so hard to be a good wife. But the bottled plums looked like specimens on an anatomist's shelves: ill-conceived, ill-formed; I pushed the bottles to the back of the pantry and became afraid even to catch a glimpse of them. But each summer I kept up the pretence that the fruit would be used and each summer I remember Michael climbed a ladder to reach the higher branches and Peter stood on the ladder's first rung, holding it steady.

I watched them from the kitchen window. If Michael was to look back at the house he would see me and he might wave in acknowledgement; he might smile, perhaps even raise his hand to his eyes to shield them from the sun. He would see how wan I appeared, ghost-like, because by then I knew that Peter had stolen him from me. They spent their days together, and in the evenings they ate the supper I prepared and talked about what they had done together. Together they went to the public house and planned what they would do the following day and the smoke from their cigarettes would camouflage them and not one of their fellow drinkers would be in the least suspicious of the young man and his blind companion, two veterans, old comrades in arms.

In the Castle & Anchor Michael will lead Peter to a quiet, out of the way corner. Although the other drinkers are becoming used to them, Michael feels that it's best if they keep to themselves; also he is protective of Peter and doesn't want drunks bumping into him not realising he is blind. So, they sit away from the bar, a little way from the coal fire at a table that seems as though it has always been waiting for them. Michael would buy the drinks, always with a kind word for the barmaid who seems to him to be in need of kindness because sometimes her eye is blackened and sometimes there would be bruises blooming around her wrists and the brute of a landlord would leer at her and wink at him, as though Michael was his ally and not sickened by his monstrousness.

Behind the bar where Michael orders two pints of beer is a herring gull in a glass case, seashells scattered at its webbed feet. He will describe the stuffed bird to Peter as he describes other odd things that appeal to his imagination. He will say,

'The gull looks as if it's about to speak.'

Peter smiles; he sips his beer and sets his glass down on the marble-topped table. 'What's it about to say, do you think?'

'I don't know. Hello?' All at once Michael wishes he hadn't begun such a whimsical conversation. He is too preoccupied. He is thinking of his wife who he has left weeping on their bed, who would not be consoled by him, who screamed at him to go, to just get out, get out, he couldn't help her, he was no use to her. A few minutes earlier he had found her tearing up rags: she had begun to bleed; her bleeding was as regular as the moon that was so bright tonight and looked so cold and full of malice.

Sitting beside Peter, the coal fire warming his back, he fumbles in his pocket for cigarettes, lighting two, handing one to Peter who is smiling to himself, happy to be here, away from the house and from his sister whose moods are so unfathomable, so volatile; he has always known that his sister is mad—has been quite insane since she had a hand in their mother's death.

Peter hates how Michael is too quiet and knows that his quiet is down to his sister, Michael's wife. He would like Michael to be unaffected by her moods, to not think about her at all when they are alone together. Of course he knows he *is* thinking about her, there is a recognisable quality to his quiet: strained, uneasy: guilt-ridden. God knows he has nothing to be guilty about—one can't help one's feelings; he has tried to explain this to Michael; he's not sure that he has got through to him.

Then all at once Michael says, 'She's disappointed, that's all.'

Peter tries to keep his voice light—he can't be heard to take his sister seriously; he even laughs a little, 'Disappointed over what, precisely?'

There is another drawn-out silence. Peter senses Michael shifting in his chair, casting his eyes around the bar, unable to look at him. He would like to rest a steadying hand on his arm because Michael's agitation makes his own heart race. Instead he sits quietly, drawing deeply on his cigarette; he will be patient; he won't scare him away or make the same mistakes his sister makes.

Presently his patience is rewarded because Michael says, 'I'm sorry. I'm sorry you heard us rowing like that.'

'What were you rowing about?' At once he regrets the mistake of asking this. 'Sorry—none of my business. Just a lovers' tiff, anyway. Nothing. I wasn't disturbed.'

'It's difficult for her.'

'For all of us.'

Peter waits for confirmation of this; he hears Michael drawing on his cigarette, imagines his face frowning through the smoke. He waits, although he longs to break the silence, to badger him into admitting that yes, he understands that it's difficult for him, too, difficult to sleep in the next room to his, listening to the noises of his marriage. Not for the first time he wonders what Michael sees in his sister, she was always such a plain child, such an earnest young woman, and a murderer at that; he should remind Michael again that she killed their mother, but this is a risky strategy so he only smokes his cigarette, reaching out with an unsteady hand to feel for the tin ashtray he knows is there in the centre of the table.

The barmaid comes to clear their glasses. Peter catches her scent and knows that she is perpetually afraid. She reminds him of his sister who, he realises now, has also come to smell like this.

Edwina is right to be afraid—they are rivals after all. Perhaps he should take action, a counter offensive. Perhaps he might after all remind Michael about how he found her standing over their mother's lifeless body and how her dress was so wet, her skirts dripping into the puddle at her feet, how her sleeves were rolled up past her elbows as if she'd prepared to thrust her hands and arms into their mother's bath water. He would tell Michael that she hadn't cried, not once, since that day. He would say, 'Don't you think that's peculiar? Don't you think she might not be quite right in the head?' And Michael would begin to defend her, but this would be a hopeless task because he would know the truth; in his heart he knew already that his wife was quite insane.

Michael says, 'Would you like another drink?' His tone is quite ordinary and man-to-man and this is how it should be in such a place as this—Michael is always careful never to give his true self away. So Peter doesn't smile at him, although he wants to, but is quite off-hand as he replies, 'Whiskey.'

Michael touches his arm discretely, he would hardly have felt it at all if he wasn't so sensitised to him. 'All right. I'll have one with you.'

Peter can hear the love in his voice, although of course it's not obvious to anyone who may overhear. To anyone else they are just two men having a drink together.

They stayed for one more drink—the whiskey that warmed Michael's guts and helped him forget that he was becoming the man he hoped he would not become when he put on that transforming khaki uniform and told Uncle that he was leaving. *My heart is broken,* Uncle had said, and indeed he had died quite soon afterwards so that it felt as though he had killed him, although he didn't hear of his death for many months, until his first leave, because there had been no one who knew enough to write to him. But one more death in the scheme of things hardly mattered and he had stood by Uncle's grave feeling only like a hypocrite, the single rose he intended to place at his headstone becoming limp in his hand, a pathetic symbol that seemed all at once too posturing; he has never been much of an actor, too ready as he is to see through to his own absurdity.

In the Castle & Anchor he is again a poor player; he is sure that the men at the bar, those drinking a few feet away, even those engrossed in their game of dominoes, know what he is. Only the pity they feel for Peter's blindness keeps him safe. But there is only so much he can stand of being on show like this. He drains his glass and says gently, 'Come on, Pete, let's get you home.'

Half way along the road to the house, Peter stops, catching hold of Michael's arm. Michael turns to him; the moon is bright and he can see clearly the anguish on Peter's face; it shocks him and his dismay is such that he doesn't think to check himself; his words come out in a rush and are too full of pity. 'Peter, I am so sorry—truly I am—I would do anything—anything at all—'

A man is walking towards them, hurrying his dog along and pulling at the creature's lead as it dawdles at a lamppost. Michael looks towards him helplessly—he knows how he must appear to this stranger: like a man who hardly knows which way to turn in his panic, and so he steps into the shadow of a privet hedge bordering a neighbour's garden. He draws Peter into this shadow, too.

'Peter—'

But Peter pulls away from him. He can hear the man's footsteps, the patter and click of the dog's paws. He calls out cheerily, 'Lovely evening for a stroll.'

The man passes him, grunting a response. Peter waits until he can no longer hear his footsteps then taps his stick against Michael's leg. His voice is flat, deadened as he says, 'Home, then. You can come out from skulking in the shadows.'

◆   ◆   ◆

Together they walked home, back to me, and Michael kissed my forehead as I placed the book I'd been reading on my lap. The fire had died and he told me that I shouldn't be sitting there, waiting in the cold, that I should have gone to bed. Peter waits in the doorway, so alert; he doesn't need to see anymore, he only has to sniff the air. We say goodnight to him, Michael and I, but I know he will stay awake, all the senses he has left so finely tuned that the house seems to vibrate and hum with his pressurised longing. I lie awake and it's as if we communicate through the straining walls until it feels the house might explode.

I get out of bed and put on my dressing gown, tying its cord tight around my waist. I am bleeding and I suspect my nightdress may be stained with blood, but even more than to hide this stain I want to stop my smell escaping: such a ripe, fertile stink—ironic when it signals only my barrenness. I am calmer now, my rage has abated a little with this show of blood but I still feel the pressure of it, it's too soon to be over the worst, I'm not yet fully purged. For a moment I stand over our bed and watch Michael sleeping. If he were to wake he would be afraid—I know what a fright I look with my face still swollen, my eyes still red from weeping and my hair in such disarray where I have been tearing at it. I reach out and my hand hovers above his head; I would so much like to touch him but if he wakes I would frighten him; I don't want him to be scared any more.

After a moment of watching him I draw my hand back to clutch at my throat, grasping my gown even tighter around me. I am tempted to sit down on the chair beside the bed, a dainty, button-backed chair that is used only to throw clothes over. I would sit and watch over him and help him slip away if he should wish to. That I should have such a thought horrifies me. I kick out at the chair, toppling it so that the heap of our clothes spills to the floor, cushioning its thud. Michael stirs and grumbles from his sleep but doesn't wake. Breathlessly I stand over him and the urge to reach out and touch him is stronger still.

I exhale and try to regain the calm I had felt a moment ago, the calm that flees from me so swiftly if I let down my guard for even one moment. Finally, breathing deeply, I tip-toe from our room.

◆   ◆   ◆

Peter is not asleep. I know this already from the hum and throb of his jealousy and spite vibrating through the house. I know even before I push open his bedroom door, before I see him sitting up in his bed, lit only by the cold moon light. It's as though he has been waiting for me and I have a vision of him waiting for me like this every night, propped up on his pillows, not sleeping but only waiting, listening, ears straining after every creak of floorboard. His pyjama top is buttoned to his throat, his hair is neatly combed, his face pale and scrubbed-looking, as though he is too young to shave; his hands rest in his lap and the bed looks as though it has been made around him, the sheet, blankets and eiderdown so straight and smooth a nurse might have just left him with a warning to remain tidy for the doctor's round. Only his eyes are chaotic and wander restlessly, giving him away.

My back to the door, I close it softly behind me and for a moment I stay there. My brother's bedroom is unfamiliar to me; this was always his sanctum, a place I was never allowed entry. I take my time to look around. The moonlight shows up a wardrobe and a desk; above the desk there is a shelf crowded with model soldiers. The unearthly light makes these toys look as though they have only paused in their battle and that they are about to spring again into animated, deadly life.

Peter clutches his hands together. He says, 'I knew you'd come.' I take a step towards him but he stops me by saying, 'Night after night I'd wait, half afraid you would come, half afraid that you wouldn't. Sometimes it was all I could do to stop myself from calling out to you. But you're here now. Thank God you're here now. Come closer.'

I tip-toe across the room and stand at the end of his bed; from this little distance I can see that he is sweating; beads of perspiration stand out on his forehead and his hand trembles as he reaches out to feel for a glass of water on his bedside table. He grips the glass tightly as though he is afraid it will slip from his grasp; when he raises it to his mouth it clinks against his teeth and his hand shakes so that a little water dribbles down his chin. He smiles shyly, embarrassed. 'I'm nervous, or scared—both, I think. Nothing to be scared of really, is there? Nothing at all.'

He turns towards the window; the curtains are drawn back to reveal the dark glass that has become an inadequate mirror where I can see myself, my eerie outline at least. 'The light is queer tonight,' he says, 'the moon must be very bright. The old enemy moon,' he adds softly, 'sniper's friend.'

He sets the glass down again. He seems to hold himself less tautly but his hands are once again knotted together in his lap and he licks his lips as though they are parched. Presently he says, 'Won't you lie down beside me?'

He moves to the edge of the bed, lying on his side so that there is enough room, and I'm reminded of Lieutenant Sparrow—of how things should have been between the lieutenant and me, if I had had the courage to let myself go with him. If I'd been brave then I would have spared myself so much pain, but I thought that there might be hope for me, a normal life to come if only enough men had the will to survive. If enough survived then one of them might marry me. We would be a normal happy couple with no one to interfere, no one to come between us, we would be happy and ordinary and normal.

I think of this ordinary life I might have had as I lie down beside Peter. I think of it with a feeling of detachment—as one might think of winning some impossible prize, knowing in one's heart that it could never come to pass. No ordinary man would marry me, nor love me enough to make the marriage happy—not after everything I had done. So I can't blame Peter, not really; instead I feel my anger dissipate and I am as calm as I always was in this situation; it might only be yesterday since I had done this: the knack has not left me, I don't have to winkle it from some awkward cranny in my heart or soul; I only have to lie there, besides my brother who wants this—of course he does; nothing could happen without him wanting it.

But then he reaches out, his fingers creeping across my mouth and nose and eyes and his expression changes, the calm that mirrored my own falls away from him and a look of horror darkens his face.

CHAPTER 25

~

Whilst David is visiting Father Purcell, Debra is visiting Gaye. I flit between the two scenes, curious about Debra's visit. She is here because over the last few days she has been worrying about Gaye, and she has an idea that for once her peculiar talent can help. This interests me—I wonder what she imagines she can do. I sit beside Gaye on the couch, the coffee table with its tray of coffee and cake between us. Debra looks uncomfortable, even shy. She says, 'I hope you don't mind me popping in like this, Gaye. Say if you're busy . . .'

Gaye hadn't been busy. She had been sorting through the box of photographs again, had begun to build up piles of pictures for each year of Emily's life. She had been absorbed in this task and quite happy, albeit the kind of happiness that is only recognised as such when it has become a memory. When she heard the knock on the front door she had been startled and her usual feeling of being timid and afraid returned. Getting up from the table and her piles of photos, she had gone to the window and stealthily lifted aside the curtain. Her surprise at seeing Debra there on her doorstep had caused her to dodge out of her visitor's sight. Her hand had gone to her heart as though she was a Victorian virgin whose suitor had come to call. She thought how ridiculous she was, how bereft of friends to behave like this. She had smoothed down her hair, her skirt—and these actions too had seemed ridiculous although irresistible—and she had gone to the door, opening it with a flourish and a bright, tense smile.

Now Debra sits opposite her and seems like a different woman to the confident, flirtatious guest she had been in Ralph's company. She is a woman who needs men to make her shine, Gaye thinks, remembering how Debra behaved at the supper party. At once she berates herself—isn't she such a woman, after all—a man's woman, interested in men's faces and physiques, in how they might be in bed. She has always liked men, whether such behaviour was fashionable or not.

Gaye says, 'I was just sorting through some photographs,' and then adds quickly, 'Mostly of my daughter Emily—it's time I put them together in an album.'

Debra smiles. 'My photos pile up in boxes, too—and in a couple of old handbags, if you're anything like me.' As Gaye hands her a cup of tea Debra asks, 'Could I see some pictures of Emily?'

Gaye hesitates, unsure whether she is ready to talk through the pictures, each one needing some explanation, no matter how brief. But the thought of not sharing her memories seems pointlessly, obliquely cold. She stands up and goes into the dining room to fetch the pictures from the table.

◆   ◆   ◆

To share the photographs with Debra, Gaye asks her to sit beside her on the couch. She has selected the pictures quite randomly, had almost not looked as she collected them up. Sitting beside Debra, only a hand's breadth between them, she hands her the photos one by one and her explanations are fluent and full of detail and she finds herself laughing and saying such things as *I'd almost forgotten that!* and *I think that was in Dorset* and *that's David, disguised as Santa.*

Debra glances at the photo of David in his red and white suit only to turn to Gaye. 'How is David?'

The question draws Gaye up short as she remembers David's brittle behaviour towards Debra. Shuffling the photos she still holds on her lap she says, 'He's fine, thank you.'

Debra hears the guardedness in Gaye's voice; it gives her pause but all the same she goes on, 'And how are you?' Then, more daringly, 'Really, I mean.'

'Really?' Gaye laughs shortly. Looking down at the photos she says, 'I don't know. This morning I was all right, I think. Hard to say.' She realises that this conversation has turned into the one she hoped one day to have with this woman, had they become friends, and there is an unreality about this, a feeling of what she had wished for coming true so that she imagines she could say anything and then wish the words away again. She looks at Debra, this pretty, well-groomed, manicured woman who has held down a decent job, who has carved out her own, independent life; who has Ralph now, if she wants him; a woman who has not lost a child. How can she talk to such a woman, even if the words could be wished away and no memory of them was left to haunt her? She realises she has been staring at her and she looks down at the photos quickly, flustered that Debra seems to be able to read her thoughts.

It's this idea she has now that Debra can see into her heart, that she knows more than her appearance might imply, that has her saying, 'David isn't fine, really. I thought he was getting better for a time, but lately . . . I don't know.'

On her lap is a photo of David and Ralph and Emily smiling in Christmas cracker hats. She can't bear to look at it any longer and she meets Debra's gaze and smiles bleakly. 'I don't know because we don't talk, not to each other, not to anyone.' Instead we have affairs, she wants to say, but doesn't—she is too ashamed of herself but also of David and she doesn't want Debra to think badly of him, not when he is so vulnerable.

She thinks of something else to say, something which suddenly seems important: 'The other night you asked me if I was happy here and I've been wondering about that, why you asked but also if this house was a mistake,' she thinks of the cold she feels when I stand close to her, remembering the feeling she sometimes has in this house that if she turns around quickly she will see the intruder who may or may not be an invention of her grief. Cautiously she says, 'Ralph says the house is haunted. I suppose all old houses are, in their way.'

Debra looks at me. I gaze back at her, challenging her to do her worst. If Debra tells the truth she believes Gaye will think she is a crank, she will warn Ralph about her and Debra doesn't want to risk her fledgling relationship with him. All the same, she looks at me and I can see that she is thinking what a fright I am in my coffin dress with my hair styled in the way the undertaker thought I suited best, a style which is too girlish for my haggard face. She looks at me and I feel ashamed: ashamed of my hanging about, of my eavesdropping. But I must be defiant—this is my house, after all.

I sit up straighter; I say, 'Tell her that if she goes into the garden and looks properly she will see me sitting on a bench beneath the plum trees.'

Debra shakes her head and looks away. My defiance has back-fired because to Gaye she says, 'This house is haunted, Gaye. And I don't want to scare you . . .' But despite her suspicions Gaye is scared; it's obvious how terrified she is.

Frantically Gaye looks around the room as if she might see if she looks hard enough. 'Is it Emily?'

'No! Oh no—no—she's not here, children don't stay . . .' She takes Gaye's hands. 'Gaye, listen—Emily hasn't stayed.'

'Because if she was here and I couldn't find her . . .'

Debra is alarmed now; she wishes she hadn't started this because Gaye is so panicked, and her face is so pale it may be that she can't withstand the shock. Holding her hands tightly Debra says, 'Gaye, it's just a feeling, a sense I have that this house isn't right for you, after all you've been through—'

Gaye draws breath; she straightens her back and pulls her hands away from Debra's, folding them in her lap. After a while she says, 'Ralph told you all about Emily, didn't he?'

'He told me that she died.'

Gaye nods. 'I'd like to tell you about what happened to her, if you have time.'

◆   ◆   ◆

Gaye begins, 'We'd decided to go on holiday to Northumbria—just a weekend away, really. David said we needed a break . . .' She won't tell Debra about the friend who had been so eager to tell her how her husband had been seen in a gay club that the friend's young son frequented. She won't tell her about Luke, because Luke was long afterwards; she realises that there is much she can't talk about because of her love for David, her desire to protect him from the judgement of others.

She decides to concentrate on that day she can barely bring herself to remember. Clearing her throat she goes on, 'We needed a break because we were going through a difficult time. It seemed possible then that we might even divorce . . .' Had she really thought that was possible? It seems now that as she had unpacked their bags in the cottage divorce was all she thought about, how she might find a solicitor, how expensive it would be, how they might tell Emily, how she might survive without him. But the events of that day had overwhelmed this memory of how she had worried as she lifted out folded tee shirts and jeans, as she hung Emily's favourite dress in the tiny wardrobe in the room her daughter had chosen. Now though, as Debra listens, the memory is clear and detailed. There had not been enough hangers and she remembers the sharpness of her irritation and how she had cursed the place for this over-sight. She had wanted to go home. She remembers how very badly she wanted to go home.

David had stood in the bedroom doorway as she slammed the wardrobe door shut and he seemed to wince—his whole body wincing as though every part of him was sensitised to her anger, cringing away from it. He'd had to stoop a little to enter the room, tucked as it was under the low eaves, and this stooping made him even more cringing, more contemptible, and she had turned away from him because he made her feel so vile, as though she could spit in his face. Perhaps if she had done this disgusting thing they both would have been shocked out of their coldness. They would have raged at each other, tore at each other, she had even felt her hands clench into claws to gouge out his eyes, eyes that had looked and looked at all those twisting, writhing male bodies.

Gaye draws breath. She says, 'We arrived at the cottage and the atmosphere between us was so bad that David suggested he take Emily out for a walk. Emily was so desperate to get outside, to run to the sea. She had always been fascinated by the sea and David was always so keen to show her things, teach her about the world . . .' She hears him say, 'Look, Emily! See this?' And his voice is young and lively; he hasn't sounded like that for so long that she is brought up short. She looks down at the photograph on her lap and laughs a little when she feels Debra's hand on hers.

'I'm not crying. I don't cry very much nowadays. I used to think that I would never stop crying, never stop bursting into tears in the supermarket, in the car, in bed at night . . .' But only when she was alone, never when David was beside her—how would that have been if she had cried in front of him? She would have set him off too—the two of them would have been hysterical, thrashing about in an anguish of grief; best to spare each other that messiness.

She says, 'I hated him that day and so I was relieved when he took Emily out. But I was worried for Emily—she hated to think there was ever anything wrong between David and me. Whenever she thought we had fallen out she would take our hands and force them together . . . Anyway, I was worried for her and so I went to the window and watched them walk along the beach and Emily was pulling at him, almost making him stumble. It looked as if he was being dragged away from me, into the sea, and I was so angry with him, so angry—and all at once I couldn't have him getting away from me like that—he had to know how angry I was. He had to face me . . . He had to face me . . .'

Debra says, 'You don't have to go on, if you don't want to.'

'No, I do . . . I was watching them and all at once I was running outside, running after him, calling his name—'

◆   ◆   ◆

In Father Purcell's sitting room David says, 'I looked back and I heard Gaye calling me. She was running towards us and her face was so wild, such an expression of fury, as though she would tear me apart, and I had to stop, I had to pull my hand away from Emily's and all I could think of was Gaye, my wife, and how much I had hurt her and I wanted to hold out my arms and let her run into me and batter me, flattening me down with all that wild fury. I wanted her to knock all the breath out of me and I wouldn't put up any defence, just take it and if she tore me apart that would be all right, it was what I deserved . . . It was what I deserved so I held out my arms to my sides and I stood and the sand shifted beneath my feet as though I was already falling and she came at me and then she stopped. She stopped a few feet away, panting and breathless—'

◆   ◆   ◆

And Gaye says, 'He just stood there, his arms out to his sides as though he was Christ waiting to forgive some poor bloody sinner and if I'd had a knife then . . .' She laughs bleakly. 'He stopped me in my tracks, anyway, and I was so out of breath it took me a while to say anything and you would have imagined I could have thought of something more profound instead of —

'I hate you.'

'I know—'

'I don't care that you know! It doesn't *matter* that you bloody know!'

'Gaye, please forgive me.'

Gaye looks at Debra. 'He asked me to forgive him, he said—'

'Gaye, I love you and I've always been faithful to you.'

'Except in your heart and in your head and when we're in bed together who are you with really? Who are you fucking in your head?'

'Gaye, please. I'll try so hard to make it up to you—'

◆   ◆   ◆

Father Purcell says, 'David?'

David looks up at him. He wipes his eyes, crying quite blatantly, not caring. 'I didn't know what to say to her—sorry? I would have said sorry a thousand times—worthless, *pointless*. What was there left to say? Nothing. All I could do was wait for her to make a decision, to stay, to leave—' he laughs brokenly—'to kill me because she looked as though she might . . . And all at once I wanted to say *what have I done really? I only looked! I looked, that's all!* And yes, the bible says that for looking I should be struck blind but really—was it so bad? And she looks—I wanted to say to her *you look—we have looking at men in common!* And maybe then she would have slapped my face like she was itching to and we could have really laid into each other, we could have hurt each other properly—real blows, real, physical pain, and then I would have fucked her . . . I'm sorry Father . . . It's in my heart and I'm ashamed . . . I would have taken her and that would have been an end to it . . . But we did nothing—just stood looking at each other and we were both breathless, as though we had been wrestling with each other, and I said it again. I said,

'I'm sorry, Gaye.'

'You're sorry for yourself—that's all.'

'No—for you, sorry that I hurt you—'

'Don't you dare pity me!'

'I don't, I don't—'

And Gaye says, 'And we just went on like this, David all full of *sorry* and trying to placate me, and me—anger making me stupid. I couldn't think beyond what he had done . . .' And she realises that Debra doesn't know what he'd done, doesn't know about that tangled pile of naked, contorted men she sees whenever she thinks about David's betrayal. But she can't tell her, there is no explanation that wouldn't make her feel that she in turn had betrayed him. And so she says, 'We were arguing over nothing, really—*nothing*, because nothing matters compared to losing Emily. I can't believe I even cared about what he did. Only what we did then in those next moments matters—it's that I can't forgive us for.'

David says, 'Father, you said that God has forgiven me, but I don't feel it. And you'll say *you must forgive yourself* but how? How? I let go of Emily's hand, I told you, but also, also . . . I forgot all about her . . . I forgot . . .'

This, of course, is his true confession and it is like spewing bile, so painful, his guts are racked by the pain of being purged when there is nothing left to purge. His throat burns and his face is swollen from crying; this has been a particular type of torture, one that when it is over will make him stronger, although light-headed for a time, unable to think of anything but the relief he feels. And when the grief creeps back it will be easier to contain and less brutal in its ferocity. But for now his voice is hoarse as he says, 'How could I forget? As though she no longer existed, as though in my secret heart I had wished her away . . .'

Gaye says, 'I forgot about Emily, my own little girl. How could I forget? I had watched her all her life. She had never been more than a few steps away from me. I forgot her, for those few moments . . .'

◆   ◆   ◆

I get up and go to the window because I can't bear to hear anymore. I look out onto the garden that was once mine and is now Gaye's—full of Gaye and her memories but also my memories and the regrets that keep me here.

But I have run ahead of myself. There are gaps in my story I can't explore easily, memories that are like ragged sores in my mouth, exquisitely painful but still begging to be probed, to be returned to.

CHAPTER 26

~

Some of those memories are of that boy, Lieutenant John Sparrow, the boy I had tried to revive with my kisses. Becoming less vivid are the memories of all the nameless boys that I didn't try to save. Importantly there are the memories of early in our marriage, when Michael would wake from his nightmares before his nightmares woke me. He would grasp my hand tightly and I would surface from sleep, the dark of our room becoming less impenetrable until the shape of our wardrobe, of his jacket hung over a chair became objects I could fix on as I waited for his heart to pound out his fear, to flush away the remembered horror in sweat and trembling.

Awake, it seemed Michael had forgotten much of what he went through, almost all of the boredom and even some of the blessed quiet days when he had time almost to convince himself he could survive. But even awake he remembered cutting the German wire, how stealthy and silent he had to be except that his heart made such a thudding racket he knew that he had to be heard. How, although he was freezing cold, he would be blinded by sweat. The sweat mixed with the blacking he'd used to camouflage his face and stung his eyes. But still he went on and the wire was cut and the enemy trench was taken and Jack—his Second Lieutenant—was wounded fatally although the boy didn't guess he was dying. 'Some knew, some didn't,' Michael told me. 'I'm sure you found that, too? I'm sure we all gave them the same old useless flannel, didn't we?'

At night, as I lay beside Michael, his hand clutching mine, I would imagine how those boys would have adored him in his leading man role. He would know all the right words: his flannel would be the very best and most convincing flannel in the whole of the army; his eyes would be the most sincere, his arm around their shoulders the strongest and most reassuring. If God had been watching surely He would've applauded. Still Michael felt that he hadn't done his best, that he had made a terrible mess of things.

I never told him about my war; it was enough for him to know that I had seen and done enough to understand him. But if he had asked me I think that mine, like his, would have been an edited and highlighted version of events. I wouldn't have told him about Lieutenant John Sparrow.

I would have told him that when I first arrived in France nothing was as I had expected but within days I couldn't imagine anything but the constant exhaustion, clamour and stench of the world I'd walked into. There were ordinary things I could tell him, that at first I shared a room with a girl called Agnes and that Agnes was the kind of girl he would have married had it not been for the war—a fair haired girl, pretty and light-hearted. She called the wounded *our brave boys*, although I might not have told Michael this because he might imagine that I made Agnes up, and also because I didn't want him to scorn her, even if he did believe she was my invention.

If I had invented her I wouldn't have put such words in her mouth. If I'd invented her she would have liked me as I liked her and we would have walked arm in arm to the grey, rain-soaked little village near the field hospital and talked as girls talk, and perhaps my invention would fail here, because what do I know about such friendships? Agnes thought I was prickly and aloof; she admired me, I think, but only for those qualities she thought were excusable for a woman not to possess: I was unflinching, proficient, stern even. The brave boys didn't affect me as Agnes felt I should be affected.

Agnes fell in love with one of our patients, Mathew Roper.

I say his name aloud, Lieutenant Mathew Roper, and this memory is strongest of all and at once I'm standing by his bed. He has been blinded by gas and at first he thinks that I am Agnes because he tries to look less afraid and more like the man who might have taken her dancing one day. Then I speak and his tried-for smile falters, he becomes the man I know better than anyone else, just as he knows me.

I say, 'Lieutenant. I'll come back later, if you wish.'

'No,' his voice is a whisper because of the gas, because he is dying, because he still believes in Christ and is afraid that we will be overheard. 'No,' he repeats, 'stay.'

I hold his hand but gently—the gas has blistered his skin—and I tell him the story of the Good Samaritan and then how Christ turned the loaves and fishes into a feast for thousands. These stories that I know from my Sunday school days comfort him, full as they are with unexpected kindnesses and the bountiful love of Jesus. I am a mother sending her child to peaceful sleep and the words come naturally, the stories remembered easily. All I do is talk softly; I'm not eager or quick, my heart beats normally. I don't even watch him only keep my eyes on his old man's hand. When he dies I hardly notice; he is the last and I'm very used to the way of it.

I was used to it, and so had become careless and hadn't realised that Agnes had been watching. When it was all over, after I had drawn up the sheet and turned away, she flew across the ward towards me, a dervish.

'You're wicked! A devil! You should be nowhere near these men!' Tears ran down her face; she wiped her snotty nose with the back of her hand and all at once she was clawing at me, pulling off my cap in a frenzy of grief and hatred. 'You shouldn't be here! You shouldn't be allowed!' Her fingers clawed at my hair and scratched my scalp. She cried, 'Murderess! Wicked, wicked murderess!'

Matron thought that *poor dear Agnes* was too fragile and that the army shouldn't have expected so much from her. Matron also disapproved of her girls becoming romantically involved with the patients and so her sympathy was somewhat circumscribed by the line Agnes had crossed. Agnes was sent home and I wasn't allowed to speak to her again.

But the matter wasn't over with; Agnes's grief had brought things to a head. I was brought before a panel—that's what they called the line-up of doctors in their Colonels' uniforms, the matron in her starched, ridiculous cap. They had me stand in front of them while they told me that 'It may be for the best if you were sent away to rest. We think you are very tired. We think that it has all been too much for you. You are not to talk about what's gone on here, not to anyone.'

I asked them what 'had gone on'? and Matron was sharp with me and said that I knew—better than they did, she was sure. She said I should look into my heart and that I should pray to God—here one of the colonels cut her off, his voice weary as though he was sick of such silliness. He sighed. 'Miss Johnson,' (already in his eyes I was no longer 'nurse') 'Miss Johnson, I think you have done enough.'

I told him I had only ever done my best.

'Yes,' he said, 'I am sure you thought you were doing what needed to be done.'

And Michael would ask, 'So they wanted to die?'

If I didn't answer he persisted, 'So they wanted to die? They didn't mind?' His terrible need to understand tantalised him—perhaps he didn't have to feel so guilty if there had been someone like me out in the world all along, clearing up the mess he had made and making everything all right again. I remember how he would implore me, 'Eddie—try and think back. Think carefully . . . They were happy—at least accepting—weren't they? In the end they really didn't mind, did they?'

He would stand over me, trying to be patient, trying most of all not to scare away my memories. He would try to make his voice gentle. 'Eddie, please. Think harder.'

To make him be quiet I became glib. I told him, 'I only gave them permission.'

He laughed as if he might cry with frustration. Those boys had been his responsibility, after all.

They were his responsibility, just as Peter was his responsibility. He loved them just as he loved Peter.

He thought I didn't know about Peter and him, how they were together. He thought that they could go on with their filthiness because I was the type of person to whom things could be done: I could be dismissed, not thought of, even sent away as that panel of fools sent me away, and it wouldn't matter. I could be told to stop and I would stop, to go and I would go, to not talk and I would be silent and not cause them any awkwardness. I could be married and would be grateful to my husband simply for the fact that he had married me and not expect fidelity; why would a man be true to me? I was too cold; in my heart, where it matters most, I was cold as the dead.

My mother left me because of my coldness; she couldn't bring herself to look at me, knowing what she had created. I thought it better that she should go; what use to me was a mother who couldn't love her children equally? Peter took my acceptance as proof of my guilt. He found me standing over her bath, soaked and freezing, so cold, and knew that I had killed her.

He knew that I had killed her and I think it was this knowledge that made him so afraid when I lay down beside him, when he reached out to me, breathing my name, using his last breath to acknowledge me. I pressed my hand to his mouth; I felt him shudder as many men had shuddered at my touch, it didn't mean that they didn't want to go, even if at first they struggled. Peter struggled, but he didn't fight me for long, it was over soon enough.

I lay beside him for a little while after he had gone; I was tired, the kind of tiredness I hadn't felt during the war with all its bustle and excitement. I was tired and I closed my eyes and slept.

CHAPTER 27

In Father Purcell's study David says, 'Father, I'm not sure I can go on.'

The good priest sits forward in his chair and takes David's hands in his own. He waits for David to compose himself. David is so fragile that anything Father Purcell says may cause him to disintegrate and so he keeps quiet, although he wonders if this may be cowardly.

At last David says, 'I dream often that I save her. And then when I wake up it's as though I've been bereaved all over again.' He pulls his hands from the priest's grasp and sits up straighter; he had slumped forward as if he was about to cover his head with his arms ready for a blow and now he gropes in his pocket for a tissue and wipes at his nose and eyes fussily, aware of how he might appear. He smiles faintly. 'Long time since I cried—oh, it must be a few weeks, at least.' Glancing at the priest to see if he might be smiling at this too, he goes on, 'Only ever in private, though. I am a *very* inhibited person.'

David has made himself awkward now, and it's possible he has done this quite deliberately because he has come too close to going on, to reaching the end. But what is he here for, after all, but to tell everything so that the priest may say, 'Is that it? Others have suffered far worse and survived.' Not that Purcell will say this, of course. No one is as cruel as David is to himself.

David hears himself sigh, a great, heavy sigh of the kind he expressed often in the days after Emily's death, although sighing seemed an all too feeble response and he would be ashamed if he ever caught himself at it. Yet this inhaling and exhaling, this gorging and purging of oxygen was a comfort for a few seconds; he would feel smothered and that was fine. He would wonder if it was possible to breathe oneself to death.

'All right,' he says, and he draws in another breath. 'All right, I'll go on.'

◆   ◆   ◆

He says, 'I had forgotten about Emily,' he pauses here, taking a moment for the pain of this to become bearable again. 'But then I had this acute sense of panic—you know that feeling you get when you realise that you've taken your eye off the road and you're about to drive into the back of another car? Like that but far, far worse—I knew that she had gone and at that same moment I knew exactly where she had gone . . . And then I was running towards the sea, screaming out to her, because I could see her, I could see her and she thought it was a game at first because instead of coming towards me she went further away . . . Further away, into the sea.'

He looks down at his hands, the tissue he'd used earlier has been shredded and he clutches the remnants into his fist. Surprisingly he laughs, but it's a harsh, broken noise. 'I'd let her put on her swimming costume before we left the cottage . . . She'd insisted and I'd thought *what harm can it do—what harm?* As she ran to the sea she'd pulled off her dress . . . But I was fully clothed, of course . . . Dressed so sensibly and warmly . . . the weight of those clothes, I can still feel it, how they soaked up such a weight of water . . .'

The sea dragged at him, and his teeth had chattered with the cold, a childish, flippant response he couldn't control. The salt water went up his nose and stung his eyes, blinding him, and it was as if the waves would batter him to death and that there was something uniquely vindictive in the way the sea came at him, from above and below, from every side, the tide pushing and pulling him further and further from the shore. His mouth filled with salt water as he struggled and he gasped and spluttered and swallowed and it felt as though all that salt was petrifying his limbs, making him seize up, making him useless; he would sink and he would drown but he was afraid only for Emily; he had lost sight of her; all he could see was water, the spray and splashes of his own limbs, greyness that could have been sky or sea or the manifestation of his own terror and his head was filled with a thunderous roar so deafening he couldn't hear himself calling his daughter's name, and he was certain that he did call her, over and over and over through his spluttering and swallowing and drowning.

And all this went on for hours, or so it seemed to him, yet he didn't move forward in time or space, only fought against this mass of water and made no progress in reaching her or in preventing her becoming lost. He might just as well have thrown a stick into the waves to save her, might just as well have stood on the beach, or ran up and down the shore screaming at the sea. But he waded into the water, knee high, thigh high, throwing himself into the waves, pitching his heart and soul—his whole, unthinking being—against the tide that was sweeping his child away.

He looks up at Father Purcell and says, 'The tide was going out. There was nothing I could do.' Although he could have done more, he could have fought harder against the agony in his chest, ignored the dreadful, disabling terror he felt—because yes—he will admit it now, he will be unsparingly honest—he was, at the end, afraid of dying. But somehow he couldn't die, his head kept rising, his mouth kept gulping after air, and sometimes he wonders that if he hadn't been heaved from the water he would have reached Emily, he would have, and he would have had the strength to pull her back towards the beach and they would have collapsed on the sand together, gasping and panting and alive.

He torments himself with this wondering; he believes he could have survived the sea, like a cork, that it would have been only a matter of keeping afloat; and he forgets how his strength had begun to give out, how each time he pushed himself to the surface the pull of the sea became more tenacious and his own limbs more weighted, more accepting of the water's drag. As time goes by he forgets more easily and so the torment is more potent. He needs to be told every day that there was nothing more he could do but there is no one to tell him; no one believes that such reassurances are necessary.

He meets the priest's gaze. Purcell seems as understanding as any man could be who has not suffered the torments of such a failure. Bravely David asks him, 'Could I have done more?'

'No. There was no more to be done.'

'I could have died. I could have done that, at least.'

'That wouldn't have saved Emily.'

'It would have saved me.'

But he was saved by two fishermen who hauled him onto their little boat with desperate, panicky effort, who said, 'It's all right, mate, all right, we've got you, we've got you.' He remembers trying to fight them off, trying to tell them that he needed to be out there, but he couldn't speak, there wasn't enough breath in his body, not enough even to say her name, and this is the worst of his failures, the very worst of all his betrayals.

David stands up, unable to keep still because his torment prods at him and its bullying won't let up and so he must dodge around in an effort to shake it off. He paces to the window, then turns and goes to the shelves, aimlessly studying the spines of the priest's books. Somehow he has lost the ability to read, or at least to shape the letters into words, and his eyes rove about, unfocused; he blinks and finds he has forgotten why he got so suddenly to his feet: this dodging succeeds like this, occasionally, making a blank of his memory, making him brainless. But even when it works, its effects don't last for more than a moment or two, and then he is closing his eyes and resting his head against the shelves of books, his hands grasped into fists at his sides. He's remembering the smell of fish from his rescuers' clothes, the bright, taunting yellow of their lifesavers; the tangle of nets and buoys he fell amongst, how the boat rose and fell beneath him, defying the sea as he could not; he's remembering how the sun was so dazzling, how the water roared in his ears. He was blinded and deafened, voiceless as a fish, gasping and thrashing.

◆   ◆   ◆

In Gaye's sitting room Debra is afraid because she has only ever seen the dead cry like this. But then Gaye takes a handkerchief from her pocket and wipes her eyes, ashamed for crying so openly. 'What must you think of me?' She asks, and she laughs a little because the question is so absurd now that Debra knows all there is to know. What must Debra think of a woman who stood safe on the shore whilst her child drowned? She should go on nevertheless, and explain to Debra how David's face was so blue with cold she had wondered if he could survive and whether she could bargain with God, her husband's life for Emily's. She imagines confessing this to Debra then asking, 'Was that wicked? Even if such deals could be struck . . .' But perhaps she will only tell her about the fisherman, their shock that somehow sped them up, made them into babbling cartoons, their words spilling out of them, too quickly to be understood. And then there was the sudden, dark busyness of the coastguard, ambulance men and police, and eventually the hospital doctor who told her how brave her husband had been.

Gaye sits up straight. Of course she can't tell Debra any of this; she feels that already she has gone too far—they are not friends after all, she hardly knows her. Debra may have discovered everything about her but she knows nothing about Debra, except that she has a silly belief in ghosts. All at once she feels nothing but resentment for this woman who has visited her without any good reason and who has succeeded in tearing so much out of her. She says, 'Thank you for coming to see me, and for your concern. And I'm sorry—I don't mean to question your sincerity—but there are no such things as ghosts.'

Debra is defeated by this. She sees how withdrawn Gaye has become and suspects that this is down to embarrassment. When she meets my gaze I say, 'Tell her she has to leave my home. Tell her I'm tired now and wish to be left in peace.'

But Debra only shakes her head. She stands up and says, 'I should go,' hesitantly she adds, 'it would be lovely if you and David could come to supper with Ralph and me one evening.'

'Yes,' Gaye says. She stands up. 'Yes, that would be nice.' And then she sees how Debra looks so lost and suddenly Gaye is saying, 'I'm so sorry—it's just that you're the first person I've ever told.'

She feels Debra's arms around her, feels herself held tightly, hears Debra's soft murmuring as she cries, and it feels as though this is the first time she has cried and that afterwards she might not cry again.

◆   ◆   ◆

David returns home. He pauses to look at himself in the hall mirror; it's obvious he has been crying, but perhaps it's only obvious to him. He tries smiling at his reflection and is appalled at himself, his horrible inhibited grin that is at once unctuous and despairing. How could Gaye bear to look at him? He peers into the mirror, wanting to face up to the true horror that is the man he's become, but this is too self-conscious, he can't be distracted like this for long. Besides, he becomes aware that the house has a different atmosphere, as though lights have been turned on and windows opened. He turns to see Gaye standing in the kitchen doorway. Her face gives her away just as his does. For a time they stand facing each other, and then David steps forward just as Gaye takes a step towards him, until, with a rush, she is in his arms.

CHAPTER 28

~

I slept beside Peter and when I woke the moon was still haunting the pale dawn sky and I thought for a moment that it was Michael beside me, sleeping soundly for once. Then I remembered and I got up, fastening my dressing gown cord where it had loosened in the night, shivering a little. Before I fell asleep I had remembered to close Peter's eyes and now I set about laying him out. When I had finished this task I covered his face and went downstairs and out into the garden. The birds had begun to sing just as if nothing at all had happened. I went to the plum trees that Peter and I had planted the year before the war, when we were still children, and sat down. The ground was hard and dry beneath the trees; a thrush flew down and began to peck at a snail shell. I rested my back against a tree trunk and waited.

When Michael came he was dressed in flannels and shirtsleeves, collarless, his braces hanging at his sides, his feet bare. He stood in the kitchen doorway, cupping a match to his cigarette before exhaling smoke out into the garden. Squinting, he raised his hand and smiled at me and if he was surprised to see me there he hardly showed it. He thrust the box of matches into his pocket then leaned against the door frame, studying the sky, assessing what the weather might hold in store for the day to come. He had promised Peter that they would go back to the farm if the weather was good.

He stepped down from the doorstep and walked towards me; he was smiling, smoking and smiling and nonchalant; for once he had slept well. A few feet away he stopped and the smell of his cigarette mixed with the damp earth smells of the garden. His smile was questioning now and I held out my hand to him. 'Sit down next to me,' I said, 'sit down.'

He sat beside me. He gazed out over the garden towards the big, solid ugly house I could never keep clean enough, tidy enough, its many dark rooms conspiring to defeat me. I saw him glance towards Peter's bedroom window, only to look away again quickly and I had an idea that he knew what had passed between Peter and me and that he understood and knew it was for the best. But then he said rather quickly, 'Peter and I are going out to that farm we told you about today. There are one or two good pieces still to be taken.'

'I should come with you.'

He turned to me, smiling. 'And who would look after the shop?' After a moment he looked away again. 'All right. Come along if you like. We'll make a day of it.'

'Peter wouldn't want me tagging along.'

'He won't mind. Besides, I'd like you to come with us.'

He went on gazing at the house, smoking his cigarette steadily, carelessly, as if he really wasn't such a liar, as if he hadn't called my bluff at all but truly wanted me there at that farm. I studied his profile; he was so handsome, too handsome, I should have realised right from our first meeting that there had to be some compensating flaw in him.

I confess that I wanted him at that moment very badly. Just as I had the first time we went to the little flat above the shop. I wanted him with a wild, gut-wrenching force that would have had me pushing him down and scrabbling at his clothes if I hadn't suppressed my neediness with all the control I could muster. But my breathing must have changed because he glanced at me, frowning a little.

'Eddie, tell me what's wrong.'

'What could be wrong?'

He laughed despairingly. 'Nothing. Nothing at all.'

He finished his cigarette and stubbed it out on the ground. 'Come with us, to the farm. It's a beautiful place—I'd like you to see it.' Getting to his feet he looked down at me. 'I'll make us some breakfast.'

He walked back to the house, following the trail he had made on his way out in the unkempt grass, the dew darkening the hem of his trousers. I thought of calling after him, and when he came back, his beautiful face all puzzled by my oddness, I would beg him to tell me the truth. I would tell him that he couldn't go on lying to me because I already *knew* the truth so he shouldn't hide it from me anymore. He would pretend he didn't know what I was talking about; he would try to placate me, denying everything; he would ask what had put such filthy ideas into my head and he would pretend to be disgusted. And then he would sink to the ground beside me, seeing how implacable I was. On his knees he would beg my forgiveness.

I couldn't think further than that—couldn't imagine what I might say to him. I knew I wouldn't forgive him and so there seemed little point in actually playing out such a scene. I allowed him to walk away, back into the gloom of the kitchen. I could see him through the window, filling the kettle, taking down cups and saucers, believing his secret was safe. In a few minutes he would take a cup of tea upstairs to Peter, gently tapping on his door. When he didn't answer he would open the door a crack and call his name softly, his voice light and jokey: 'Wakey wakey, old man . . .' He always used this tone if he thought I might over-hear, never let the act falter, never dropped the mask; if I had been a little less perceptive they might have got away with their vile infidelity.

I thought of Michael and Peter at the farm, the last time they had visited, how they had held each other on the farmer's stripped-bare bed. They trembled, afraid to go too far too soon, as if they might spoil everything. But the tension between them was too great, the want and the neediness, the intense, animal-like urge to have it over and done with; the next time it would be easier, and the time after that and the time after that, easier and easier and easier until the act was as natural as breathing and Michael would no longer think of me, as he had at first, with such paralysing guilt; he wouldn't think of me at all. I couldn't have allowed them to go that far; I had to put a stop to it before I was so humiliated.

But now Michael is opening Peter's bedroom door; he had called out softly, 'Wakey wakey old man,' but there was no reply. He goes to the window to draw back the curtains; he says, 'It's another fine day. We'll go to the farm,' and, as though this is hardly a disappointment to him at all, as though he must keep up the pretence even when I am out of ear-shot, he adds, 'Eddie's coming with us. We'll take a picnic, I think.'

He turns towards the bed . . . He turns towards the bed and at first he thinks that Peter is playing some terrible joke and he laughs as one laughs when a joke is in such tremendously bad taste. And then there is a looseness in his guts, that primitive feeling that signals he should run, but he takes a step forward, and then another and another until he is beside the bed; he can see the outline of Peter's face through the sheet, the sharpness of his nose, the fullness of his lips; he can see that his eyes are closed and so still, he has never seen them so still before. His hand moves to uncover him only to stop; he steps back; he has seen too many dead; he realises that his wife has spared him the sight of this one.

After a moment he turns away; there is nothing more he can do except wonder at the relief he feels; for the first time he feels that the war is over, not just an armistice but a final peace. He exhales the breath he has been holding and walks quickly from the room.

◆   ◆   ◆

Beneath the plum trees I think about Michael, his kindness that might have been enough, that might have helped me to over-look the wrong he did me if only I had led a different life. I think about the life we might have had together, our marriage going on and on contentedly without interference or complication, about the children we might have had if my body had proved less stubbornly resistant to the very idea of another life growing inside it. Life has always defeated me; death has always been my forte ever since I was a child, my constant, good companion offering its easy escape.

I close my eyes and my mother's face rises from her bath water and her eyes are wide with fright as her body fights against her heart's desire, but she will slip beneath the water again, try again, and she will stop fighting. For all that her eyes are wide and staring, she won't see me or care that I am there.

I should follow her; I've put it off too long.

◆   ◆   ◆

I am dead. Michael finds me hanging from the sturdy bow of a plum tree, my dressing gown cord tight around my neck. I watch from one of the dirty windows of the house as he runs across the lawn, as he bundles me into his arms, lifting me up inelegantly to take the weight; I hear his voice from my small distance, how he murmurs my name, how he tells me that he's got me now, that I am safe, *silly girl—safe!* His voice breaks but he keeps up his stream of encouragement and admonishments. He hardly notices how black my face is, how swollen, my tongue protruding obscenely. He unties the cord and lays me on the ground and pushes my hair back from my forehead; he is crying; his tears fall on my face and into my eyes so it seems that I am crying too and he wipes the tears away and laughs painfully, thinking that he will tell me later about how odd it was that his tears should fall in such a way.

But then I see him clutch me in his arms; I see how he rocks me back and forth, holding me so tightly, his face buried in my neck. 'Eddie,' he cries, over and over, 'Eddie my sweet girl, my one true love.'

He is a liar to the last.

◆   ◆   ◆

I am dead, a ghost, and Gaye and David live in my house now. They are upstairs in the bedroom that once belonged to Michael and me. Normally I would have followed them inside, curious about each look and move that passed between them—I have been making them my study. But now I don't have the heart to; I feel that something has shifted inside me and I hold out my hands and they are less substantial than they were. I stay in the garden and wait; I have an idea that if I wait long enough my patience will be rewarded at last.

Time passes; the fruit swells and ripens on the plum trees and falls to the ground where the grass has grown tall and thick with daisies and clover. The frosts come and the branches are black against the winter sky as though they have been etched in charcoal, and then come the brief blossoms that scatter on the wind, the green leaves that darken and become dusty, the hard green nuggets of fruit that hold such promise. Each year grows into another and another and I wait and watch and am so patient, more patient than I have ever been so that I find I'm quite calm when first I see his shadow appear, and then more of him until he is fully there before me, an old man now but still handsome, still with the bearing of the young officer who rode his horse with such amused aplomb. He steps closer and I see that he is very old, that only his long, long life has kept him from me until now. He smiles and holds out his hand. 'Eddie,' he says, 'my sweet girl, my one true love.'

I am calm, calmer than I have ever been so it seems unthinkable that he might be lying still. I stand up from the grass and smooth down my skirts, giving myself a little more time to compose myself. Then, ready at last, I take his hand.

ENDING

∾

The plum trees have been delivered and lie on the lawn, their roots protected by hessian so that they have an old-fashioned look. The man from the garden centre also brought bags of compost and blood and bone and he stayed a little longer than he normally would to advise Gaye and David about planting the trees. He remembers what Gaye had told him about her daughter and it's important to him that these trees grow well; he almost begins to dig into the earth himself, but he realises that they are impatient for him to go: this is something they must do alone.

The man is gone and David picks up a spade and begins to dig. This is hard work because there are roots to be cleared first. Gaye takes another spade and they work together and make slow, steady progress, both absorbed in the physical effort of digging and hacking and pulling at roots that have been buried so long and are stubborn despite their redundancy. Worms recoil from the intrusion, creatures that might never have seen the light of day and are so vulnerable that Gaye is moved, and tries to avoid harming them, even the woodlice that curl defensively or scatter in panicked haste. And then David is on his knees, heaving at the final root, and he looks up and catches her eye and for a while they are still, catching their breath, their chests heaving and then David smiles and wipes away the sweat from his face with his forearm. 'Almost there,' he says, 'one last effort.'

The roots are cleared. The trees are stood in the holes and staked and the holes are filled in, the earth compacted. Gaye and David stand back, satisfied although the trees look smaller now they are planted and more vulnerable, trembling a little from the trauma of their transplant. Gaye thinks how they must be watered now, and she turns towards the hosepipe coiled in readiness, but David catches her hand and holds it tight.

They stand together like this, close and quiet, and it's not long—no more than a heartbeat—before Emily appears. To David she is five years old and she is asking him about the moon that is pale and full in the sky although it's daytime and the moon, she believes, should have been put away. He lifts her into his arms and they look up at the sky's errant planet. 'I don't know much about the moon,' he says, and it's the first time he's admitted ignorance to her so that she stares at him, her eyes so wide he laughs and says, 'I love you, Emmy,' and she is haughty, knowing this already.

To Gaye Emily is three, sat on a tartan rug beside her on the lawn as Gaye plants snap-dragons. They are peaceful together, good companions, and Emily is singing a song she's learnt from the television. When the flowers are planted, Gaye scoops Emily into her arms and carries her into the house. Daddy will be home soon, she tells her, they must wash and prepare supper, and Emily is content with this, and later, nearer the time, she will go to the window and watch for Daddy's car.

David slips his arm around Gaye's waist and she rests her head against his chest. The afternoon has grown chilly. After a few moments they turn together and go inside.